THE
DRAGON
SPY

Also by Bill Blume

Gidion's Hunt

Gidion's Blood

West of Apocalypse

The Deadlands: And Other Stories

THE DRAGON SPY

BILL BLUME

Time Killer Publishing

First Time Killer Publishing trade paperback edition October 2024

Chapter 1: Lynna

Friday, 21 January 1983

Not even night could conceal the sins of East Berlin. Lynna landed on the cobblestone streets a little before midnight. The tainted air of industrial smoke choked its way into her throat. Buildings of crumbling grey bricks wore their scars from World War II as if the race between the Allies to claim this city had ended a week ago.

The black trench coat she slipped on only offered a little protection from the cold. She turned up the collar to shield the back of her neck, which her shoulder-length hair did little to protect.

She circled the block. This time of the evening, she only shared it with a white Wartburg, parked on the street next to an office building. The auto resembled a frog with wheels. Two slender pieces of black tape were placed on top of the car, above the front passenger seat, in the shape of an "X." Smoke drifted out of the driver-side window which was cracked open enough for the driver to stick his cigarette out and tap off the ash.

Satisfied no unwelcome eyes were focused on her or the Wartburg, she climbed into the car. The driver's startled look suggested he'd expected someone different than Lynna. At seventeen, she wasn't much younger than him.

The clinking of glass from the back seat greeted her as she shut the car door. Boxes containing tall-neck bottles sat directly behind the driver on the floor and the seat.

"Good," Lynna said as she reached behind her to lift one of the heavy bottles. "You brought them."

"Weirdest damn thing I've ever been asked to do." His cigarette dangled between his lips as he spoke. "Thirty quarts of water. You wouldn't believe what it took to get all those bottles for it. What could you possibly need that much water for?"

"If you're lucky, you won't find out."

She looked out the front window towards the other office building across the street. The cracked exterior with boarded up first-floor windows made it look like some home for vagrants, a la *Escape from New York*. Lynna knew that wasn't the case, though. The building still functioned, and according to her briefing, the office where her contact worked was halfway up on the third floor. She counted four windows over and waited.

"Do your parents know you're out this late?"

The German's joke missed her funny bone by a good mile. She answered him with silence and stayed focused on the office building.

"Seriously," he said, oblivious to her irritation or perhaps egged on by it, "how old are you?"

"If I wanted to be questioned, I'd have arranged a meeting with the Stasi."

He took that as an invitation to talk about himself. Lynna failed to tune out his rambling stories about how he and his elderly uncle ran a small smuggling operation shipping pornos and cigarettes from West Berlin. "You wouldn't believe what my uncle has managed to get in here by shoving them down his pants. Of course, those border guards aren't worried about stuff getting in here, just people getting out."

During his storytelling session, he'd offered her a cigarette. Now, she was twice as glad she'd refused.

Lynna wished she could have brought her chemistry textbook. She had a test on chemical bonding in Mrs. Black's class on Monday. Of course, if she got killed on this mission, she wouldn't have to worry about the test. Going to a normal high school with other students who couldn't set things on fire with their minds, project lightning from their fingers, or feed on blood had fallen short of her expectations.

Of course, she wasn't exactly normal either. She was half-dragon, and that's why the CIA had her here and why this prick's joke about her parents made her want to hit him.

"Wall has been a blessing to my family. Wouldn't make so much money off of our imported goods without it. I'm getting a tall stack of D-marks for driving you from here to the Wall."

She didn't bother to point out he was here more to provide the water and to give her a place to wait for her meet that wasn't out in the open.

He flicked the stub of his cigarette out the window and lit another. "So why are you working for the Americans? I mean, what are you? Japanese or something?"

"I am an American." She didn't bother sharing that at least one of her parents had been of Chinese descent. Although, having been taken by the CIA right after being born, she didn't know if her mother or father or both were Chinese. If she had a dollar for every idiot at school who asked her if she was an exchange student or why she didn't have an accent, she'd be set for life.

The light in the third-floor office turned on, saving her from anymore of this German's jabbering. Someone, backlit by the lamplight, came into view. They placed two strips of black tape on the window in an "x," like the one on top of the car. The sign meant they were alone and clear for Lynna to make the pickup.

Her heartbeat quickened. In theory, this was a simple knock on the door once she got inside, take the photocopied documents, and let "Motormouth" drive her to a building near the Wall. From there, she could leap off the roof and then glide over the "Death Strip" that separated East Berlin from West Berlin.

She leaned into the backseat and pulled out two bottles of water. "Be ready to go as soon as I get back."

He answered with a wiggle of his eyebrows and a smile that somehow held his cigarette in place.

The wind picked up as she got out of the car, sending a shot of cold through her body as if the coat wasn't even there.

She marched up to the front door of the building. Her eyes shifted in all directions, especially with an eye towards any open windows on the neighboring buildings which could suggest a sniper, but they were all shut. She'd gone on plenty of milk runs like this for the CIA, and they had a flow to them. When they were face-to-face, the other person always hesitated, usually thrown by meeting a teenager. They'd study her. She'd give whatever coded greeting she'd been told to use. They'd shake their head and sometimes wipe their brow and hand her whatever they wanted the Americans to see. Then she walked away, never running and never showing excitement. Agent Mills taught her that. *"Never look like you're in a hurry, because that makes people ask questions about you. Walk like you belong there, and everyone will assume you do."*

She did belong here, having trained for spycraft since she was five. She knew multiple forms of hand-to-hand combat and how to use a variety of firearms including the East German MPi-KM assault rifle. Motormouth had been nice enough to speak his heavily accented English, but she could have answered him in German, French, and Mandarin. She couldn't speak fluently in Russian yet, but she was getting better.

Her footfalls echoed on the steps as she climbed to the third floor. Before exiting the stairwell, she glanced up for any hint of movement. Satisfied, she walked down the dark hallway towards the door, keeping her steps as light as possible.

Less than ten feet from the stairs, she stopped. Something was wrong. She couldn't say what, but Agent Mills had also trained her to trust her gut. She stayed still and studied her surroundings for some sign of danger.

Then she saw it, or rather, she didn't see what should have been there.

The third door down was her destination, the clock repair shop. The dark brown wooden door had a bland black plate at eye level with the rather basic name of "Uhrmacherwerkstatt" inscribed in white text. The door sat in its frame wrong, with almost a half an inch of space between its bottom and the floor. The light from the lamp should have spilled out of that wide crack, but no light showed.

There was a signal to warn her off, if she'd made it this far, but that was supposed to be a blank slip of paper sticking out the bottom of the door. Technically, turning off the light didn't signal anything.

Lynna's back tingled from the dueling urges of fight and flight. A look over her shoulder confirmed no one was there in the narrow hallway. With slow, silent movements, she set the two bottles of water on the floor. When she slid off her coat, she lowered it into a careful pile.

Stopping short of the door, she knelt low enough to press her hand flat, feeling for any vibrations in the hardwood surface then pressed her ear to the wall to listen.

Nothing, and under the circumstances, that was the most alarming thing of all.

Taking the two quarts of water, she placed them in front of the office, one bottle before the other to make a noise like someone stepping in front of the door and stopping. Crouching to the side again, she took a deep breath and centered her will. The world around her shimmered in a yellow haze that only she could see as she grasped the mystical energy that infused her body. She hovered on the edge, close enough to look human but altered enough to access her powers. The bottles shivered as her mind gripped the water within each of them.

She knocked. When she spoke her scripted greeting in German, she concealed the strain of the pain coursing through her bones.

"Mr. Marquardt, could I have seven minutes of your time?"

She didn't finish the question before a volley of bullets exploded through the door into the space where she would have been standing.

The destructive percussion deafened her until the gunfire cut a hole the size of a baseball in the door.

Lynna tensed as her body embraced the transformation she'd held back. Even though the overall shape of her body remained human, her skin changed to pale blue scales with wings sprouting from her back. Her hands and feet shifted into something more like talons, which thankfully didn't ruin her sneakers.

The knob turned, and the door eased open. Lynna burst into the room, slamming the battered wood against a lithe figure, who fell to the floor.

Fresh gunshots thundered within the clock repair shop. She kept moving, not letting herself become a sitting target.

Enough light from the half-moon outside cut through the window for her to assess the scene. The woman she'd knocked to the floor was scrambling to her feet. Two other women stood deeper in the room: one armed with a rifle and the other a handgun. A vacant-eyed man lay prone on the floor in a dark pool of his own blood. The left wall held a large number of tools tailored to the dead man's craft with an array of spare parts on the right. A desk sat beneath the far window with a dark lamp on it and a folder she hoped would contain the packet she'd come to get.

The fight paused long enough for all involved to stare at the unexpected. The three women facing Lynna were grey-skinned with pointed ears. Whatever they were, they weren't human.

Neither was Lynna.

The tallest of the three got her rifle back up first. "Dragon!"

Lynna launched at the woman who got off a few shots, two of which bounced off Lynna's steel-hard scales while putting a hole in her tank top. The third shot nicked the left side of her stomach, above the waistline of her jeans, and chipped off some of her scales to expose the more tender flesh beneath. One of her wings swatted the rifle out of the woman's hand as she slashed forward with her razor-sharp nails. She missed the tallest one's throat, but she forced her back towards her companion, turning her into a shield to block attacks from the other two.

Fortunately, the tall one didn't block Lynna from attacking the others.

Water shot out of the bottles she'd left in the hallway. The twin streams spiraled into the room at their targets. Water blasted one in the face, but the other stream hit the mark, burrowing into the woman's open mouth, pushing down her throat to choke her.

Who were these people? What were they? Lynna didn't stand around to ask them. She turned and went straight for the desk. She snatched up the brown folder she'd been sent to collect, closed her eyes, and leaped through the window.

Glass shattered and rained onto the street as she plummeted. She pulled her wings in tight to speed her descent. A three story drop might have threatened her in her human form, but as a dragon, it posed no challenge. She hit the ground, rolling to distribute the force of her landing and launch back onto her feet, a task not made any easier by the folder flapping in her hand.

She came back upright, restored to her human form, because if her driver got a look at her all dragonfied, he might panic and leave her in the cold with nothing but her tank top and jeans. She could fly, but not faster than a bullet.

The two pointy-eared women not choking on water followed. Whatever they were, the drop didn't threaten them either.

Lynna jumped into the passenger seat of the Wartburg and slammed the door shut. The entire car shook, causing all the bottles of water to rattle.

"Go!"

Motormouth didn't answer her demand, didn't even move. His eyes stared straight ahead with his jaw hanging open, almost as wide as the bloody slash to his throat.

Someone grabbed a fistful of her hair from behind and jerked her back against the seat. A dagger pressed against her throat.

The two attackers who had leaped down after her strolled towards the car. The tall one smirked.

The one in the car growled in her ear, her breath a mix of flowers and honey. "If I see a hint of smoke from you, dragon, I'll slice you open."

This shouldn't have made her heart go berserk and want to jump up into her throat, but this wasn't a training room with a CIA-approved, thick-necked soldier ordered not to damage the "test subject."

Lynna barked a nervous laugh at that thought. She tried to keep still, but her body shook so much she feared she might accidentally cut herself on the knife.

"You think this is funny?" The Grey Woman in the back seat tugged harder on Lynna's hair.

"Actually, yes." Lynna tapped into her power, the world shimmering for her again. "I'm not that kind of dragon."

The smirk on Tall, Dark, and Grey outside the car changed to panic when she got close enough to see the bottles of water stacked in the back seat. She shouted a warning to the one with the knife, but Lynna couldn't make it out as a twist of her thoughts shattered every bottle behind the driver's seat and in the trunk of this cheap Eastern Bloc wind-up. A second thought, and the complex shape she gave the water pushed the knife away from her throat and flung back her attacker. Then the car blew up around Lynna like a hurricane in a balloon with her safe at the center of the storm.

Lynna dropped to the street, landing on her feet. The attacker in the car was flung back with Lynna's seat landing on top of her. The passenger door had smashed into the shorter of the two outside the car. The tall one stood unscathed and drew a long, curved dagger identical to the one that had been pressed to Lynna's throat.

Transitioned back into her dragon form, Lynna held onto her control of the water which returned to her, spinning around her in a spiral that acted as a shield.

The tall woman twirled the long dagger in her hand. "Give me the file, and I might let you live."

The file! Lynna dropped it when the car exploded.

The tall one must have registered Lynna's panic. Her eyes shifted to the road, scanning left and right for the file. Lynna did the same. The paper had scattered onto the street to Lynna's left near her driver's body.

They both raced for the paper, with Lynna too slow to get there first. These Grey Women moved like cats. A shift of thought, and Lynna sent two threads of water spiraling after the tall one's ankles. The first tendril missed, but the second wrapped around the woman's right ankle and spilled her face first onto the cobblestones.

Lynna didn't slow her run. She leaped over the woman and snatched up as many of the scattered sheets of paper as she could with her talon-like hands. She shoved the damp pages into her pants pockets, and then sprinted for the nearest building. She jumped with all her strength. Her nails dug into the brick, getting enough of a hold to keep her from falling back to the street, but her tennis shoes slipped against the flat surface.

Something hard slammed into her right shoulder blade. Pain exploded through her back and down into her arm, causing her to lose her grip on the wall. She plummeted with her wings flapping limp around her. The ground crashed against her back, her head bouncing off the cobblestones, leaving her dizzy. She regained her senses in time to pull her wings in tight and roll out of the way of the tall one's boot which stomped onto the street where her face had been.

Lynna got to her feet. The tall one snatched her dagger off the street. In hindsight, Lynna realized the hilt of the dagger must have been what hit her in the back. She tried to summon up the water from the street, but it was distributed too far and her mind was too fogged from her fall to control it. If she could get away from this woman and get enough height, she could take to the skies, but the woman pressed her advantage. The dagger slashed through the small bit of space between the two of them. Lynna batted the swing away with her hands and wings, but she wasn't gaining enough separation to turn and run.

Another swing of the dagger and Lynna swatted with her wing, but the Grey Woman's attack had been a feint. She grabbed Lynna's wing before it could pull back. She raised the dagger, ready to bury it in Lynna's chest.

Instinct asserted itself, and Lynna flipped backwards. The move slammed the bottom of her foot up into the woman's jaw. She let go of Lynna's wing to try to block the kick, but the Grey Woman's muffled shriek of pain and surprise proved she'd been too slow.

Lynna landed on her feet and ran for it. She rounded the nearest corner and spotted a black car parked on the side of the road. It would have to do.

She sprinted for the car and leaped up onto the back of it. Then she jumped with all her strength off the top of the car. The jump pushed her up a good two stories. Her arms and legs went limp as all her thoughts turned to her wings, which beat down hard to catch the wind and push her higher into the sky. The pain in her right shoulder didn't help matters, but she clenched her teeth, fighting back the sensation of bruised flesh and muscle.

Swimming through the air, she banked right to turn the next corner taking her out onto one of East Berlin's major streets. Bullets whistled through the air from her attackers. One shot pounded into the building she'd rounded. The office building shielded her for a moment as she pushed higher into the sky. She couldn't get high enough to be out of range of their guns, but the more distance she gained, the less likely they were to hit her.

The searchlights of the Wall came into view, sweeping across the ground along the Death Strip. Only God and the communists really knew how many people had died trying to get through that obstacle field of barbed wire, bricks, and cement in hopes of making it into West Berlin. Never mind the soldiers with guns and dogs on constant watch for anyone fool enough to make a run for it. Of course, this was why the CIA deployed her for these missions.

Lynna didn't need a plane or a bribe to slip past the Wall and its defenses. She could soar right over all of it without making a sound.

She flew high above the street of Zimmerstraße towards Checkpoint Charlie, though not as high as she would have liked. Given the women chasing her, she preferred to take her chances with the guards, who focused more on the ground. They didn't have a chance of spotting her until four gunshots chased her and sent her spinning to her left. Not one of the bullets came close. She never even heard the hiss of their flight path try to intercept hers. As she rolled, she spotted one of the Grey Women on a nearby rooftop. Even from here, she could see her struggling to catch her breath through a satisfied grin.

The witch hadn't worried about hitting her. The dozens of armed soldiers on the ground and in the lookout tower at the border crossing would take care of that. The searchlights swung in Lynna's direction, cutting through the dark sky until they caught the shimmer of her pale blue scales. Shouts of "Segelflugzeug!" went up from all directions, the border patrol of East Berlin mistaking her for a glider. A storm of bullets drowned out the rest of their cries and sent her turning hard in retreat.

Flapping her wings, she forced herself into a climb. If she could gain enough elevation, she could then dive like an attacking peregrine falcon on the hunt, not for food but for safety. At that speed, the guards wouldn't have a chance of hitting her as she raced over the Wall.

Her shoulder protested, and she worried the blow to her back might have hurt her more than she'd realized. She screamed as she struggled for more altitude. Bullets hissed around her. One passed within inches of her head. She flinched, and the mistake sent her tumbling too soon into her dive.

She tucked in her wings and let gravity pull her. The dark streets rushed up. Searchlights blinded her as she neared the point where she needed to stretch out her wings. Trusting to her instincts and the feel of the wind rushing around her body, she threw her wings wide and pushed up, praying she wouldn't smash into a building or the road.

Shouts and more gunfire erupted from the ground. Her vision adjusted in time to see the Checkpoint Charlie watchtower rushing at her. She'd all but gift-wrapped herself as a target for the rifleman. The only thing that saved her was the shock he got as she came into focus and he saw the truth, that she wasn't some fool trying to get over the Wall with a hang glider but a thing of myth.

Twisting to her left, she missed the watch tower by inches. The guard shot after her, but the attempt came too late for him to get a decent aim.

The Death Strip vanished from beneath her, replaced by the more brightly lit streets of West Berlin.

Her efforts to avoid the watch tower sent her flying too fast and too low down a narrow street off of Zimmerstraße. Buildings, street lamps, and utility lines thrust into her path like a maze being built around her with cars and people zipping along its floor to deny her a safe landing.

She lost height. Her wings fought in vain against the tug of the planet. A dark colored car moving slower than her came up beneath her and she did the only thing she could think to do. She tucked in her legs. Her feet neared the top of the car. Just as she was about to hit it, she kicked up with her feet, bouncing off the roof and back into the air. Beating her wings, she fought her way up until she could place herself safely above the buildings. Without the obstacles of West Berlin threatening to crush her, she let her flight slow to a less perilous rate until she found an alley to descend into and land. Her legs churned so that once she landed, they took over for her wings.

Finally stopping, she leaned against the side of a brick building next to a dumpster. Her body shook as her pounding heart refused to believe she was safe. Shifting back into her human form, her body trembled more from exhaustion than the cold. Sweat rolled down her face. She clung to the wall as she headed towards the street.

Emerging from the alley, she leaned against the front of what turned out to be a hotel. A few stared at the fool girl standing outside in the cold in nothing but a tight, black tank top and a light pair of jeans. The cold didn't touch her—not yet. Whenever her internal war of "fight or flight" passed, she'd want to crash, but she couldn't do that before she found true safety.

She spotted a yellow phone booth on the far corner of the hotel and staggered towards it. Nausea hit her, but she forced it down. A couple approached her, asking if she needed assistance. She waved them off. "Nein," she said and repeated that word until they were gone from view.

As she entered the phone booth, the stench of stale cigarette smoke and things she didn't want to recognize punched to the forefront of her olfactory senses. She pulled a coin from one of the smaller pockets in her pants, lifted the receiver off its cradle, and dropped the coin into its slot. Her hands shook as she dialed the number she'd memorized for this and several other missions in and out of East Berlin.

After one ring, a woman with a deep voice answered in an American accent with a hint of New York to it. Her tone suggested she expected nothing but the most boring conversation of her life to follow. "Endeavour Bookstore."

"I'm looking for a copy of *The Deadlands* by Paul Starnes."

Lynna heard the faint spin of a rolodex on the other side of the call. "Do you know its ISBN?"

She took a deep breath, forcing her brain to pull up the code number. "9798218199395."

"ID confirmed. Please state your request."

She covered the handset's mouthpiece to hide her laugh of relief and then said, "I'm at the corner of Trittstein and Schwarzer Dornbusch, and I need an extraction."

"Standby." The phone clunked in her ear as the woman on the other end put down her handset.

Several minutes passed. The cold, which all of her physical efforts had staved off, finally took hold. She leaned against the inside of the phone booth and hugged herself as she searched the passing cars and the pedestrians for a sign of the Grey Women who'd attacked. Who were they? What were they? What if they could change their appearance the way she did? What was taking this lady on the phone so long? If those Grey Women could track her, this phone booth left her too exposed.

The welcome sound of the phone clunking again let her know the other woman had returned.

"White and yellow Volkswagen van three-two-three-Whiskey-Bravo-niner-six. Ten minute ETA."

"Got it."

The line went dead. She dropped the handset back into its cradle and waited.

Three hours later she was strapped into the back of a military transport heading straight across the Atlantic to Langley Air Force Base. Before they took off, she ate a ham-and-cheese sandwich and washed it down with a bottle of Coca-Cola, which she also used to swallow two acetaminophen. The last thing she saw before she fell asleep for the entire flight back home was the grim face of the CIA agent strapped in across from her. He'd looked less than pleased ever since she handed him the fruits of her labor, which were the wet pieces of paper with the smeared ink from typed Cyrillic letters. There might have been as many as five pages in what she handed him, but it was hard to tell given they almost fell apart coming out of her pockets.

Hopefully the Grey Women wouldn't get anything better from the pages she'd left on the streets of East Berlin. Once she got back to the Greenhouse campus, she needed to study for her chemistry test and take her dog on a long walk to make up for being away from him so long.

Chapter 2: Lynna

Monday, 24 January 1983

In true Mrs. Black fashion, the witch had crafted a multiple choice and true/false test just as tough as if she'd made it fill-in-the-blank. Lynna would have struggled with this test, even on a good day. Lynna's skull ached from being yanked to Berlin time and back. The gunshots hadn't left any marks once she shifted back to her human form, but the strike to her shoulder still hurt.

Most of the other students had finished the test within the first half of the fifty-minute class. Five minutes later, another wave of people walked up to their teacher's desk and handed in their tests, along with their green and white scantron sheets with pretty little grids of number-two-pencil-filled-in ovals.

Lynna glanced at the clock on the wall above the blackboard, giving her a brief moment of eye-contact with her teacher. Mrs. Black was a short, stick-thin woman with harsh lines on her face and brown hair that sat on her head with all the elegance of a football helmet. The little troll probably harbored an unnatural fear of Bunsen burners because of all the hair spray she used.

With ten minutes remaining, Lynna called it quits and turned in her test. Without a word, Mrs. Black glanced at the answer sheet as if she expected it to give her a bacterial infection and then pointed to the blackboard behind her, which instructed them in pale yellow chalk to start reading the next chapter in their textbook, reminded them their notes on the chapter would be due tomorrow, and warned them not to talk while others finished the test.

Trudging back to her desk, Lynna straightened when she saw Patrick smiling at her. He sat in the desk in front of hers, and she considered him her only real friend at school, outside of the handful of students who also lived with her at the Greenhouse. Patrick Rogers wasn't the best-looking boy in school, but he was one of the cutest and nicest, the kind of guy who was popular partly because he had no clue how popular he was.

He'd left a note, folded up to take up less space than a quarter, on her desk. Lynna didn't unfold it until she'd pulled out and opened her chemistry textbook and her spiral notebook, filled with various doodles of elaborate line art far more than chemistry notes. In her defense, Mrs. Black made what should have been an interesting class as boring as stale bread.

Patrick's note didn't contain any words. Their notes to each other kept the words to a minimum, because they both knew if their teacher ever caught one of their exchanges, it wouldn't leave her anything to read out loud to the class if she decided to go the "shaming" route for punishment. He'd make a great spy thinking like that.

The note showed a drawing of a piece of paper, followed by a plus sign, then a pencil burning at one end like a match, followed by a sad face.

She scribbled next to the sad face, "Same."

Then she drew a guitar followed by a plus sign and a drum with another plus sign and a sandwich with a bite taken out of it. After the equals sign, she drew a square with Tuesday written at the top and a question mark in the middle of the box.

She folded up the paper again, stole a glance at Mrs. Black to make sure she wasn't looking, then slipped the paper onto Patrick's right shoulder. Her fingers brushed his dark brown hair before she pulled her hand back, less because she liked his hair and more as a silent cue that she'd left the note. The first time she'd slipped him a note near the beginning of the school year, she'd done it without brushing his hair. He hadn't realized she'd placed the note there for several minutes, so she'd started doing the hair thing. Of course, if she was being completely honest, she did like his hair.

Before he could draw a reply, the bell rang to signal the end of fourth period and the start of lunch. Mrs. Black shouted a reminder about their homework being due tomorrow.

Free at last to speak, Patrick turned to look at her as he slipped on his grey windbreaker. "I'll save us a space in the band room for lunch tomorrow."

"Cool!" She smiled back at him, trying to not let it show how glad she was he'd agreed to it. They sometimes got together at lunch to make up songs. He performed in the marching band, so he always had his drums on campus, but she had to plan ahead to bring her guitar.

She hissed in pain as she pulled on her backpack.

"You okay?" Patrick asked as they walked out into the hallway.

She nodded. "Fell down this past weekend."

The bruise on her shoulder looked ugly with hues of purple and yellow. She'd never before taken a hit in her dragon form that had injured her enough to carry the wound over to her human form.

"You do look really tired."

She mock-glared at him as they headed towards the cafeteria. "I look that hideous?"

"What? Oh! Uh, no. I mean, you just—it's that...you look..." His eyes couldn't have gotten any wider, and she couldn't keep herself from laughing. They'd stopped in the middle of the hallway, with people pushing their way around them.

"I'm only messing with you." She couldn't help herself. He was such a goody-two-shoes that he made it impossible for her to resist finding ways to shock or startle him. He liked her. At least, she hoped he did. The question weighed on her whenever she thought about him. He made her least favorite class something she looked forward to, and while she enjoyed finding ways to shock him, she also panicked whenever his expression turned sad or troubled. Was it a reaction to her, or was he thinking of something else? Worse, what if he was thinking about someone else he was interested in more than her?

The circle of questions choked her. Getting to talk with him, here at school or on the phone before curfew at home, was the most normal thing in her life. At least, she assumed it was normal. She didn't know of a life before being taken to the CIA's Greenhouse, and Patrick offered her the closest thing to an escape from her sheltered life.

Her worst fear and her most frequent fantasy involved him. They'd be alone. He'd take her hand, pull her close, and then they'd kiss. She wondered what that would feel like, but she didn't dare press him to cross that line. If anything, she did her best to discourage him.

When the CIA arranged for them to go to classes at West Chester High School, the arrangement came with a long list of rules. One of them was a hard "No" on any after-school activities. They also weren't allowed to go off-campus at lunch, because if a mission came up that required them to deploy immediately, they had to be accessible. Technically, they weren't forbidden from dating, but all the regulations they had to obey made that impossible. Patrick once invited her to go dancing at this teen club downtown called "New World," and turning him down had been one of the worst things ever. Months later, that memory still stung.

Fortunately, the unwritten rule against dating didn't stop her from bringing her guitar to school and being alone with him to play their music.

"I'll go save us the room for tomorrow." He grinned as he headed towards the band room. "See you later!"

He disappeared into the chaos of other students, and the smile melted from Lynna's face. This was when the fears of their awkward dance troubled her most, her heart vibrating with worries—thinking if she'd said something wrong, that he might expect more than playing music together tomorrow and that their friendship would fall apart. "Normal" would end, and she'd lose the only real friend she had outside of the Greenhouse.

A blast of cold air disrupted her spiraling thoughts as she stepped outside into the breezeway and headed towards the center of campus. West Chester High's courtyard stayed packed with students at lunch, no matter the weather. Some preferred to hang out in the breezeways making them a slightly less challenging obstacle course to maneuver than the hallways. Bathing in the welcome sunlight added a few degrees compared to the shade.

The floor of the courtyard was made up of large square stone tiles with a few round benches forming incomplete circles with bushes behind them for a little privacy.

Lynna and her friends from the Greenhouse always staked out one of those cement benches for lunch. Her friends Maria and Nevada waited there, already eating the sandwiches from their bag lunches, prepared by the Greenhouse's kitchen staff. Most of them had unique dietary needs.

Back when Dr. Howard had proposed the idea of them getting part of their education from a public school, she'd convinced the CIA that Lynna and the others would learn how to interact with people in the "real world." Lynna had expected to make so many friends here. They all had, but it hadn't taken long to realize how superficial those potential friendships were. The students here were nice enough—well, some of them were—but Lynna and the others were expected to maintain their covers as orphans from a school for the gifted. Only, that lie didn't go far when faced with a real conversation, because they weren't allowed to discuss anything that happened in their classes at the Greenhouse. In less than two weeks, they had discovered it was easier to cling to each other.

Lynna, Maria, and Nevada had been close before they started attending West Chester, but their friendship had gotten stronger since then. Lynna dropped her backpack to the ground, got one look at Maria and knew something was wrong.

Maria's features were pinched, adding deep lines to her round, tanned face. "What's the problem?"

"I failed my test on *Frankenstein*. We're talking nuclear bomb failure here."

Nevada sat on the other side of Maria and hand-signaled the grade: five fingers followed by eight.

"But you read the book. Devoured it in a single weekend!" While it wasn't exactly a question, Lynna couldn't hide the unspoken "How?" Nevada scowled at Lynna, silently demanding how brain dead she was to pour salt on an open wound.

"Yes." Maria flung her half-eaten sandwich back into the brown paper bag on the ground in front of her. "I read it in time for the test two weeks ago, but then Mr. Roof rescheduled it. I started reading another book, and I couldn't remember half of the crap I'd read for the test. I'm struggling wildly to think of the name for Victor Frankenstein's best friend, and all I can come up with is Roland Deschaine and the Man in Black." She roared her frustration, then paused to chug what was left in her can of Mountain Dew. "By the way, *The Gunslinger* is one serious acid trip. After I finish it, you two gotta read that so we can talk about it. Stephen King has got some seriously rabid cats rolling around in his head."

Lynna and Nevada laughed. Whenever Maria got going, her rants rolled out in an avalanche.

"I'm serious! You two better read it." She sat straight and stared down her thin nose at them. "I really, really, really need to talk about this book. Don't be mocking me!"

Nevada held up her hands in surrender. "Lynna and I will spar this weekend to see who reads it first."

"Good." Maria smiled as if she'd won an argument.

"Loser has to read it first," Lynna said.

Nevada snort-laughed as Maria's victorious expression transformed into a wide-eyed glare of betrayal.

A shadow fell over them as one of the few boys from the Greenhouse joined them. Lynna took a moment to recognize Pockets. This past weekend, he'd traded in his short afro for a buzz cut similar to the one Agent Mills had.

"Is it safe to sit, or should I run for it while I still can?" Pockets asked, probably noticing Maria looked upset. His tortoise shell Ray-Bans hid his eyes, but they all knew he was looking at her.

She smirked. "Enter at your own risk."

Lynna scooted over so Pockets could sit next to Maria.

Pockets and Maria kissed as soon as he was settled. Sure, the school had rules against that, but as long as students weren't giving each other dental exams with their tongues in the hallways, most of the teachers never said anything.

Of course, getting time alone to make out was harder back at the Greenhouse campus. Pockets and Maria had started "jogging" in the woods within the fence line a lot more often since they became an item. That they were going together (couldn't really say "going out," since the CIA never allowed them to go anywhere together outside of school or the Greenhouse campus) was the worst kept secret in the unit. If Dr. Howard or any of the other staff knew about it, none of them had said anything yet.

Maria caught up Pockets on her disastrous test grade while he destroyed his sandwich in three large bites.

"Don't sweat it," he said around a mouthful of cheese and bologna. "Not like Doc Howard and Mills really care about our grades."

"Yes, but I really, really care."

"Then I'll kiss and make it better later," Pockets said.

Nevada gagged as loudly as possible. The only reason Lynna wasn't joining in was that she wished she had the opportunity to be mushy. Within the unit, there was only one other option for her and Nevada, and neither one of them had any interest in "Captain Ego" no matter how hot he was.

Before any of them could say anything else, the public address system beeped way too early to signal the end of lunch.

"Attention, students. Rowan Beltrami, Raymond Bennu, Nevada Brandle, Lynna Harrison, Ava Lanier, and Maria Sanchez, please report to the Main Office."

The office secretary repeated the announcement, but they'd all heard it the first time with their eyes widening and backs straightening with each name added to the list.

Pockets found his voice first, though he kept it to a whisper. "It's an Alpha callout." His words held a question in their tone, because this had never happened. The most the CIA had ever done was extract two of them from school at one time, a Bravo callout. Usually, it was one of them, a Charlie, as they had on Thursday to get Lynna to East Berlin in time for her op.

"Daemons on the move," Pockets said as they grabbed their book bags and went straight for the main office. He'd given the team their nickname a couple years ago when they'd first started going on missions. He was big into comic books and insisted they needed a proper "superhero" name. Lynna didn't care for the label, but "Daemons" had managed to stick, partly because it was a somewhat accurate description for all of them: half-human and half-myth.

Plenty of eyes followed them. Lynna didn't doubt the other students traded lots of rumors about the "special kids," speculation about what happened at their private school. Much as the talk behind her back annoyed Lynna, what troubled her more today was the fear she might not be here tomorrow to jam with Patrick.

Chapter 3: Lynna

Monday, 24 January 1983

The ride from West Chester High to the Greenhouse offered no answers. The driver fell into the same category as most of their campus guards: buzz cut, no-neck freaks who silently screamed "military" even wearing a dress shirt and khakis. These guys rarely spoke and typically knew even less.

Lynna sat next to the driver side window in the back row. Maria and Pockets had taken the middle seats with Nevada riding shotgun in silence.

Her "little sister" Ava sat next to her. The freshman had adapted best to high school life out of all of the Daemons. Her numerous calls to classmates after school and on the weekends had single-handedly provoked Dr. Howard into placing limits on phone usage, which included a signup sheet. That only turned blocks of phone time into a form of currency that some of the unit children sold off to get out of chores. Ava cleaned the bathrooms a lot.

"They've only ever called me in one time for that Charlie to West Berlin." Ava vibrated with an enthusiasm that Lynna's sore shoulder didn't share. "This must be as big as the Atlantic."

Lynna understood her reaction. The CIA had pulled her out of school for her first Charlie more than a year ago. Sure, she'd been excited to put all of her life's training to the test, but getting to walk in the open without some agent shadowing her every step had offered even more excitement. She'd gone to Spain and tracked a high-priority target as they drove and walked around Madrid. The agents on the ground never realized a teenage dragon acted as their "eyes in the sky," radioing in the target's movements. They'd given her money to spend in the event of an emergency, but instead, she'd used it to buy three empanadas from a street vendor. She'd only intended to buy one of the savory snacks, but the pastry and beef filling were unlike anything she'd ever eaten at the Greenhouse. Fortunately, that was after the operation ended, because she might have had trouble getting airborne after all that food.

"If we're lucky, it's nothing." Lynna did her best to sound like she believed it, but judging from Ava's raised eyebrows, she wasn't buying it.

"It better be more than nothing." Raymond slouched on the opposite side of Ava. A pair of aviator sunglasses hid his eyes. Sadly, nothing could hide the stench of cigarette smoke coming off of him. "I was making out with Constance Wilson in the chemistry lab."

Pockets reached back and high-fived Raymond.

Lynna rolled her eyes. "In the chemistry lab... Yes, that would be an appropriate place for a walking petri dish like you."

Raymond flashed a ready-for-his-close-up smile. Only he would take an insult like that as a compliment.

The trip to the Greenhouse campus took another fifteen minutes and placed them at the westernmost edges of Chesterfield County, near the border with Powhatan—so basically in the middle of nowhere. Their driver turned onto a long private road with a red, black, and white "Restricted Area/No Trespassing" sign halfway down it that included a lot of small print spelling out that under federal law violators could have their heads and other body parts shot off—not in those exact words, of course. Tall trees crowded in the narrow driveway on each side. A ten-foot tall chain-link fence, complete with razor wire winding its way along the top, added another layer of deterrent. The gate parted for their van after the driver hit a button on the dashboard.

Almost as soon as they were through the gate, the driver turned left towards the main campus. The buildings lined up in perfect right angles, but other than that, no effort had been made to make them fit together. Four barracks buildings, including the one where Lynna lived, sat along the left side of the parking lot. The actual headquarters for the Greenhouse loomed to the right, a gothic mansion shaped like an uppercase L, when viewed from above. The mansion had belonged to one of Virginia's nineteenth century tobacco kings, but his family's fortune dried up before they finished construction. The government had snatched it up at a pittance, or so Dr. Howard claimed. The two-story house included a third, underground level. The CIA had converted most of the space into classrooms, exercise rooms, offices, and a large dining hall where most of the hybrids and staff got their three meals.

The van stopped in a space near the mansion's entrance.

"You're to report to the second floor, west wing conference room." The military driver didn't bother with a look over his shoulder or even a glance in the rear-view mirror. He turned off the engine and climbed out, heading for the barracks building reserved for campus security.

Lynna and the rest of them hopped out and headed for the mansion. Dark red bricks formed the mansion's façade with the inside done in dark wood. An attempt at decoration was made, mostly during the past five years, with some large paintings, flags, and rugs.

The inside resembled a maze, because the government had finished the construction without the benefit of the original blueprints.

The smell of fried chicken followed them upstairs. Lunch would have just ended, and most of the younger students would be in the sublevel classrooms, going through foreign language classes before their combat training.

The quiet didn't last as they neared the conference room. The door sat open and before they got close enough to look inside, Lynna noticed three distinct voices. Dr. Howard and Agent Mills she recognized, but the third voice, a man's, eluded her.

Lynna entered the room with the rest of the group behind her.

"Daemons are in the house!" Pockets announced, his voice trailing off as he realized too late the mood in the room wasn't receptive to his enthusiasm.

A man in a black suit and a red paisley tie sat at the head of the table. Angry lines wrinkled his forehead. Some men lost their hair in a dignified fashion, but the way he'd grown five paltry strands long enough to reach across his scalp from ear-to-ear warned of some serious denial. That or he was very proud of those five overachieving strands of hair.

The stranger's pale eyes shifted over each of the hybrids as they entered. His scowl didn't change as he did so.

"Is this all of them?" he asked.

Dr. Howard stood on the far side of the table with her chair knocked back and her fists planted on the table as if she'd jumped to her feet to argue with this stranger. Her eyes softened as they met Lynna's. The doctor had been with the Greenhouse from the beginning, and she'd done her best to protect Lynna when the program's methods had become more aggressive and deadly. These days, Dr. Howard called the shots, but even Lynna recognized that the CIA had been undercutting her authority more during the past two years since they'd started sending the Daemons on missions.

"Take a seat, please," Dr. Howard said, also following her own instruction.

The conference room table was varnished wood with enough space to seat sixteen. Blue fabric covered the "spinny" chairs, and the wheels squeaked as Lynna pulled hers back. None of the Daemons took the seat next to the stranger.

Agent Mills pointed towards the man of the five proud hairs. "This is Associate Deputy Director Donald Brand from the CIA."

Mills kept his tone civil, but in the five years he'd been affiliated with the Greenhouse, they'd learned most of his tells. The way he sucked in his right cheek when silent warned of barely contained anger. The dark-skinned, well-groomed agent intimidated people, even when he wasn't pissed. He stood a solid six foot four with the kind of upper body that scared linebackers. Normally, he had kind eyes, but they were narrowed in a threatening manner.

"Atlantic huge," Ava whispered to Lynna. She pivoted her chair back and forth with her excitement.

ADD Brand didn't seem to notice Ava's comment. Instead, he pointed to the stack of manila folders in front of Agent Mills.

"Show them."

Agent Mills stayed silent as he clenched his jaw and passed around the folders to each of the Daemons. Lynna recognized the top sheet in the thin folder from the pages she'd smuggled out of East Berlin, although this copy was riddled with handwritten notes.

"A few nights ago, Ms. Harrison went on a mission into East Berlin to retrieve a packet of transcripts from a defection interview conducted by the KGB. Four unknown subjects killed our contact and attacked Ms. Harrison as she tried to escape."

The other Daemons all stared at Lynna. The CIA didn't permit them to share any details of their assignments, but they tended to slip each other fragments of the more exciting things. The look on Maria's face from across the table suggested she was upset Lynna hadn't confided in her about the Grey Women.

"Ms. Harrison failed to retrieve the entire packet. We only have the handful of water-damaged sheets she delivered to our analysts. Only fragments of information could be translated, but what we've learned suggests that the defector knows about the Greenhouse and its purpose."

The CIA trained their regular agents at the Farm, which was why someone higher up the food chain got the idea to call their unit the Greenhouse, since the children abducted at birth and placed here were cultivated in a more controlled and scientific environment.

Lynna ran her fingers down the top sheet of paper. Light grey smears with clusters of Cyrillic characters covered the sheet. Each legible portion included notes from a translator. Her breath hitched as she spotted a name no one here had dared to speak in years.

"Zach," she whispered and choked on the dusty memories her voice had stirred. In the brief silence, she shifted her attention back across the table to glare at Raymond. He'd taken off his aviator sunglasses, and the ambivalence in his blue eyes only pissed off Lynna even more.

"We don't know who the defector is." Brand flipped through the pages in front of him. "The information we retrieved only includes the most tedious of details. It contains a list of names that includes staff members, many of whom are no longer affiliated with the Greenhouse. The list is out of context, so we don't know if the defector was simply supplying a list of people the KGB could look into or if they were mentioned for other reasons. We are investigating the activities of all mentioned, though, to make certain."

The names included Dr. Howard, and Lynna wondered if that was why she'd been so angry with Brand when they'd entered the conference room.

"One name on the list doesn't have an obvious connection to your unit, though." He held up a sheet near the bottom of the thin stack, a brief bio that included a photo that had been attached by a paperclip to the upper right corner when it was photocopied. The picture, rendered black and white by the copier machine, looked taken from a driver's license. The man had short, light-colored hair, bright eyes that his profile described as blue, and a pleasant smile and a well-trimmed goatee. "We believe Dr. Calum R. Taggart refers to an English professor in South Carolina. Not only has he never been affiliated with the Greenhouse, but he has no direct or secondary connections to the CIA."

Lynna studied the professor's picture more closely. Did he look familiar? Did she want him to? Something stirred in the dustbin of her brain, but she couldn't make it click.

"Ms. Harrison?"

Lynna looked up at the ADD whose grey eyes appraised her in a disapproving fashion. What had she done?

"Would you share details about the subjects you encountered in East Berlin?"

She cleared her throat, not sure what to say now that she'd been given permission to share. What she eventually said came out in a random pause-filled jumble.

"There were four of them. All women. They weren't human, or they might have been hybrids, like us. I'm not sure, but they stepped out of a third story window and landed like it was as easy as taking the bottom step on a set of stairs. They had grey skin and black hair and pointed ears. I'm not sure if they always look like that or if they're like me and can change to a more human appearance. They were all armed with guns or rifles and long, curved daggers. They could move fast and were trained to fight." Pain rippled through her shoulder blade, reminding her of the strength behind the dagger throw that had knocked her off the side of a building. "They were stronger than a human, too."

She'd avoided looking at anyone as she shared the details, but their collective silence drew her eyes back up to them. The Daemons responded with a mixture of shock and fascination. After all, there was a strange comfort to know there were others like them out there.

But the contrast of Dr. Howard and ADD Brand's reactions chilled her. The doctor's features pinched with worry. Brand, though? The smug curve of his lips suggested he'd just won an argument.

"There's every reason to believe," Brand said, "that these subjects might have been working with the KGB or East Germany's Stasi."

Agent Mills clenched his fist so tight it turned his dark brown knuckles a few shades lighter. Crap. What had Lynna done?

Whatever had Mills so ticked, he kept silent, letting Brand continue. "An agent we have in Moscow has tipped us off that the KGB will be flying this defector into West Berlin tomorrow. Mr. Bennu, Ms. Harrison, and Ms. Lanier, we're deploying you to provide backup to our agent in West Berlin." Ava's chair squeaked as she hopped in place with a muffled "Yes!" loud enough for only Lynna to hear her. "The rest of you will accompany Agent Vale to South Carolina to look into Dr. Taggart."

"Director Brand, I'd like a word alone before you go any further." Dr. Howard kept her tone polite, but she chewed out the words and glared at the director.

Brand rolled his gaze over towards Dr. Howard and made no effort to hide his impatience. "I don't believe that will be necessary."

"I do." Dr. Howard stood and turned her attention to the Daemons. "Children, please step out for a moment."

Lynna and the others didn't say anything as they stood and slipped out of the room. Pockets and Raymond exchanged nods before they got out of their chairs.

As soon as the door closed, Raymond went straight for Pockets and spoke in a fast whisper. "Where to?"

"What are you two up to?" Lynna placed herself in their path to stop them.

"The game room. Hurry up!" Pockets ran past her and down the stairs.

Realization hit Lynna and near choked her with panic. "Pockets! Tell me you didn't!"

"Of course he did." Raymond glanced over his shoulder at her like she was an idiot.

Lynna hesitated at the top of the stairs, but the rest of the Daemons ran past her to follow Pockets and Raymond. Looking back towards the conference room, she didn't see Agent Mills or anyone else following them, so she ran down the stairs to catch up to the others.

Chapter 4: Lynna

Monday, 24 January 1983

When Lynna reached the game room, she spotted the others hunched down on the far side of the pool table. As she joined them, she noticed faint voices, but they weren't coming from any of the Daemons. Maria held a finger to her lips for Lynna to stay silent while her eyes pleaded for her not to snitch on them.

A black circle floated up against the side of the pool table. The small void, one of Pockets' creations, measured at least six inches in diameter. This was one aspect of his powers, the ability to create a pocket from one place to another and eavesdrop on someone. What troubled Lynna most about his pockets was how they let sound travel between places, but light didn't. If they threw a tennis ball into the hole on this end, it would bounce out on the other side in the conference room, but you'd never see the ball until it emerged from the colorless void between the two holes.

Now that she was closer, Lynna recognized Dr. Howard's voice coming from it. "—full well they might be facing an enemy they know nothing about?"

"We know enough thanks to Ms. Harrison's intel."

"Intel!" Dr. Howard's fist slammed on the table. "Lynna was nearly killed! I was guaranteed these children would be allowed to enter into normal lives once DeWare was removed from his position."

A shiver shook Lynna's body at the mention of Dr. DeWare. The geneticist had founded the Greenhouse, selecting the children he wanted based on DNA samples taken from newborns in every hospital in the U.S. since testing had secretly started back in the sixties. He was one of only two people she blamed more than Raymond for getting Zach killed.

"That was under the Carter administration," Brand said. "Things have changed."

"That's bullshit." That retort came from Agent Mills. "The decision to make these kids operational was supposed to be limited to milk runs and long-distance surveillance. That was decided less than two years ago, well inside of the current administration."

"And who do you think gave the green light to push ahead with this? I'm acting on orders direct from the president. Did you suddenly go deaf while Harrison gave her report? The Soviets have made the first move! They're using their own hybrids. We've been pushing along like we're the only ones trying to develop these agents, and now we know the Soviets have not only been doing the same, they're ahead of us!"

"These are children whose lives were stolen from them." Dr. Howard's voice kept calm, but the hint of a shake to it sounded clear enough, even with her voice muffled by Pocket's circle being placed under the table. "This country owes them a debt."

"They aren't children, Ms. Howard. They're weapons, and this country has invested tens of millions of dollars for more than fifteen years into making them operational." The sound of shuffling papers could be heard. Brand packing up to go? "I have an obligation to the American people and a mandate from the president to do whatever it takes to ensure the safety of this nation and its people."

"Just not these kids," Mills said as one of the chairs squeaked from someone standing. "Right?"

"These 'kids' aren't even human." Brand then cut off what sounded like the start of a protest from Dr. Howard. "Fine. They're half human."

"That's more than you," Mills said, and then everything went silent. Lynna could feel the heat from the exchange of adult glares she couldn't see.

Ava squeaked with excitement. Maria threw a hand over the girl's mouth to muffle the noise.

The adults on the other end of the pocket didn't say anything to suggest they'd heard Ava. That didn't stop Lynna from glancing into the foyer to make certain none of the staff walked in on them.

Brand broke the silence. "Let me make something very clear. I expect Agent Mills to have Bennu, Harrison, and Lanier delivered to Langley Air Force Base by 18:00 hours for their flight to West Berlin. A car for Beltrami, Brandle, and Sanchez will arrive here at 15:00 hours. If they aren't dispatched on time, I will personally see to it that both of you are removed from this operation. And if any of these hybrids refuse to carry out their duties, I will go one step further and have all funding to this operation cut."

More papers were shuffled, followed by the snap of what sounded like a briefcase being closed.

"Agent Mills, walk with me. Ms. Howard, good day."

"Director Brand, you will address me as *Dr.* Howard."

"As you like, *doctor*." Lynna heard the eyeroll in Brand's reply.

The sound from the other side of the pocket ended. Then they heard two pairs of feet pounding their way down the stairs into the foyer. The steps came to a sharp halt, punctuated with a squeak of dress shoes on the marble floor.

"You weren't given this assignment as a reward, Agent Mills."

The Daemons scrambled to the edge of the doorway connecting the game room with the foyer. Lynna dared a peek around the edge of the white beveled frame. From this angle, she could see Brand's profile and most of Agent Mills' back.

Brand looked so caught up in delivering his lecture that he didn't notice the six pairs of eyes stealing looks from the other room.

"If you've gotten confused about why you were put here, then we can find someplace even less pleasant for you to learn the chain of command and the fine art of keeping your mouth shut. Your duty within this operation is to make certain CIA interests are being prioritized and carried out. Are we clear?"

Agent Mills' answer came out in a deep growl. "Yes, sir." His glare followed Brand all the way out the door. He didn't say anything until after the heavy wood slammed back into its frame.

"Shouldn't y'all be retrieving your mission bags?" He turned his head to look at the six of them.

Ava muttered an "Oops!" and Raymond cursed under his breath. They all scrambled to move at the same time, which only got them tangled in each other's way.

"And, Pockets," Agent Mills pointed at him, "you better hope the doctor doesn't find that hole you planted in the confer—"

"Rowan Beltrami!" Dr. Howard's voice came from the top of the stairs.

Pockets groaned. "Aw, man."

Lynna placed a hand on Pockets' shoulder. "It was nice knowing you."

"Raymond, Lynna, Ava!" Agent Mills snapped. "Mission bags. Now! We're rolling out in thirty minutes."

Lynna glanced over her shoulder as Pockets marched up the stairs to Dr. Howard. The doctor's anxious eyes met hers, and Lynna smiled to her, a silent promise she'd return safe and sound.

As soon as Lynna and Ava stormed into the second floor of Barracks Bravo, a light brown and black terrier raced out of Lynna's room and down the hall to greet them. Chewie circled Lynna until she scratched him behind the ear and then followed her back into her room.

The fifteen-pound furball had somehow dug his way under the fence and onto the Greenhouse campus a little more than a year ago. Lynna found him during one of their "capture the flag" games. His cute face with his big black eyes had distracted her and gotten her "killed." She immediately took him back to her room in the barracks. She feared Dr. Howard or Agent Mills would make her get rid of him, and while they weren't thrilled about it, Chewie's adorable face made it impossible to deny Lynna's pleas. She couldn't imagine living here without him now.

Chewie stopped celebrating over her coming home early as soon as he saw her pull out the army green duffle bag. He hopped onto the bed next to the duffle bag and pouted, giving her a guilt trip that would follow her all the way to West Berlin and back.

After she'd finished packing, she picked him up and hugged him.

"I'm sorry, little guy." He answered by licking her face. She laughed and set him back on the bed. "Thank you for the kisses."

Knowing better than to interrupt the classes in the mansion, Lynna wrote a detailed note for one of the girls on her floor to care for Chewie while she was gone. Normally, she'd have left her dog in Ava's care. Until now, they'd never been sent on a field assignment together.

Frustrated grunts and shouts came from Ava's room as Lynna took Chewie out to do his business. Seemed she didn't have her mission bag packed. By the time Chewie finished and Lynna had gotten back into the barracks, Ava was waiting in the hallway with her mission bag slung over her shoulder.

Chewie stood outside the open door to her room and stared after Lynna with a look accusing her of abandonment as she and Ava left.

They climbed into the van with Agent Mills in the driver's seat and Raymond riding shotgun. From the back of the van, Lynna watched the patch of rooftop above the front door. She remembered Raymond's blood rolling down the stone steps. The tinge of red had finally vanished a month later, but hints of the burn mark remained even after five years.

When the trees obscured her view, she turned her attention back towards Raymond. The boy leaned back in the seat with his eyes closed and jaw hanging open as he fell asleep. He had better hope she didn't need to save his ass, because she doubted she would.

Chapter 5: Nevada

Monday, 24 January 1983

Nevada got shotgun thanks to the two lovebirds wanting to sit with each other. Nothing against Pockets and Maria, but the more they whispered and muffled their laughter in the back seat, the more relieved she was to be sitting up front.

The only drawback to sitting up front was Agent Vale. The man driving the black Crown Vic resembled a recruitment poster for spies, with smartly trimmed black hair that had a hint of a wave to it, tanned skin, a black suit and tie, and a smarmy smile that suggested he thought he was the shit. He'd tried to strike up a conversation by asking about the Greenhouse. Nevada had answered with a flat "We're not allowed to discuss it" and slid on a pair of black frame Ray-Ban knockoffs.

That shut him up for about a half hour until they hit the interstate and left Richmond in the rearview mirror, not that they could really see any skyline from where they got onto I-95 south of the city.

"So, how old are you, Brandle?"

"Sixteen."

"Jesus," he muttered to himself as if she couldn't hear him. "Jailbait."

Could this lousy peacock be any more gross? Raymond said he'd worked with Vale a couple times and liked him, which should have been her first warning.

"So you all got drafted into the Agency from birth." He said that like it was some kind of hilarious, private joke.

"I think you're confusing 'drafted' with 'abducted from our parents,'" Nevada said as she pulled off her black leather jacket.

He hit her with a sidelong glance. His right index finger had been tapping at the steering wheel the entire way, but the beat kicked up a notch.

"Surprised they let you wear that," he said, clearly meaning her Union Jack t-shirt.

"Are you kidding?" Pockets laughed. "Nevada there has at least three more shirts with the British flag on them. She's a hard core England-phile."

"Anglophile." Nevada pulled off her sunglasses to glare back at him. "If you're gonna mock me for it, at least get the word right."

Pockets shrugged. "You're just annoyed because I got to go to London twice last year."

Maria slapped him on the chest. "You know we aren't supposed to be sharing stuff like that."

Pockets muttered a curse. "Pretend you didn't hear that, Vale."

Vale didn't say anything, focusing on the drive down I-95 instead. The CIA would have told him the bare minimum about what each of them could do, but even when the Daemons worked with field agents who were "in the know," they weren't allowed to share anything about their previous missions.

Maria tapped Nevada on the shoulder and pointed at the radio. "Turn on some music."

"Whoa!" Agent Vale planted his hand in front of the radio, blocking it from Nevada. "I'm driving, so I get to choose the music."

He reached towards Nevada's knee. Reflex kicked in. She snatched his wrist and slammed his hand on the dashboard.

Vale screamed and the car swerved right onto the shoulder filling the car with a deafening grinding vibration. Pockets, Maria, and Vale all shouted. The agent jerked his hand back as she let go of him and slid the car back into the lane.

She took some satisfaction in the way he studied her with wide eyes. He wouldn't treat her like some pretty plaything after this.

Nevada felt the demon stirring in her as she spoke. "Don't touch me."

He held his right forearm against his chest, flexing his fingers as if to check if they still worked. When he spoke, the words came out with angry precision. "I have cassettes in the glove compartment." Under his breath, he muttered, "Christ on a cracker."

She pulled open the glove compartment to the jangle of plastic cases shifting against one another. There were at least ten cassettes shoved in there, each one a mix tape, labeled and with the playlist written on the paper insert. Her eyes settled on one labeled Led Zeppelin. At least the fop had decent taste in music. She slid the cassette into the deck, and it picked up in the middle of *Babe I'm Gonna Leave You*.

"Rewind it to the beginning," Vale said with his lips twisted in a snarl, then leaned slightly in her direction, although he kept his wounded wrist a little closer to his chest. "Please."

"I like this song."

"This drive is gonna take five to six hours, you'll get to hear it from the beginning."

Maria cleared her throat in that way that made it clear she wanted Nevada's attention to turn to her in the backseat. She didn't say anything and neither did Pockets, but the look on their faces clearly begged for her to relax.

"Fine." Nevada stabbed her finger at the rewind button. While the tape hissed its way to the start, she reached into her purse and pulled out a pale green thermos.

"No, no, no!" Maria snatched the thermos out of Nevada's hand.

The loud click and opening bars of *Kashmir* drowned out the faint growl in the back of Nevada's throat as she turned on her friend. She wanted to blame her reaction on the "demon" in her, but she knew better than to think it was an actual demon. That hunger and anger was "grade A" Nevada Brandle.

"Don't you dare even remotely think of opening this in here." Maria pointed the thermos at Nevada.

"Seriously." Pockets would take Maria's side on this. Guys always thought with their dicks. "You'll stink up the entire car."

"Fine." The word came out minced through her clenched teeth. "I'll wait until the next rest area." She took the thermos from Maria's hand and shoved it back into her purse. God's teeth, she needed a hit.

"Jesus, what's in that thing?" Vale's eyes shifted from Nevada to the lovebirds in his rearview mirror.

Nevada answered in a saccharine sweet voice. "Warm pig's blood."

"Sure." He drew out that single word enough to give it a couple extra syllables. Seems the CIA didn't think his "need to know" extended to her eating habits. That or he didn't believe it yet.

Blood charged her powers, but the docs in the Greenhouse had stopped short of letting her try human blood for fear it would turn her feral. They'd experimented with a lot of other options. Pigs had proven the most practical option for fueling her abilities. They'd once imported some chimp's blood for her to try, and that stuff had been the bee's knees. Never mind the rush she'd gotten from it, but she'd bench-pressed six hundred pounds without breaking a sweat. The hangover the next morning had sucked, a migraine brutal enough that Doc Howard had let her stay home from school and chew on pain pills like they were M&M's.

As loud as the music was, Nevada still heard what Agent Vale said under his breath.

"This mission is screwed from A to Z and back."

On that, they both agreed.

Chapter 6: Lynna

Monday, 24 January 1983

Lynna had never gone on a mission with Raymond, and the past six hours had impressed on her how much she never wanted to again.

"Do you think the water itself might have hurt them in some way?" He'd sprawled out on top of a wooden crate and tossed a baseball up towards the ceiling in the rear of the plane.

For all Lynna knew, this might even be the same aircraft she'd ridden in to get back home after her mission. They all smelled the same, with grease and years of collected body odor competing for dominance.

Her gaze burned over the top of her sketchbook. When the doctors in the Greenhouse had learned about her ability to manipulate water, they'd made her learn dozens of shapes she could form to maximize the physical force of her attacks, which was how she destroyed that car in East Berlin. She'd hoped that practicing her line drawings would deter the attention whore from talking to her. No such luck.

"If you mean, did they start collapsing into grey puddles going all 'I'm melting!'" she said, including a bit of flailing with her arms, the sketchbook providing some added effect, "then no."

"No, not like that." He rolled his head to the side to look at her. His expression softened as a quiet snore to Lynna's left shifted his attention to Ava, who'd fallen asleep within two hours after takeoff. The only reason she hadn't fallen out of her seat was the shoulder straps holding her tight. Raymond laughed and then looked back to Lynna. "What I meant is, did they appear weakened in any way by the contact with water? Some mythical creatures are supposed to have trouble with water, so I'm wondering if it's an advantage we can exploit."

"I think choking them with a stream of water shoved down their throats suggests they need to breathe air, so if you'd like to get close enough to place them in a chokehold, you have fun with that."

She'd recounted her run-in with the Grey Women in East Berlin during the car ride with Agent Mills to Langley. Raymond, with Ava as an eager accomplice, had pressed her into going through it another time shortly after takeoff. Since then, he'd circled back many times with different questions. He'd even pressed her about the Grey Women's clothing, whether they appeared to be wearing uniforms or if they might have been wearing something name brand or tailored to them.

He sat up, his legs dangling over the edge of the crate as he tossed the baseball back and forth between his hands. "What is your problem?"

She bit out a curse to herself as she gave up on drawing and flipped her sketchbook shut. "My problem at the moment is that I've started this same drawing five times now, because some jackass keeps interrupting me."

The ball stopped jumping between his hands. "We used to be friends. What changed?"

Her heart fluttered, not the way it did when she was alone at school with Patrick. No, the shakiness running through her entire body mimicked the panic from when she'd fought for her life against the Grey Women. This insufferable dick was so wrapped up in his little world that he couldn't even make out what should be as obvious as a full moon on a clear night.

"Zach happened." She flung the sketchbook and pencil into her seat as she stood.

He hopped from the crate and stepped closer to meet her eye-to-eye. "What happened to him wasn't my fault." The way those words twisted his face suggested he believed otherwise.

"They beat him to death." She refused to cry. Dammit, she wouldn't show this bastard the tears that hadn't run out yet.

"*They* beat him. *They* did it!" He kept his voice lowered with an anxious twitch of the eyes towards Ava, but that didn't hide the emotions burning behind his words, nor the way he pointed an accusing finger towards the rear of the plane, towards the West, in the direction of the United States and the Greenhouse. "I never touched Zach, and you know that. We're all in the same cage, so what makes me the one you blame? Why does a stupid guard pounding the shit out of Zach to turn on whatever powers he might have had fall into my lap?"

"Because you gave them the idea!" She grabbed a fistful of his red t-shirt and pushed hard, but he didn't budge, just stood there with his mouth hanging open in dumb confusion. "If you'd never taken that stupid swan dive off the top of the mansion..."

She'd never forget that morning, the guards shouting after the kids had fallen into formation with Raymond absent and nowhere to be found after they searched the barracks. Raymond had shouted the guard's name, the same one who later beat up Zach, from the top of the mansion and then flipped the bird at him with both hands. He'd fallen head first and cracked against the front steps, blood pouring out of his nose and ears. More screams followed, but then flames consumed Raymond's body with a slap of air like a hammer strike and a loud shriek. When the flames snuffed out, they left a confused thirteen-year-old Raymond sitting up with his hands stretched out in front of him and his entire body aglow in yellow light.

In the here and now, Raymond grabbed Lynna's wrist and pulled her hand away from his chest. "You act like I knew I'd survive. I was trying to kill myself."

"And if you had, Zach would still be alive."

He stumbled back from her until his back hit the crate. The wounded look on his face told her she'd hit the mark, and the sight of it couldn't have been less satisfying. When he looked ready to speak, his attention went to something past Lynna.

"What's going on?" Ava's drowsy voice floated over the low hum of the plane.

"Nothing." Raymond forced a smile as he shook his head. "We were discussing strategy in case we run into those grey things."

He met Lynna's gaze for a moment, those blue eyes almost glowing in the dim interior of the cargo hold. Then he headed towards the rear of the plane, taking a seat farther away from them.

Lynna forced down her anger and turned to face Ava. She hoped her reassuring smile looked more natural than it felt.

"Sorry we woke you, little sister." Lynna ruffled Ava's dark brown hair as she sat down beside her.

Ava didn't stay awake long, lights out again in a matter of minutes, but with her head leaning against Lynna's shoulder. She kissed the top of Ava's head. Her gaze fell on Raymond, whose head was tilted back with his eyes closed. He'd donned a pair of headphones connected to his red Walkman.

They had been friends. She and Zach were the first two children brought to the Greenhouse, and a few months later, Raymond followed. As the population grew, the three of them became known as the "First Years." Almost all of the others who followed were brought in when they were about two years old or younger.

Ava was the exception, brought into the Greenhouse a few months after Zach's death at the age of ten. No other child at the Greenhouse could remember a life before coming there, not that Ava ever spoke of it. Dr. Howard had placed her under Lynna's care, and she'd resented the responsibility at first. Didn't take long to realize Ava understood what she was going through in the aftermath of losing Zach. All the things they didn't need to say tied them together.

She struggled to remember when she and Zach and Raymond had been that close. What hurt most was that as much as she wanted to forget those times with Raymond, she couldn't do it without forgetting about Zach.

Chapter 7: Pockets

Monday, 24 January 1983

Pockets felt near-blind by the time they reached the outskirts of Columbia. Agent Vale took them down a dark stretch of highway labeled 277. Of course, Pockets had a skewed definition of dark, but with the time a little after nine at night, the green grass and trees on the shoulders of the interstate had turned into a wall of black. He'd tried to take the sunglasses off, but the headlights of the cars coming in the opposite direction and the brake lights of the cars in front of them blinded him.

"Quit fidgeting," Maria said as she fussed with the knot of his tie. "You don't have it right."

He tilted his head back to give her better access. "Have you ever tried to tie one of these things?"

"No, but I know what it's supposed to look like."

Reflex caused him to jerk back anytime her fingers got close to his Adam's apple. Each time, she would growl and mutter, "Stay still."

A ways back, they'd stopped at a rest area past the state line so Pockets could change into a suit and tie. Pockets had worn a tie before, but never for more than a few minutes. Years ago, the Greenhouse had wasted a week teaching them how to dress for different occasions. He'd decided then and there he never wanted to do anything that required a tie and loafers.

Agent Vale shook his head, his eyes visible for a moment in the rearview mirror. "If you two were any more precious, I might be sick."

Nevada snort-laughed. Apparently, her hate for Agent Vale didn't stop her from laughing at Pockets' suffering. Not that he cared much more for Vale. The guy's ego could fill the entire car, trunk included.

He couldn't hold back his relief when Maria stopped messing with his tie and patted him on the chest. "Much better," she said.

"Thanks."

She grinned as she leaned back and admired him. "I could certainly get used to you like this. You look awfully good in a suit."

"This car belongs to the Agency, so you lovebirds behave back there."

Did this guy ever turn off that mouth? Maria placed her hand back on Pocket's chest, this time as a silent cue to keep calm. He hoped Agent Vale could push this Dr. Taggart's buttons as easily as he seemed to with all of them.

The bright street lights of downtown Columbia were a welcome sight. Not that Pockets didn't prefer things dark, but at least if the overall brightness stayed more consistent, he could see better.

The city looked smaller than Richmond, but he supposed catching it at this time of day didn't provide the most accurate impression. Even with multi-story buildings on both sides of the street, this place lacked the claustrophobic impression that Richmond's downtown possessed. He could see where Columbia's Main Street ended at the front steps of South Carolina's statehouse with its green dome.

"That's the place." Agent Vale pointed to an eight-story building of grey bricks to their left. He swung their car around to pull into an angled parking space in front of the apartments.

He pulled out his handgun, giving it a quick check before sliding it back into its shoulder holster beneath his black suit jacket. "Ladies, do a 360 on this place and keep an eye out for our friend, in case he tries to climb out a window or walks out while Shades here and I go up to his place."

Nevada pulled open the glove compartment as if searching for something. "You got any two-way radios?"

"Nope, but you can lay on the car horn if you need to get our attention." Agent Vale didn't wait to discuss it. He climbed out of the car and headed towards the building.

Maria gave Pockets a quick kiss. "Go get 'em, Tiger," she said before getting out of the car.

Pockets took a deep breath and got out on his side. He'd expected this city to smell different somehow, but he supposed urban places all wore that same bland combination of exhaust fumes and dust.

Agent Vale's whistle echoed down the sidewalk. "Come on, Sunshine."

Pockets gritted his teeth and followed him through the front double doors of the building. He glanced through the glass door as it closed behind him to see Maria sitting on the hood of the car. She blew him a kiss, and he pretended to catch it before he went deeper into the lobby for the elevators.

Agent Vale leaned against the wall next to the far elevator door. The button for "up" already glowed a dull yellowish white.

"So, tell me, Peanut," Agent Vale said as he pressed the "up" button again, "how long have you and Little Miss Muffet been doing the dirty?"

"Pockets."

"What?"

"My name is Pockets, not Sunshine, not Shades, and certainly not Peanut." Now that they were both standing, he could see that Agent Vale wasn't that much taller than him. He offered the jackass his best glare and wondered if his sunglasses hurt or helped the effect.

Agent Vale broke into a smile. "That's what I'm looking for." He pointed straight at Pocket's face. "That right there. Just without the mouth working. I want you to look all tall, tense, and brooding. Want this Taggart guy off-balance, and you looking like that is just what the doctor ordered. Walk around his apartment, touch things, move them around a bit. Make him wonder what you're looking for without lingering on any one thing." He leaned closer towards Pockets. "Think you can do that, Sweetheart?"

Pockets gritted his teeth again.

"See?" Agent Vale clapped his hands in mock applause. "That's not so hard."

The idea of opening a pocket under Vale's feet sounded like a perfect plan right now.

They didn't say anything on the ride up. Fake wood paneling and uncreative, ballpoint pen graffiti born from bored minds during their thirty second rides covered the elevator's interior.

They stopped on the fifth floor. The narrow hallway included more of the cheap wood paneling on the walls but with a dark green carpet floor. Long, plain white light fixtures sticking out of the ceiling bathed the hallway in fluorescent light. Bass pounded from the nearest apartment to the elevator. The door vibrated in its frame and had a brass "E" screwed into the middle of the door, below the peephole.

Vale pointed to their right. "He's in G." They found Taggart's apartment next to the door to the stairs.

Agent Vale stopped in front of the door and cracked his neck before knocking. His fist pounded on it as if he had a grudge. After a minute, a pair of loud clicks could be heard as more than one bolt unlocked. A chain jingled as the door opened a couple of inches. From his angle, Pockets couldn't see the person inside.

Agent Vale held up his credentials. "Dr. Taggart, I'm Agent Elliot Vale with the CIA. My partner and I would like a minute of your time. May we come in?"

"CIA? Is this some sort of joke?" The Scottish lilt to Dr. Taggart's voice suggested his time in the U.S. had tamed his accent without killing it.

"No, sir. We have a few questions we'd like to ask."

"About?"

Agent Vale snapped shut the wallet holding his credentials and slid it back into his jacket's breast pocket. "I'd prefer not to discuss that in a public hallway."

"And I'd prefer to go to bed."

Vale sighed with unhidden irritation. "We aren't here to arrest you or charge you with anything. We just have some questions. Fail to cooperate and that could change."

"I don't see how, when I've done nothing illegal." The doctor sounded more amused than perturbed. If Agent Vale had hoped to intimidate him, he'd missed the entire target.

Vale stepped closer to the open door. "You were mentioned in a list of names contained in a report taken from a KGB agent last week, and Dr. Calum R. Taggart isn't exactly hitting any top ten lists of popular names in the U.S. or Scotland, or any other country for that matter."

The resulting pause made Pockets really wish he could see the look on Dr. Taggart's face. When the man answered, the words came out in a slow, considered pace. "What kind of report?"

Agent Vale swaggered as he stepped back from the door. "Sorry. Public hallway."

"Fine." The way Dr. Taggart said the word added an extra syllable to it.

The door shut for a moment as the chain rattled free of its track and then jerked back open.

Pockets followed Agent Vale into the living room of the apartment. He and Dr. Taggart exchanged surprised looks as they got their first impressions.

The English professor had traded in the well-trimmed goatee in his driver's license photo for a carefully sculpted beard. His dark blond hair contained white streaks above his ears and in his chin beard.

As for the perplexed look on Dr. Taggart's face, Pockets hoped that had more to do with his sunglasses and less with how young he looked.

"This is my partner, Agent Beltrami," Agent Vale said as he stood in the center of the cramped living room. Pockets contained his surprise that Vale had used his correct last name. With all the annoying nicknames, he'd suspected the guy couldn't remember.

Pockets hesitated as he tried to figure out where to stand. Agent Vale had instructed him to nose around the place and rifle through Dr. Taggart's belongings. Only, the room didn't contain much for him to mess with. A wooden desk with a chair was in front of a window with its blinds shut on the left wall. A round kitchen table, with enough space for four, sat in front of the kitchen. The desk had a black, metal lamp with an adjustable angle neck and a plain orange coffee mug packed with pens, but that was it. The walls didn't contain a single bit of decorative art, not even family photos or a calendar. This heathen didn't even have a television, unless he kept one in his bedroom. The door to the bedroom was shut.

"Recruiting you boys young, aren't they?"

So much for Dr. Taggart not noticing his age. Pockets nodded and added a "Yes, sir" as he walked over to the desk and picked up one of the pens from the large coffee mug.

"So, Dr. Taggart," Agent Vale said, pausing to clear his throat, "any idea why the KGB would have an interest in you?"

"No." Dr. Taggart crossed his arms and stayed close to his front door, not offering for them to sit.

Agent Vale responded without a word, staring at the man with the obvious expectation for him to say something else. Pockets abandoned the staring contest to walk over to the kitchen table. The kitchen looked as absurdly tidy as the rest of the place. Other than a French press and a knife block, the kitchen had an abundance of available counter space.

Pockets turned back towards the other two when Dr. Taggart caved and spoke again.

"I suppose there was that paper I wrote years ago calling *Lolita* a rubbish book with a narrator as unreliable as an alcoholic in a liquor store, but then again, Nabokov was more American than Russian by any stretch of the imagination."

"Can't say I've ever read it." Agent Vale made a show of pulling out a notepad and clicking a ballpoint pen to scribble something. "How long have you been living in the United States?"

"Moved here in…oh, 1963 after I finished college."

They already knew that. The bio on Dr. Taggart in their mission briefing packet had offered plenty of dates. Agent Vale was testing how honest the professor intended to be with them.

"And was that when you moved to South Carolina?"

Dr. Taggart nodded. He kept his arms crossed and one of his eyebrows inched up in obvious irritation at these questions.

"What brought you here?"

That produced an unexpected laugh. "There was a girl, of course."

"You two marry?" Agent Vale made a show of glancing at the obvious lack of a wife's touch to the apartment.

"No."

"Why's that?"

"Well, there was another girl. The first one didn't take too kindly to that."

The two men laughed at the joke.

"So when did you first meet Dr. Rudolph DeWare?"

The question murdered Dr. Taggart's smile into a hard line. "I don't know who that is."

Pockets walked up to the desk again, sitting on the edge of it. He grabbed the top half of the lamp and moved it up and down and side-to-side with lots of squeaks to accompany it. He hoped his anger at the mention of DeWare wasn't too obvious. To be sure he hid his anger, he stuck his fingers in the blinds and parted them enough to look down into the alley behind the building.

"Really? Funny thing that." Agent Vale tapped his pen against the edge of the notepad. "The KGB listed his name along with yours."

Dr. Taggart unfolded his arms and shrugged as he responded. "Well, apparently we are both doctors."

"Somehow I don't think a doctor of English literature has much in common with a geneticist." He pointed the pen at Dr. Taggart. "So why don't we try that answer again?"

"Then let's make this my answer." Dr. Taggart opened his apartment door. "I'm going to bed. Get out of my home."

Agent Vale sighed in melodramatic fashion as he slid his notepad and pen back into his jacket. He pulled out a business card and tossed it onto the desk.

When Pockets followed Agent Vale out the door, Dr. Taggart grabbed him by the arm. Pockets almost punched him but somehow restrained the urge.

"Beltrami," Dr. Taggart's eyes glared at him as if he could see through Pockets' sunglasses. "Unique name that. Don't recall you showing me your credentials."

"No, he didn't." Agent Vale had reached inside his coat, with his hand wrapped around the grip of his gun. "And if you don't take your hand off my partner, we'll arrest you for assaulting a federal officer."

"Is he one?" Despite the skepticism backing Dr. Taggart's hard gaze, he released his hold on Pockets' arm.

As Pockets walked out of the apartment, Dr. Taggart slammed the door shut.

While they waited for the elevator, Agent Vale rocked back and forth on his feet. "Well, that was somewhat productive."

"Is that sarcasm?" Pockets didn't think it sounded sarcastic, but he couldn't see any reason for this guy to be so cheerful.

"Are you kidding?" Agent Vale stopped rocking and then dipped into an accent that sounded closer to Sean Connery than Dr. Taggart. "'Beltrami... Unique name that.' Schmuck might as well have admitted to knowing all about your unit."

As they got in the elevator, Pockets realized why Dr. Taggart had shown his hand. "He wanted to see my reaction."

"Might have wanted to see..." Agent Vale's voice trailed off. He shrugged and then hit the button for the lobby. "I don't know, maybe to see if you recognized him?" He leaned against the back wall of the elevator.

Pockets cursed under his breath. Why would he recognize Dr. Taggart? The staff for the Greenhouse had changed little prior to Dr. DeWare getting booted from the place. Even after Dr. DeWare got canned, most of the staff stayed the same. Doc Howard got rid of some of the bad eggs, but as covert as they were, the CIA didn't seem to relish the idea of letting too many in on their secrets.

"Well, I don't recognize the jerk," Pockets said, his conscious mind fighting back a maelstrom of memories of needles, knives, and blood. "But it's obvious that man has something to hide."

"Yeah, and I want to find out what it is."

The elevator clunked and shimmied as it hit the bottom floor. The doors opened with a ding.

"So what's next?" Pockets asked.

"I think it's time to go back to school, buddy boy." Agent Vale waltzed out of the elevator.

As Pockets followed, he got the feeling that didn't mean getting them back to Richmond.

Chapter 8: Lynna

Tuesday, 25 January 1983

While most Greenhouse field ops involved working with agents who had no idea about the Daemons' abilities, one of the few exceptions worked in West Berlin.

Lynna considered Agent Victoria Morgan her favorite field operative to work with, and not simply because she was a six-foot tall, brunette badass.

Vicki returned to the safe house, a sparsely furnished two-bedroom apartment inside a fourteen-story building in the military's Sundgauer Family Housing area, shortly after noon. "I see you're all awake again," she said as she kicked the door closed behind her.

Lynna dropped her open sketchbook on the coffee table. Ava waved a hand in greeting to Vicki but remained fixed on the television, claiming she was trying to improve her German.

Vicki stepped around Ava on her way to the kitchen where she put down the three paper cups she'd carried in with her.

"This one's yours." Vicki offered Lynna one of the pale green cups with its white spill-proof top. She always knew the best way to keep the Daemons fueled.

"Black with a little honey?" Lynna peeled off the top and inhaled the steam. "You are the best."

"I look out for my agents." She lifted one of the smaller cups and held it out in Ava's direction. "Hot chocolate."

Ava jumped up and ran over to grab it, shouting "Gimme!" a half dozen times before chugging half of it. "Thanks!" Then she ran back to plant her butt in front of the TV, taking the occasional sip. Lynna was impressed Vicki had known what to get, since Ava's previous field op happened in October.

"Where's the pretty boy?" Vicki asked.

"He's been sleeping almost the entire time." Lynna had tried to do the same, but the sleep she'd gotten on the plane had her body baffled. That it was still only seven o'clock back in Richmond only added to her confusion and made the coffee all the more welcome. Making this trip twice in less than a week didn't help matters. She'd mainly wanted to avoid Raymond, given their conversation on the flight.

As if knowing he'd been invoked, Raymond strolled out of his bedroom wearing a white v-neck t-shirt and blue jeans.

"Oh, now this is unacceptable." Vicki held the last cup out of Raymond's reach as she examined him. "Bad enough you keep getting taller, but what's with this peach fuzz on your face?" She grabbed him by the chin with her free hand and added a "Tsk! Tsk! That is not regulation, mister."

"I'll do twenty Hail Marys after I've gotten some caffeine in me."

"I should make that thirty push-ups, but somehow I think you'd enjoy the excuse to show off." She handed over the hot tea as she muttered, "Making me feel old."

At twenty-eight, Vicki acted less like a supervisor and more as the merger of a surrogate big sister and a mother figure.

"What's the story on the defector?" Lynna asked as the three of them sat at the table. Ava stayed glued to the TV. Raymond took the seat directly across from Lynna, and that was fine by her. She didn't want him next to her.

If Vicki noticed the tension between them, she didn't show it. She stayed all business and pulled out a folded sheet of paper from the breast pocket of her brown leather jacket. "The flight from London he's supposed to be on will board in a little more than an hour. Should land at Tegel around 19:00 hours."

"Still no word on who they are?" Raymond sat with his left leg slung over an arm of his chair.

Vicki unfolded the sheet of paper and set it in the center of the table. "These are all the names on the flight's manifest. None match anyone associated with your unit or the CIA. You two can take a look. Maybe you'll spot a name we've missed, but I doubt it."

They both reached for the sheet of paper. As their hands landed on the page at the same time, they exchanged glares. He let go of the sheet but moved to the empty chair next to her, so they could look at the list at the same time.

This close, Lynna caught the scent of chemically fabricated pine that came from his deodorant.

The list of names didn't offer any surprises for them, not exactly. They didn't recognize any of the names, but one person was marked by a thick line from a yellow highlighter.

"Who's this?" Raymond asked before Lynna could.

"That's why we're still confident the defector is on the flight. Ivan Trotsky is KGB. Used to be the cultural attaché in the Russian embassy in D.C. He's stationed in London now."

"Why not take him into custody before the plane takes off?" Raymond asked.

Lynna rolled her eyes. "It's called diplomatic immunity, idiot."

Vicki scowled at her but didn't voice her disapproval. "He plays things smart, too. Rarely does anything to dirty his hands."

Raymond leaned back in his new chair but thankfully kept both feet on the floor this time. "Why can't we detain the person traveling with him?"

"We've got agents keeping an eye out for that, and if we spot the defector before they board, we'll take him then and there."

"You don't think they'll be that sloppy, though," Lynna said, "do you?"

"Trotsky isn't a rookie." Vicki shook her head. "There's also a good chance the Russians know we're on to what they're doing."

Lynna looked over the flight's manifest again, but none of the names caught her attention on the second go. "Any news on the murders of Mr. Marquardt and the guy who was driving the getaway car? Anything that confirms the Grey Women are working for the Stasi or the KGB?"

"Your pointy-eared friends? Next to no clue on all counts." Vicki rested her chin in the palm of her hand. "We know the Stasi went to the clockmaker's shop after a patrol unit found your driver's body in the street. They only removed his body and Marquardt's. If you killed any of the ones who ambushed you, they took the bodies with them."

Ava turned off the TV and wandered over to sit at the table. "So what's the plan for today?"

"We go to the airport, set up camp outside the British Airways gate, and wait to see the passengers after they clear customs. There are plenty of places to sit and watch. I brought some hooded sweatshirts for the three of you to wear." She must have noticed the confused looks on their faces. "This defector has intel on your unit. There's a good chance he'd recognize you, and we don't want to tip our hand."

"What about security cameras? Could we watch from the security office?" Lynna asked.

Vicki shook her head. "There aren't any security cameras at Tegel, and we aren't working with Berlin Police on this one anyway."

"Why not? Don't they have guards set up inside customs?" Raymond sipped some of his tea.

"Not my call. The higher ups think there's too great a risk of someone inside the Berlin Police tipping off Trotsky."

Ava jumped in her seat and clapped her hands. "We get to grab the bad guy?"

Vicki shook her head. "Sorry, kiddo. I've got two other agents already posted in the terminal. We'll have concealed comms for all of us. If you spot our defector, then you give the description to me and my agents so we can grab him outside the terminal and shove him into a car I'll have waiting."

Raymond glanced at Lynna, making no effort to hide his annoyance. "That's all we're doing here?"

"I want to keep you three hands-off. You only come in-play if those Grey Women make a move to interfere."

"Fighting fire with fire?" Ava wiggled her fingers in anticipation of using her powers. Considering Ava's powers generated a massive beam of light, watching her get excited about using them made Lynna nervous.

Vicki answered Ava with a wicked grin. "Exactly."

Lynna didn't look forward to a rematch with the Grey Women. Her shoulder had finally stopped hurting this morning.

"All right," Vicki said as she stood. "Let's grab your bags and load up. Time to snag ourselves a defector."

Chapter 9: Nevada

Monday, 24 January 1983

One advantage to visiting the campus of the University of South Carolina a little before 11pm was that street parking didn't offer much of a challenge. The campus was spread throughout downtown Columbia. Finding the Humanities Office Building took a while, though.

Agent Vale acted like he knew where he was going until he started backtracking. The limited signage didn't help, and all of the trees blocked most of the lamplight. After going in circles for a half hour, they ran into a guy wearing a white shirt and black dress pants. He smelled of garlic and looked like a server who'd gotten off work and was walking back to his dorm.

Nevada had feared the server dude might prank them and send them in the wrong direction, but five minutes later, they found the Humanities Office Building. From what she could make out of the building at night, it was about ten stories tall with a beige concrete exterior. Rectangles of the concrete stuck out on the right and left sides of each window, and the overall effect reminded Nevada of a four-sided cheese grater.

Agent Vale made quick work of the lock on the front entrance, picking it with two slender pieces of metal. Nevada got the easy part of the job, keeping an eye out for campus security.

Once inside, they stuck with the stairs. Dr. Taggart's office was on the second floor. Picking the lock on the office door took even less time than the main entrance.

Floor-to-ceiling bookshelves covered two of the walls in the office. Taggart had crammed so many books on them that he'd piled some books on top of shorter ones at any angle that allowed them to fit.

Two wooden chairs, avatars of discomfort, sat in front of the wooden desk. The desk itself wouldn't win any ergonomics awards either with its fake wood and slender metal legs.

The only expense belonged to Dr. Taggart's chair, a plush leather thing that creaked as Agent Vale sat in it. He flipped a switch on a power strip on the floor to turn on the computer. "While I'm doing this," he said, "you check the shelves."

"Sure," she said, drawing out that word, "because how long could that take one person? Hel-looooo... he's an English professor."

She went to the right side of the room and started on the far left of the middle row, pulling out books and flipping through them to look for any notes that seemed out of place or if anything might be hidden in them. She'd barely made it halfway across the middle row before the computer's irritated beeps and Agent Vale's cursing distracted her.

"Having a problem over there?" she asked.

Agent Vale rolled his eyes at her. "The bastard has his computer set up to require a password. I checked the computer and the desk for anyplace he might have kept the password written down, but no luck."

"Why don't we trade?"

There must have been something in the way she asked, because he fell back into the chair and slumped as if he'd found out the universe hated him. "You're one of those computer genius kids. Right?"

"Yeah, one of the benefits of being abducted right after birth by the CIA."

He stood without a word and offered her the desk chair.

When she sat, the leather creaked as it molded itself to her body.

Dr. Taggart's computer looked like some custom-made, IBM knock-off. The fat beige monitor sat on top of the hard drive, which took up a third of the desk.

Judging from how much the fan struggled, the stupid thing probably contained half of its weight in dust.

As she placed her fingertips on the home row of the keyboard, she checked if Agent Vale was watching. The Greenhouse had instructed all of them on how to hack computers and kept them up to date on all the latest changes. This past fall, the CIA even forced a hacker from the infamous 414's to instruct them as part of a deal with prosecutors to avoid jail time for hacking into multiple federal agencies, including the Los Alamos Labs. Nevada wasn't as good at this as Maria, and she'd never used these skills in the field. After taunting this arrogant suit for his ineptitude, looking equally incompetent in front of him would suck.

While Mr. CIA perused Dr. Taggart's dusty tomes off to Nevada's left, she tried the old standbys for logging into a computer. She plugged in "password," "123456," and a host of other overused passwords. No surprise that none of them worked, but she wanted to be sure before getting into all of the coding nonsense.

Five minutes later, she'd hacked into the computer. She didn't celebrate, though. She checked the two disk drives, one of which still had its boot disk in there. Agent Vale had already gone through the desk drawers, having unlocked the two that had a lock on them. The bottom left drawer had a large plastic container with about two dozen 5.25" by 5.25" floppies. All of them were labeled by year and class. A few of them were programs, including one for spreadsheets.

She went through all of the disks quickly enough, pulling up a list of files for each of them. Almost all of them were for the spreadsheet program, and if the labels on the disks and the file names were any indicator, then none of them had anything out of the ordinary.

"What is it?" Agent Val asked as he slid a book onto the shelf. "That computer insult you?"

"No, I'm wasting my time. If he has anything that vital on this computer, he's not keeping the disk in the same place as these others. For all we know, he's got what we need in his apartment."

"And that's our next move, if we don't find anything here."

She slammed a fist down on the desk, pulling back on it enough at the last second not to damage the desk. Sometimes, her strength got away from her. "This is stupid. Why don't we beat the information out of him?"

Agent Vale crossed his arms, leaning against the bookshelf at his back. "Because we don't have any proof he's done anything illegal."

"We don't? His name's on that list."

"So are the names of other people on staff with your unit, including Dr. Howard. Has she done anything illegal?"

The look on her face called him an idiot. "She's a conspirator in the abduction of several dozen children. Last I checked? Pretty illegal."

That only provoked a disinterested shrug. "I don't understand you kids. You all act pissed about being taken from families you've never even known, but here you are working for the people you blame the most."

The chair creaked as she leaned back into it. "And where would we go? We're teenagers, and it's not like we have bank accounts. Some of us have very specific needs, too, the kind that aren't cheap or easy to come by. Even though we depend on the unit doesn't mean we have to like it."

"Specific needs, huh?" He asked the question in the way that recognized he probably didn't want the answer, and she didn't offer one.

"At the moment, I want to get this over with." She pointed at the desk. "He's not hiding anything here, so if he has a slick in this room somewhere, then it's somewhere else. That leaves only his shelves."

Agent Vale pulled out a thick hardback book and flipped through it. "Well, if he's hiding something important in here, then he'd still want it easily accessible."

"Assuming he even has anything here. Why wouldn't he keep it at home? He might store it in a briefcase he carries everywhere."

"I'm not sure this guy would have anything hidden in here, but if he does, then this is our only likely time to find it. After our little visit this evening, I'm half-surprised he didn't come straight here to get anything he has hidden."

"Probably already knows we're watching his building." Nevada glanced under the desk and pointed a flashlight at the bottom of the drawer. She'd already felt around, but she wanted to make sure nothing was taped to the bottom and that there weren't any seams to suggest a hidden compartment.

She went through the drawers again. "Pockets said you're sure he's dirty."

"Oh, trust me. You didn't see the way this guy grabbed your friend's arm when we—son of a bitch." He hit his forehead in the most melodramatic fashion with the palm of his hand. "He's right-handed."

Nevada looked up at him from where she was on the floor. "So?"

He pointed to the shelves behind him. "So, if he's hiding anything on his bookshelves, then I'm probably on the wrong side of the room. These books are to his left when he's sitting at his desk."

He walked around the front of the desk to the shelves on the right side and stood next to where Nevada was. "Probably not the middle shelves. Too likely for some student to pull out one of those books," he mused to himself.

Nevada looked past him, first at the bottom shelf and then at the top. Once she saw it, she couldn't stop herself from laughing. "That's got to be it."

Agent Vale glanced back at her. "What?"

She stood and walked past him. Reaching up for the top shelf, she grabbed a beige dictionary with a spine at least three inches wide. "No one is gonna casually pull this monster off the top shelf."

The book thudded as she dropped it onto the desk.

She opened it and smiled.

"Jackpot."

Chapter 10: Pockets

Monday, 24 January 1983

Pockets got excited when Agent Vale placed him and Maria on a stakeout outside Dr. Taggart's apartment building. Then he found out that meant him marching around the outside of the building in the freezing cold. Okay, maybe it wasn't technically that cold, but his teeth still chattered. Would have made a great excuse for making out with Maria for body warmth, but she'd taken the building's heated lobby. He couldn't stay there, because Dr. Taggart would recognize him.

About fifteen minutes after Nevada left with Agent Vale, Pockets had set up camp in the back alley, staring up at Dr. Taggart's apartment window. The blinds being closed didn't hide the light still on inside, but no shadows moved in Taggart's apartment. Maybe the man had made good on his word and gone to bed while leaving on his living room's lights.

The alley stank of mold, and some of its puddles looked old enough to have developed their own ecosystems. The building had a single door with no handle on it, leading into the alley, most likely a fire exit. No one probably came out here unless tossing trash into the dumpsters. He wondered where the people living here parked.

Something moved out of the corner of his eye. He jumped back, fingers splayed open on both hands, the gesture he formed whenever he opened one of his pockets. Not all of the portals he opened led somewhere here in the "real" world. He'd learned to store things in whatever nether place served as the pathway from one hole to another. Among the things he'd stored were steel harpoons fired out of a cannon, a volley of bullets from a machine gun, and even hurricane-force wind gusts. That last one had been fun to capture when the scientists took him to a wind tunnel and strapped him into a chair nailed to the floor. When he released the items, they always came out with the same momentum and strength they had going into the pocket. When he'd started, he'd only been able to store up to about a dozen things, but thanks to some memorization training techniques, he'd taken that up to fifty. The docs were even discussing letting him experiment with storing living things, starting with mice and moving up to attack dogs, because while in the pocket, the items never aged. They'd tested it by tossing a stopwatch in a pocket and then pulling it out an hour later. He couldn't exactly explain how he tracked the inventory, but some instinct helped him recall what he needed, when he needed it.

His thoughts reached for something potentially non-lethal, a set of throwing sticks flung into his pockets by one of the Greenhouse's strongest guards, but he stopped short of opening the portal.

Maria appeared, seemingly out of thin air, next to the building about ten feet away from him. That was part of her power, the ability to turn invisible and pass through solid objects. She also moved a lot faster when she turned intangible—maybe not all DC Comics' Flash fast, but still superhuman fast.

He relaxed his posture, releasing his grip on the pocket he'd planned to open. "Thought you were guarding the lobby." He couldn't resist a smile at her that confessed he was glad to see her.

Maria got close enough for him to see the taught lines of her face, not scared or troubled—just determined. She walked straight up to him and pulled him into a kiss. He didn't fight her. Her body pressed against his, and he melted against her. They'd been going together for a year. They'd managed to have sex by occasionally sneaking out into the woods on the Greenhouse campus. Their lust for one another wasn't anything new by now, but an unfamiliar need filled

Maria's embrace. He forgot the cold and focused on that kiss and then the next and the one that followed that as his lips moved down her throat.

When they finally stopped, Maria's forehead rested against his as they struggled for breath.

In spite of himself, Pockets laughed. "We probably shouldn't mention this in our debriefing."

She kissed him again, a gentle peck that assured him she didn't mind the timing of his joke.

"I love you, Rowan."

The words came out of her as a hard fact, and her determination caught him off guard. He leaned back to look her in the eyes. "I love you, too." He stroked her back with one of his hands, keeping her close. "What's going on? You know our assignment is to—"

"Screw the mission." Her eyes narrowed, and the way she said this held all the venom of a viper. "When are we ever going to have a moment alone to talk like this?"

"To be fair, we weren't really talking just now." He couldn't hold back his smile again, especially when she grinned back all bashful.

"Well, that's your fault. You distracted me." She pressed her fingers over his lips to stop him from anymore playful banter. "I'm serious, though. We need to talk, and this absolutely might be the best chance we're ever going to get."

He pulled her hand up to his face and kissed her fingertips. Then he nodded for her to go ahead.

"I've been thinking—really thinking—about what we overheard today, what that baldheaded CIA suit said to Dr. Howard and Agent Mills. I was glad you planted that pocket for us to listen in on them, because I've been considering this for a while now." She paused, shaking her head and no longer meeting his eyes.

"Thinking about what?"

She let out a long breath then tilted her head back to look up into his eyes.

"We need to run."

"What do you mean 'run'?" The question tasted like a lie as he voiced it, because he knew exactly what she meant.

"I love you." She placed her hand on his chest, above his heart which was still racing from making out. "Dr. Howard and Agent Mills… they treat us like people, but ever since the CIA started sending us on missions, it's getting more obvious we're nothing but property to the government. I know the Doc and Mills will do whatever they can to protect us, but what eventually happens when the CIA yanks them out of there and replaces them?"

Maria's question sucked all the warmth out of Pockets. The chill should have forced him to cling more tightly to her, but instead, he pulled back so he could pace as he thought through this. He loved going on their missions. He wanted to do more, a lot more than providing support to field agents. Dammit, he wanted to be the field agent.

"I don't think there's any point to this line of thinking." He held up his hands to stave off her counter-argument, but that didn't stop her.

"Really? Do you honestly think they'll ever let the two of us be together?" She snapped out the question as hard as a slap to the face. "No. They'll treat us like lab rats. And God forbid I get pregnant. What would they do with our child?"

"Whoa! Okay, nobody is getting pregnant." They'd been careful enough. Early in the school year, he'd paid a guy at school to purchase a pack of condoms for him. "Let's be honest, there's a solid chance we might not even be able to have kids together, because of whatever mythical what's-it's we have in our DNA."

Maria cursed under her breath, hands pressing against her forehead. "Dammit, Rowan. That's exactly it. I might want to have a kid someday. With you. At a minimum, I want you. I've known you all my life, and if our little experiment at being in a public school has taught me anything, you're the only one I'll ever truly want."

He walked back up to her and wrapped his arms around her, pulling her back into him. "No one is going to keep us apart. I won't let it happen."

"There's only one way to make completely certain of that." She rested her head against his shoulder. "We have to run. Not tonight, but we have to get a plan together soon, because after all we heard today, I'm pretty sure we're on borrowed time."

A pair of headlights blinded both of them, and somehow, things then got even brighter as more lights joined the first. Only these lights were blue.

"Oh, man..." Pockets muttered under his breath. It was the police.

"Hey!" A man's voice thundered down the alley towards them as two officers climbed out of the squad car. "Step away from that girl. Now! And keep those hands where I can see 'em!"

Pockets did as told, taking five long steps back from Maria who also raised her hands.

The two officers, both large white men in uniforms that clung to them like shadows, either black or a very dark blue, approached them. Both had their hands resting on the guns at their sides in their holsters.

One walked straight towards Maria. "Ma'am, this boy hit you?"

"What? No! Why would you think—?" She turned to look at Pockets and the look on her face explained it all. He hoped she was wrong, but the next words out of the officer's mouth confirmed it.

"We got a report that a man was assaulting a woman in this alley."

Dr. Taggart must have realized they were down here and called the police to sideline them. Odds favored he'd already made a run for it.

Their debriefing was going to suck.

Chapter 11: Lynna

Tuesday, 25 January 1983

Lynna pitied the traveler who tried to nap while sitting in one of the many blue cushioned chairs positioned outside the departure gate at Tegel Airport. They were designed to offer an illusion of comfort and little else.

The fog of cigarette smoke irritated her even more. The nearest offending cigarette belonged to Raymond, who sat beside her. He lit a second one shortly after they learned the defector's flight was delayed a half hour, in spite of Lynna's glare of protest.

"What? It's not like they'll kill me." The words came out in a mutter as the slender smoke dangled between his lips.

Lynna fought down the urge to snatch the cigarette out of his mouth. "Keep it up, and I'll test that theory."

His grin widened, and her scowl deepened.

"Fine." He stabbed out the cigarette in the ashtray next to his seat. "Of all the dragons in the world, I get stuck working with one who doesn't care for smoke or fire."

She didn't respond to his taunt. What she wouldn't give to have her sketchbook to doodle in, but she'd opted to keep it in her duffle bag while waiting in the airport.

Ava played solitaire with a deck of cards she'd owned since before she came to the Greenhouse. The cards weren't technically marked, but many had worn and bent corners. Some were torn. Ava growled her frustration as she flipped through the cards and lost every game. Lynna had taught her this version of solitaire shortly after they met. The rules were simple enough. She started by drawing four cards from the back of the deck, flipping them over. If the first and fourth card were the same suit, she could remove the second and third card. If the first and fourth card were the same face value, she could withdraw all four cards. The goal was to finish flipping through all the cards, one-at-a-time, without any left in her hand. The best game she'd managed today finished with eight cards. Judging from the small stack on her chair, with their red backs that included an intricate design of two angels riding bikes, this latest hand wasn't going to do any better.

"Look alive, troops," Vicki's voice cut in over their radios, the ear pieces hidden beneath their sweatshirts' hoods. *"The passengers are finally going through customs."*

A slight distortion made it difficult to understand Vicki, and Lynna wondered how well her radio would work while in flight. The lightweight headset fit over her ear and clamped into place. It pinched, but if it stayed on in flight, it was worth the discomfort. She struggled to use handheld radios while flying. The cords ran beneath her clothing with the microphone clipped to a bracelet underneath her right wrist.

She scratched the bridge of her nose to bring the microphone up to her mouth. "We're watching."

Lynna strained to look at the people going through the line. A glass wall separated them from the people inside, but she sat so far away that reflections of the lights in the terminal bounced off the glass, making it near impossible to make out details of anyone in there. The large crowd on both sides didn't help. The flight delay had placed the defector's arrival in the middle of the evening rush.

A pale man in a brown suit with a blue and green paisley tie hanging loose around his neck emerged from the gate. A girl who must have been close to three or four rushed at him shouting "Vater!" A woman in a black dress with white polka dots came up behind her and kissed him. Lynna wondered what that was like. Had her parents loved her? Would she have loved them back? Were they still together without her? The notion of a life where you went home from school and did nothing but homework and watched TV puzzled her. What could possibly occupy the minds of people like that without combat training and intelligence reports to study? Much as she envied that little girl, Lynna knew living like that would bore her.

Lynna glanced at Raymond. He glared at the open door as people walked through it. His words from the plane kept coming back to her. *"You act like I knew I'd survive. I was trying to kill myself."*

She'd never thought of it that way. The whole thing that day had been out of character for him. He'd always been the golden boy, and his being the first to manifest powers only added to his status. When it came to the Greenhouse staff, Raymond could do no wrong. Prior to last night, she'd only once voiced her thoughts about how Raymond's actions had eventually gotten Zach killed. Maria hadn't agreed and told her she needed to let it go, but Lynna had refused to. She remembered overhearing an argument between Dr. Howard and that bastard Dr. DeWare. Dr. Howard had argued against using physical violence to force the rest of them into manifesting their powers. She pointed out that Raymond's ability to revive himself might go hand in hand with an urge to make the process happen, that his abilities might have forced their way into being by instinct. That meant letting the rest of them develop at their own pace made more sense. Lynna pushed the memory aside, not wanting to let the thought reach its inevitable conclusion.

Lynna watched as more people came through passport control and customs. The process of going through both didn't take as long as she would have expected.

Vicky's voice came over the radio. *"The guy in the light grey fedora. That's Trotsky."*

Trotsky wore a heavy wool coat over a black suit with a solid red tie. His round head didn't turn to look at anyone. He had a large, flat nose and big ears.

If anyone had traveled with him, he wasn't worried about watching them.

"The bald man," one of the male agents transmitted. *"The tall one in the dark leather jacket. That's Sergei Sobol."*

"He's a big one," Ava whispered to Lynna. The guy stood a foot taller than Trotsky.

Lynna struggled to keep up with the sea of faces rushing out of customs. A few wore hats, which didn't help matters. A tanned man with a bushy mustache and a dark-red newsboy pulled low stood out, because he kept his eyes somewhat hidden by looking down at the floor. He didn't sprint but moved much faster than the rest of the foot traffic in the terminal. His path didn't take him right past them, but Lynna still got a split second look at his face before the crowd hid him from view.

The glance had been enough. Lynna's breath caught. In spite of all her training to not freeze up, the memory of the guards dragging Zach's body into the barracks overwhelmed her. The remembered stench of blood and urine hit her as fresh as the night she sneaked over to Zach's cot to check on him. Only one of his eyes had met her concerned gaze, his left one too swollen to see anything. He'd died an hour later, and even five years removed, she choked back tears.

Lynna grabbed the arms of her chair to steady herself.

"Did you see—?" Before she could finish asking, Raymond launched out of his seat.

"Stay here!" Lynna snapped at Ava before taking off behind him.

She navigated the crowd a step behind Raymond as she brought the radio's microphone on her wrist up to her mouth. "Detain the man in the dark red newsboy cap! White male, short black hair, mustache. He's moving fast towards the terminal's inner ring"

Vicki kept her voice controlled, but that didn't hide her anger. She must have realized Lynna and Raymond were going after the defector. *"Do not engage. Stay in the waiting area. That's an order."*

Lynna and Raymond ignored her.

The defector was Tobias Graham, the guard who'd beaten Zach to death.

Chapter 12: Lynna

Tuesday, 25 January 1983

The flock of travelers and airport staff clogged Terminal A of Tegel Airport. They moved with all the reason of ocean currents, finding the fastest way around each other as they sought gates, food, and exits.

Raymond could run faster than Lynna, but his broader shoulders made this crowd harder for him to navigate. She'd always been small and lithe, allowing her to flow through the travelers with greater ease.

She caught up with Raymond in that organized chaos. He turned in place, searching for Graham. Most of the people in the terminal were white men, businessmen commuting back into West Berlin from their day jobs in West Germany and other places.

"I have eyes on him," one of the male agents said. They could hear him moving quickly through the crowd. "I'm right behind him. He walked out into the inner ring and is heading for the taxis."

Raymond and Lynna ran for the nearest door leading outside. Terminal A of Tegel Airport was shaped like a hexagon with the gates running along the outside of the ring on five of the six sides. All the car traffic circled on the inside of the hexagon. It was easily one of the weirdest airport designs Lynna had ever seen but also remarkably efficient.

"Graham." Raymond growled the guard's name as if to speak it made him nauseous.

Tobias Graham had overseen security at the Greenhouse. None of them had liked him, even before he beat Zach to death. He treated them like prisoners. In a strange way, that was his only redeeming quality, because unlike the scientists and teachers, Graham never bothered with a pretense that they were guests or students.

"I lost him!" the agent transmitted. *"He went past the taxis and then I lost him in the crowd."*

Lynna and Raymond rushed out into the winter air. She couldn't half-see anything for all the people out there.

"Got eyes on him," Vicki transmitted.

One of the male agents answered. *"Same."*

"Move in. Now!"

Lynna spun in place, looking for Vicki or Graham.

"Crap! Where are they?" Raymond jumped in place, trying to see over all the travelers.

Some shouts went up far to their left.

"Got him!" Vicki transmitted. *"Subject is detained. Marino, get the van."*

"Come on," Raymond said as he walked through the crowd in the direction of the disturbance. He sounded deflated. Lynna understood. She'd wanted to make the capture for Zach. Even now, she couldn't promise she wouldn't blacken one of Graham's eyes or worse as payback.

She lightly gripped Raymond by the arm. "I know it wasn't your fault."

He stopped to look back at her, his eyes narrowing in confusion. He nodded once he'd pieced together what she meant. "It's fine. I've blamed myself. Sometimes, I even blamed you for reasons I knew were just as stupid."

She looked away to start working through the crowd again. "I've blamed myself a lot. Dr. Howard... I overheard her arguing with DeWare, saying he shouldn't start with me because she felt I'd made the most progress out of anyone at that point."

Raymond hesitated before he responded. His voice sounded strained in a way that had nothing to do with the prospect of facing Graham.

"It'd be nice to have a friend at home again."

She couldn't hold back a smile. "Sounds nice, but I don't like you."

He laughed. "Feeling is mutual, dragon lady."

They bumped their fists together.

The moment ended as they spotted Graham's dark red hat. Then Lynna made eye-contact with Vicki, who nodded to her. Vicki's lips were pressed tight, not likely to celebrate until they had their prisoner on a plane, headed back to the U.S.

Graham had his back to her and Raymond as they approached. When they got within arm's reach, Raymond lunged forward. He grabbed Graham by the arm and jerked him around to face them.

"Bet you never thought you'd see us again, you son of a–" The words stopped short, as did the swing of Raymond's fist.

"What's wrong?" Vicki demanded, but judging from the panic contorting her face, she'd already guessed.

This wasn't Graham. They'd apprehended another man wearing the same coat and hat.

"He's a decoy," Lynna said.

Raymond pushed the man away from him and forced a path through the crowd towards the edge of the sidewalk. Lynna followed.

"I don't see him," Raymond said.

Lynna focused her power. That yellow haze filtered her gaze for a moment as she only allowed her transition into her dragon form to reach her eyes. When she changed, her eyesight improved, allowing her to see more details.

The cars, taxis, and buses went through the center ring of the airport. Even with her improved eyesight, the traffic overlapped, making it difficult to get a decent look inside each passing vehicle.

"There!" She pointed to the far side of the inner ring. She hadn't spotted Graham, but she saw the tall man with the bald head, Sergei Sobol, climbing into the back seat of a black, four-door. The car jerked into the traffic, headed straight out towards the main road.

"Dammit!" Raymond took a step into the traffic and jumped back before a bus almost ran him over.

Lynna grabbed him by the arm to stop him from trying again. "I'll get airborne. You let Vicki know." They weren't allowed to mention their abilities over insecure comms, especially with agents monitoring who didn't have clearance. It also meant Vicki wouldn't get a chance to protest before Lynna got airborne.

Raymond bumped fists with her again and then ran back for Vicki and the others.

Within five minutes, Lynna was flying through the night. She'd taken too long and hadn't a chance in hell of spotting that car from above the airport. Odds favored their destination would take them into East Berlin through Checkpoint Charlie. She had to get within sight of it in time to spot the black car when it went through. She prayed they didn't go to some safe house in West Berlin or change cars.

Chapter 13: Nevada

Monday, 24 January 1983

The giant dictionary Nevada had pulled off the top of the bookshelf offered more than definitions. A white sleeve taped to the inside of the back cover contained a single disk labeled "Hunting."

The disk contained a lot of files with lists that weren't that long. Nevada opened each file. They were titled by the year and went back as far as 1961. The spreadsheets didn't offer any specific information, not exactly. Nevada started with the most recent file, which was for 1983, and worked her way backwards. One column appeared to contain letters with no clear meaning to them. Other columns used a set of abbreviations that didn't make any sense when taken out of context. The only column that didn't require much explanation was the third one. Each line of that column started with a dollar sign.

Agent Vale let out a low whistle. "Somehow, I doubt he's making that kind of money from publishing essays that call Tolstoy a hack."

Nevada nodded her agreement as she worked her way through each file, which were more of the same. If she'd taken anything from her economics lessons at the Greenhouse, crime not only paid, but it paid damn well for the more competent breeds of criminals.

"Can we make a copy of that disk?" Agent Vale asked as he drummed his fingers on his forehead.

"Probably, but I'm not sure how long it'll take. Our professor might be bringing in the money, but he's still working with a computer that's a knockoff piece of crap."

"If he's got a blank disk in there, let's copy as much of this as we can." He turned back towards the bookshelf. "I'll see if this guy is hiding anything else over here."

Nevada got to work on that. The floppy disk case in the desk contained about four blank disks. Odds favored this guy wouldn't miss one of those as quickly as the original disk he'd hidden in the big ass dictionary. Copying the disk did take a while. After a half hour in which the dual disk drive went through a variety of grinding sounds, Nevada got all of the spreadsheets saved onto the borrowed disk.

"Got it." She pulled out the finished copy and handed it to Agent Vale, along with the original disk.

"I'll let the analysts get their hands on this and see what they make of it." He took the disks, sliding the original back into its sleeve in the dictionary before putting it back on top of the bookshelf. His search through the shelves hadn't produced anything else of interest.

Nevada turned off the computer, the fan whining to a stop.

Agent Vale glanced at his watch. "Let's get out of here. We'll pick up the lovebirds and head to the hotel."

He cracked open the office door and peeked into the hallway.

The door flew open. The edge smacked Agent Vale's face and knocked him to the floor, toppling one of the chairs in front of the desk.

Nevada jumped back, knocking over the other wooden chair.

Standing in the hallway, outside the door, Dr. Taggart glared at Agent Vale and then Nevada.

The professor attacked her and moved fast. When his first swing missed, he shifted straight into the next attack. He could dismantle the average person with this speed and skill, but Nevada had trained in hand-to-hand combat since she was five.

They dodged each other's attacks until she grabbed his arm on one of his swings. Before she could slam her foot down on his knee, he grabbed her arm and flung her at the bookshelf next to where Agent Vale had landed.

A dozen books spilled around her, two landing on her chest. None hit her head, thankfully.

Agent Vale flailed in slow motion on the floor. Dark red lines flowed down his face. The smell of his blood teased Nevada's senses and filled her with an urge she knew on a first-name basis.

Dr. Taggart charged at her and slammed his foot down, aiming for her stomach. She rolled out of the way and then swept his legs while his balance was off.

They both scrambled back to their feet with Dr. Taggart retreating back towards the door.

Nevada ran her fingers along the trail of blood on Agent Vale's face, then licked her fingers clean. The shot of blood didn't kick in right away, but that taste invigorated her. Her breath shuddered as a tingle started in the back of her neck. A split second of vertigo purred up into her brain.

The chimp's blood dropped to second place, because human blood...that was far more than the bee's knees. That was the whole bee.

Nevada leaped up as Dr. Taggart came at her. She revelled in the rush of her heightened senses. Her brain burned in the most pleasant fashion, each thought zipping along twice as fast. Dr. Taggart's movements no longer matched hers. She danced around him, and her fist slammed into his temple. The pain should have brutalized her knuckles but didn't faze her. The scent of even more blood, Dr. Taggart's, called to her.

She finished him with a kick to his torso. He flew back into the hallway. Blood spit out over his lips as he landed on the floor. He gaped up at her.

A growl whispered up from the back of her throat. The urge to rip out a chunk of his neck and drink deep screamed for satisfaction, but the idea of being that close to this old man made her stomach turn.

She kicked him across the head. He dropped to his side. Eyelids fluttered as he fought to stay awake, but then they shut. The tension vanished from his body as he released a long breath.

"Please tell me you didn't kill him." Agent Vale groaned as he grabbed onto the side of the desk and pulled his way up onto his feet.

"He's alive." The urge to change that condition caught Nevada by surprise. The idea of killing someone thrilled a primal part of her, the half that didn't belong to anything remotely human. "What do we do with him?"

Agent Vale laughed. "Leave him. We were conducting an illegal search."

"But he attacked us!"

"Yeah, and he can claim he assumed we were criminals who broke into his office. That's not a conversation we want to have with the local cops and certainly not the FBI. "

Nevada swallowed the urge to kick Dr. Taggart again. "He's up to his neck in this. He has to be."

"At best, this guy is a hired gun. He's not what we're after, and leaving him loose to run might lead us to the person we really want." He flapped the disk in his hand. "This is what we want, and it won't involve playing cat and mouse with this guy in an interrogation room."

Nevada stared down at the dark red line running down Dr. Taggart's face from his temple. She wondered if his blood would taste as good.

"Let's go." Agent Vale stumbled into the hall, heading straight for the stairs.

Nevada hesitated, her inner debate still roiling. That they needed to leave Dr. Taggart here didn't trouble her, though. She leaned down and ran her fingertips up the side of Dr. Taggart's face, collecting as much of the tiny river as she could. She licked the blood off her hand and savored the rush. Oh, man. Forget the bee. That was the whole damn hive. She grinned as she walked away and followed Agent Vale down the stairs.

Chapter 14: Lynna

Tuesday, 25 January 1983

Lynna reached Checkpoint Charlie, but the black four-door never made it. Ivan Trostky and Tobias Graham entered East Berlin inside a red Trabant. Sergei Sobol's hulking body behind the steering wheel gave them away as they crossed the border, not that anyone else without an exceptional pair of binoculars could have seen him at Lynna's distance. She'd flown over the border crossing before the defector got there. With the night to cover her and no Grey Women to call attention to her, she perched on the roof of a five-story building two blocks from the infamous death strip.

"I'm going to follow them," Lynna said over her radio.

"We're still a few blocks from the checkpoint." Raymond's transmission came in faint. Their comms weren't designed for long distances. Lynna knew that might be a problem, even if Vicki got them across the border.

"I'll try to keep you updated on where they go," she said.

"If we lose contact, our rendezvous will be St. Nick's." The church had recently undergone reconstruction, and for Lynna, the church's twin spires provided an easy-to-see landmark from the skies. Raymond's next comment came in muffled, but she understood him. "Vicki's really pissed." Little surprise there.

Lynna didn't answer. Instead, she ran across the rooftop, leaped off the building and let her wings do their thing. Her dragon hide protected her from the cold.

Two hours passed with the red Trabant heading northeast out of East Berlin. She frequently back-tracked enough to get a decent signal on her radio to update Raymond without risking losing sight of the Trabant. She'd feared the others wouldn't be able to follow, but somehow, Vicki got them out of East Berlin and onto the A11. The long stretch of road helped with their communications, without any tall buildings to block their transmissions.

Lynna savored the cleaner air beyond the city limits. Her shoulder still ached. The strain from such a long flight didn't help with the pain, but she loved these rare opportunities to explore the skies. She never got to indulge in them at home. Dr. Howard feared someone might spot her or that a hunter in the woods might take a shot at her. Virginia didn't hurt for gun nuts.

As Lynna started to wonder when Vicki might decide to call off the pursuit, the red Trabant pulled off the A11.

"They're heading into Melzower Forst." Lynna circled over the highway before continuing the chase.

"Wondered if they might." Vicki didn't sound pissed anymore. She'd always been good at adapting to ever-worsening conditions. *"We've had reports they use a cabin there as a safe house."*

"I'll see where they end."

"We'll wait near the main road. You figure out what kind of security they have and then rendezvous with us. I'll decide what's next after that. Work quickly."

"Okay." Lynna hoped the radio and the wind hid how much she didn't trust Vicki to go in after Graham. Now that they were inside enemy territory, it created a lot of problems without easy answers. Given their special abilities, Lynna and the others could tear into that safe house and drag Graham out of there without much challenge. That's when the real problems began. Getting someone out of East Germany was hard enough when they were a willing participant. Graham would fight them the entire way. Even if they turned around to head back to West Berlin, they'd be cutting it close to get back over before midnight, which East Berlin required for anyone from the West visiting on a single day pass.

She ignored the potential problems and focused on following the red Trabant. Even with trees obscuring her view, she didn't lose it. The car stopped in front of a lone cabin in a clearing along the shores of a river.

The building was rectangular, but it hadn't always been that way. The main structure had been square and the additional rooms to the right were added much later, judging from its less weatherworn, darker shade of green. Someone had boarded over a window on the addition from the outside with what looked like leftover bits of wood. If the KGB agents planned to stash Graham anywhere, then it was in that room.

Lynna landed atop a tree within view of the cabin's front door. She watched as Trotsky and Sobol ushered Graham inside the cabin. The good news? No lights were on inside until they entered it. No one was waiting here for them.

Part of her wanted to go in by herself and take Graham. She knew she could do it, but she also knew it wouldn't be smart.

What would she do if Vicki called it off? They couldn't let Graham get away, not after all he'd done. He killed Zach, and the CIA only fired him. They should've thrown him in a cell, locked it, and lost the keys. She wished Nevada was here. If anyone would back the idea of storming this place to kill Graham, Nevada would.

She swore an oath to Zach's spirit not to pass up this chance, no matter what.

Lynna launched into the sky, the push of her legs causing the tree she'd perched on to sway. She flew over the river, and then regained enough altitude to clear the treetops of the forest.

She'd only flown a few hundred feet before she noticed something moving across the ground beneath her. Curiosity drew her back. Someone was walking through the forest, the movement little more than a shadow in the dark. Her heart stuttered at what she assumed she'd seen.

No birds cried out and no insects clicked their night song. The forest held its breath. In that stillness, Lynna found the source of the movement she'd noticed.

A thick tree branch near the roof of the forest provided a place to land and watch. Her spot placed her between the person walking through the woods and the cabin.

A ray of moonlight revealed a Grey Woman's face, crowned in long black hair. Going by the many faint crunches of footfalls on grass and the forest floor detritus, this one wasn't alone and there were far more of them here than when Lynna had faced them in East Berlin.

Lynna launched back into the sky. She struggled to gain enough altitude so the Grey Women wouldn't hear her speak. She hoped those pointy ears of theirs didn't mean they had heightened hearing. She pushed another hundred feet up to be safe.

"We've got company. How far out are you?"

"We're stopped outside the forest," Vicki said. "What kind of company?"

"The grey kind, and I estimate at least a dozen of them." When that news was met with silence, Lynna decided to add what else she'd noticed. "The one I saw is armed with a handgun, and—no kidding—a sword. They don't look like they're guarding the place. From what I can tell, they're preparing to attack the cabin. I think they're also after Graham."

A pair of pauses followed, separated by a clipped transmission from Vicki that took Lynna a moment to decipher as *"Stand by."* Not only had Vicki cut off the first part of the transmission, but Raymond's angry voice in the background almost drowned her out. Vicki planned to call off the op.

Backing off was the smart play. The odds stank to high heaven, even if their opposition had been the plain human variety. Even worse, the Grey Women were operating as a third party, so there was no guessing what their real objectives were. If they intended to kill Graham, then Lynna would happily let them do the deed. Retreating now saved their asses, but what if the Grey Women were hunting for the Greenhouse? Lynna and the others might save themselves today, but if Graham gave up what he knew, that placed everyone back home at risk and waiting for an attack that could come at any time.

That sickening sensation of her stomach floating in rough seas hit her as the reptilian part of her reached the obvious answer.

She had to get Graham first, and failing that, she needed to kill him.

The CIA had trained her from an early age to take that last step. They started with cockroaches, then frogs, and then cats. 'Make it swift,' they'd tell her. 'It's more merciful.' That's what they said, but she'd learned the lesson hidden within it. When you killed them quickly, you gave them less time to save themselves or to kill you.

Swift.

"Vicki, I'm going in, and Graham won't be coming out. Going radio silent."

She turned off the radio and dove.

Chapter 15: Ava

Tuesday, 25 January 1983

Minutes earlier, Ava woke as Vicki parked her grey BMW on the shoulder of the entrance to Melzower Forst. Even though she'd conked out through most of the flight to Germany, Ava had no trouble flaking out in the back seat of the car. She'd even managed to sleep through most of Checkpoint Charlie. Sleep was the best drug ever.

"Are we there yet?" she asked through a yawn that unhinged her jaw.

"Almost. Hang tight, kid." Raymond smiled back at her from the passenger seat. The moonlight and dashboard offered enough illumination for her to see his face and the way he rubbed the pads of his thumbs against his index fingers. He always kept his fingers moving, as if the urge to release his soul fire required him to burn off the energy another way when he wasn't igniting the world.

Ava felt something like that. In her case, the butterflies in her stomach burned off her energy. The need to move and act drove her crazy. Sleep was better, by comparison. In her dreams, she could tap into all the power she wanted and let those beams of light explode from her palms.

Vicki turned to look over her shoulder at Ava. She tried to smile, but the effort only heightened the tension on her face. Did people realize how much power flowed through their bodies, the way it twisted against lies and feints? The light of life moved like raging waters, shaping the land into its desired path.

Probably why some old people got more wrinkles than others, too much effort pretending to think and feel something they weren't. Ava liked Vicki a lot, but she was gonna get a whole lot of wrinkles. Well, if she got to old age.

Lynna's voice on Vicki's handheld radio disrupted the uncomfortable silence inside the car.

"We've got company. How far out are you?"

Vicki thrust the radio up to her mouth. "We're stopped outside the forest. What kind of company?"

"The grey kind, and I estimate at least a dozen of them."

Vicki cursed under her breath.

Raymond's hands went statue still. That, almost more than Lynna's report, warned her they were about to move on the cabin.

Vicki brought the radio back up to her mouth, but she hesitated. Her eyes narrowed in indecision. Before she could respond, Lynna transmitted again.

"The one I saw is armed with a handgun, and—no kidding—a sword. They don't look like they're guarding the place. From what I can tell, they're preparing to attack the cabin. I think they're also after Graham."

"We gotta get in there." Raymond slapped his hand on the dashboard twice and pointed down the dark road into the forest.

"Like hell." Vicki glanced back at Ava, as if hoping for a sign of agreement. Ava did agree...with Raymond.

"Lynna's not gonna back down, and I sure as hell won't either! That son of a bitch doesn't get to walk out of here!"

"That's enough!" Vicki pointed at him with the radio. Then she brought it back to her mouth as Raymond plowed on with his protests. "Lynna, stand by."

Ava leaned back. Was Raymond serious? Lynna never made a risky play. She always pestered Ava for being reckless when they played capture the flag in the woods around the Greenhouse mansion. If anyone went for risky moves, it was Raymond.

When the argument between Vicki and Raymond reached a level to hurt Ava's ears, Lynna's voice crackled over the radio.

"—cki, I'm going in, and Graham won't be coming out. Going radio silent."

"Lynna, no!" Vicki shouted into the radio. Silence answered. "Lynna!"

Vicki cursed multiple times, slipping through French and German and back to English, as she hit the steering wheel.

"We have to get in there." Raymond didn't shout this time.

Vicki clenched both hands. "We don't even know where the cabin is."

Ava took a deep breath and closed her eyes. She felt the beams of life all around them. The trick had always been ignoring them, not letting anyone realize she saw a second layer to everything. Relaxing the mental muscle that kept her third eye shut, she sifted through the noisy chaos of light. She found the beautiful blue and green pattern of Lynna's thread easily enough. The pattern resembled her mother's, something she'd never admitted to Lynna. While Lynna could never replace Mom, the day Ava saw Lynna's thread, she knew her heart had found a new home.

No one and nothing would take Lynna away. Not like Mom. Not again, and sure as the night sky was dark. Not. Now.

Ava sat forward and pointed down the road. "Straight ahead," she said, without opening her eyes. "Then take the third right."

Chapter 16: Lynna

Tuesday, 25 January 1983

Unlike the Grey Women, Lynna didn't worry about making noise moving through the woods. She flew over it, straight towards the cabin. Her mooncast shadow chased her over the water of the river.

Flight offered her only advantage against these Grey Women. She could still reach the cabin before them, but if they realized she was here and making her move, they'd probably abandon stealth and rush the cabin.

Be swift, she told herself. *And to hell with mercy.*

She reached high into the sky and then looped back, twisting in midair to plunge at the back door of the cabin.

The descent took less than three seconds. At the last moment, she tucked her wings in tight and twisted. Her feet smashed in the back door. She landed in the kitchen on a floor covered in reddish-orange linoleum.

Trotsky and Sobol were in the den. She'd caught Sobol tossing wood into the fireplace. Trotsky sat in an old chair. Graham wasn't with them.

Sobol reacted faster. He flung a piece of firewood at Lynna. She swatted the projectile aside with a swipe of her taloned hand.

Trotsky stood and snatched up one of two Makarov handguns on the coffee table. He squeezed off two shots as Lynna charged at them.

His first shot missed, and the second bounced off her left shoulder. The Makarov lacked enough power to pierce her scales.

Lynna feinted to Sobol's right and then leaped at him. She flew over his left shoulder. Her razor-sharp nails shredded his left ear, ripping off most of it and sending out a spray of blood. She landed in a crouch behind him, and the bald man ran towards the kitchen.

She barreled at Trotsky. He shot at her again. Both shots hit her in the center of her chest and knocked the breath out of her. She stumbled back a few steps. Dropped into another crouch and launched at him.

His next shots all missed and shattered the cabin's front window.

She jumped over him. Her nails slashed his face, drawing deep red lines in his flesh and gouging his right eye. Trotsky crumpled to the floor as he screamed.

The front door burst open. A Grey Woman rushed into the room with her gun drawn. Sobol found his courage again and shot at the new intruder.

Had any doubt remained as to whether the Grey Women were working with these KGB agents, it now ended.

Choosing to pursue her true target, Lynna ran into the hallway leading towards the cabin's addition. The doors to both rooms were closed, but she knew which one to open. The sounds of gunfire from the living room didn't drown out Graham's shouts demanding to know what was happening. Of course, the bolt on the outside of the door didn't hurt.

Be swift.

She repeated the two words in her head five times as she steeled herself for the kill. Her memories of the two cats the CIA instructor had ordered her to kill howled in her mind, almost pushing her out of this moment. The first one had been the easier of the two. The snobbish, grey beast had only focused on the CIA instructor. Lynna had walked into the room, grabbed the cat by the scruff and twisted its neck until it snapped.

The second one hadn't gone so well. The cat they'd chosen for her was a small tabby with greenish-yellow eyes. She still had nightmares of that cat and the way it looked at her. Those eyes stared up at her in a way that said, *"I know you'd never hurt me. I'm a good cat, and I just want your love and scratches on my back."*

She didn't remember killing it. Lynna recalled the instructor yelling at her to "Finish the fucking assignment!" Then she was in Dr. Howard's room, the same room she'd run to for help the night the guards beat Zach to death. She cried so long and hard that she fell asleep in Dr. Howard's arms. Part of her wanted to lie to herself, saying that if she didn't remember killing the cat, then it didn't happen.

Only it did.

Somewhere in the void between those two moments—between the instructor's shouts and Dr. Howard's hugs—the sensation of fur on her palms and that snap lived forever. The only sound worse than that was Zach's sneakers squeaking as the guards dragged him across the cement floor of the barracks the night he died.

That cat's trusting, betrayed eyes were the only reason Lynna didn't tear Graham's throat apart when she opened the door to his room in this cabin. He staggered back at the sight of her. When he'd last seen Lynna, she'd been thirteen and six inches shorter. He'd only gotten the one look at her in her dragon form, the night he'd beaten Zach. The bastard had dropped her best friend on his cot like a bag of rotting potatoes. Lynna had panicked and run out of the barracks in defiance of the strict curfew. She'd changed into her dragon form for the first time that night, the stress and terror that pumped her blood like a bullet train running through her heart had found its trigger. Graham had chased her towards the mansion, grabbed her arm. Then she'd changed, not even knowing she'd done it. All her combat training kicked in, backed by a strength she'd never possessed until that moment, and she flung him to the ground.

Five years later, Lynna was almost as tall as Graham. He'd always loomed over her and all the other kids in the Greenhouse. She learned in the stories they read for English class at school how people feared ghosts and bogeymen. Most of the Daemons didn't fear that stuff. They'd grown up with enough real-world monsters in their home. The way Graham looked at her now, she felt as if he saw her as the monster of his nightmares, and the thought pleased her. What she said next tasted like moldy air and sickened her.

"I'm your only way out of here alive. You have two seconds to decide." She didn't share that the alternative meant adding something bigger and more awful to her tabby cat nightmares.

Chapter 17: Lynna

Tuesday, 25 January 1983

Lynna led Graham back towards the den. The gunshots stopped. The only sound coming from the other end of the cabin belonged to Sobol's choked off attempts to breathe.

"We run out the back," Lynna said, "and you stay with me."

Graham answered with a weak nod. Sobol's death rattle held most of his attention.

Despite her warning to Graham, Lynna froze as she dashed out of the hallway towards the kitchen. The sight of the tall Grey Woman from East Berlin holding Sobol's lifeless body more than a foot off the floor startled her, but it was the six-and-a-half-foot-tall man striding through the front door that captured Lynna's gaze. Black hair flowed from his head in an unruly mane. His skin matched the Grey Women. He carried a black handgun in a holster on his right hip, and the golden hilt of a sword jutted out over the back of his right shoulder. His pale blue eyes narrowed on Lynna.

"Daughters," he said in German, his voice a deep rumble that echoed in a way that suggested he stood within a vast coliseum and not a cramped wooden cabin, "take them."

Lynna realized she'd stopped running. Graham had also halted, keeping Lynna between him and these strange beings. He must have realized the mistake first, because he bolted out the back door. Lynna raced after him. Less than ten meters out the door, the tall Grey Woman tackled Lynna from behind.

They tumbled across the ground, strewn with broken branches that snapped under their combined weight. The tall one recovered much faster, smashing an elbow into Lynna's face. The strike didn't draw any blood, but the inhuman strength of the Grey Woman knocked the wind out of her. A kick landed hard into Lynna's stomach, launching her off the ground. Her back slammed into a tree's thick trunk and sent her spinning across the forest floor.

A small voice in the back of Lynna's mind shouted to get up and defend herself. An entire river flowed less than thirty feet away, waiting for her to summon it to her defense. Only the notion to call on all that water came too late, because the tall woman descended on her again in a flurry of punches and kicks that gave Lynna no chance to get off the ground, much less fashion a line of attack with the river.

"You killed Katya, you monster!" A strike to Lynna punctuated each word from the Grey Woman. Didn't take much for Lynna to realize Katya must have been the one she'd choked with a stream of water hammering down her throat in the clockmaker's shop.

Another kick sent Lynna flying again. She landed deeper in the forest, pushing her farther from the water. Lynna's only consolation was that she didn't strike any trees this time. The distance she'd flown gave her a few seconds to get up onto all fours, and her effort produced a fit of coughs that spilled dark blue blood over her lips. Dizziness kept her from getting to her feet, causing her to sprawl onto the ground again.

"Father wants at least one of you alive." The Grey Woman loomed over her and drew a black Smith and Wesson from a holster on her hip. "It won't be you."

Lynna looked up into the barrel of that large revolver. A stupid giggle interrupted her coughs as she imagined this woman quoting "Dirty Harry," asking if she felt lucky.

No, she didn't.

That voice in her head screamed for water, but the shadow in the muzzle of the gun scared off the ability to summon the river to her defense.

She shook as she scrambled back on all fours, a task complicated by her wings. The last thought as the Grey Woman pointed the gun between Lynna's eyes was that she hoped she'd see Zach on the other side.

Then a light blazed through the air, blinding Lynna to anything for a few seconds. A welcome heat pulsed through the forest, followed by a scream cut short and the smoky stench of wet tender set afire. A sickening, burnt scent of spoiled meat followed.

As Lynna's eyes readjusted to the moonlight, she recognized the short figure striding up to her from deep within the woods.

"Vicki is super-ticked at you right now." Ava offered a glowing hand for Lynna to take and pull herself back to her feet.

"I got Graham out of the cabin." Lynna coughed up more blood and spit it out. "Where's Raymond?"

Loud pops and the whistle of bullets burned past them. The Grey Women rushed towards them.

Ava let go of Lynna and raised her hands, palms up. Energy thrummed out of the ground, up the girl's legs into the rest of her body and formed spheres of light above her open hands.

"Ljósálfr!" One of the Grey Women shouted.

The light from Ava's spheres met and then burned through the night in another large beam of blue-white light.

The Grey Women screamed as they dodged Ava's attack. Then a pillar of flames shot into the air from the front of the cabin, answering Lynna's question about Raymond's whereabouts.

"Are you okay to run?" Ava asked as she fired two more shots. One sizzled into the river, creating a large cloud of steam. The other toppled trees that groaned until they crashed to the ground.

Lynna got upright. Little chance of her flying, not until the damn world stopped tilting to her left. She considered changing back to her human form so she wouldn't need to worry about her wings snagging on the trees, but she feared the strain of the change might knock her out cold, that and her dragon form healed more quickly than her human one.

"I'll be fine." Lynna stumbled into the forest. Bullets whizzed past them and embedded themselves into the trees.

"I've got Lynna!" Ava transmitted on her handheld radio before putting it back on her belt.

"Get her out of here, and I'll catch up when I can," Raymond said. *"I'm gonna play for a bit."*

Ava ran ahead of Lynna. "Vicki's got the car waiting."

"We've got to find Graham." Dammit. She refused to leave empty-handed after all this.

"No, you don't." The answer didn't belong to Ava. It came from Graham, who emerged from the shadows. "I don't want those things getting me, and neither do you."

"Right, because we both know you'd give up everything about us." Even tired and hurt, Lynna still wanted to slice open his throat with her nails. At least they had him as a willing passenger now. If they could reach the car, then they might get him back across the border.

Ava fired more blasts of light to cover their retreat, but some of the Grey Women appeared to have followed Graham along the river bank. Wouldn't take them long to converge on all three of them.

"Keep in front of me." Lynna pushed him and Ava forward. "My wings can shield us from the bullets." At least, she hoped they would.

The gunshots from the Grey Women became less frequent. The bright, white circles of flashlights bounced through the woods at their backs. Ava's firepower had forced them to keep their distance, but the same glow from Ava that allowed Lynna and Graham to see where they were going also revealed them to their enemies.

"Ava, knock down some of the trees as we pass them. We need to make it harder for them to follow us."

Blasts of light sliced through the tree trunks. A particularly large tree took a hit near its base and whined as it tumbled. Curses went up at their backs.

Two lights that didn't move appeared ahead of them. The headlights and rumble of the BMW's engine greeted them as they emerged from the trees and onto the dirt road.

Vicki sat in the driver's seat, her body slumped over the steering wheel. She didn't move.

Panic hit Lynna with a burst of adrenaline, giving her the strength to sprint past Graham and Ava to the driver side door. She jerked it open and yanked Vicki back so that she sat upright. Vicki moaned. Her eyes fluttered open. A large bruise discolored the left side of her face.

"She was so damn fast." Vicki's words slurred.

"Are you all right?" Lynna asked as Ava pressed in beside her.

Vicki grabbed at her left side. "Dammit. She got my—got my…"

"Her gun."

Lynna looked up from Vicki to see the Grey Woman who'd spoken. She held Vicki's High Standard HDM up against the back of Graham's head. The former guard kept his hands held up as if the worst she planned was to cuff him.

"If I try to hit her, I'll hit him, too," Ava whispered.

"Get in the car," Lynna whispered so only Ava would hear her, "and move Vicki into the passenger seat."

"You're on the wrong side of this fight," the Grey Woman said.

"And what side would that be?" Lynna asked.

"We don't have time to discuss this here." The Grey Woman looked over her shoulder into the woods as the shouts of her comrades echoed towards them. She lowered her voice so that only Lynna could hear her. "If you want answers, then meet me Friday night in Washington, D.C. at the Lincoln Memorial. Midnight. Don't let your human handlers know. You come alone."

Lynna recognized the voice this time. "You were the one in the car with the knife to my throat."

"You need to leave now!"

"I'm not leaving without Graham, and we're waiting on a friend."

"The phoenix fighting the Erlking? Your friend is as good as dead."

Lynna laughed. "Our friend doesn't die."

"Nothing lives that the Erlking cannot kill. Leave now."

"I want Graham."

She shook her head. "I can't go back empty-handed, but don't worry. This one won't tell them anything."

The Grey Woman fired Vicki's gun twice, planting two bullets in the back of Graham's brain. He dropped to the ground with his eyes wide and blank.

Lynna screamed as the Grey Woman slipped back into the forest, leaping up into the treetops before she disappeared. She'd dropped Vicki's gun, which Lynna retrieved before making a quick check of Graham's pulse, which was nonexistent. He'd deserved worse than a quick death.

"Ava!" Lynna ran back to the driver side of the car. Ava had gotten Vicki into the passenger seat and buckled her into place.

"Take this!" Lynna handed Vicki's gun to her. "Drive her out of here. Raymond and I will catch up. I'll radio you so we can figure out a place to rendezvous."

"I can barely see over the steering wheel!" Ava reached towards her as if to pull her inside the car.

"Go! I have to get to Raymond now!"

Lynna slammed the car door shut and sprinted down the road. Fighting down her dizziness and nausea, she launched into the air where the road dipped. The way the Grey Woman had insisted Raymond wouldn't survive his fight with this Erlking hadn't sounded like bluster, more like an instructor scolding a student for failing to complete their homework.

Chapter 18: Raymond

Raymond sprinted up the road towards the cabin, the hood of his sweatshirt flapping behind him. He felt the souls around him. Everything resonated for him. People, animals, insects, trees, even the land, all whispered to him. This forest screamed with plants, making it all the easier to sense the Grey Women. What bothered him most was how much they reminded him of his fellow Daemons. If he hadn't lived with Lynna all of his life, he wouldn't have detected her so easily among all the noise.

The way he saw the world made it easy to navigate the nighttime forest. He never got a feel for the subtle details of a person's face in the dark, but he could see where they stood as easily as in daylight, even if he'd been blindfolded.

Gunfire erupted from the cabin. Lynna had started the party without him. He hoped one of those bullets hit Graham and killed him.

A Grey Woman spotted him less than a hundred feet from the cabin's clearing at the end of the road. Perched on a thick branch twenty feet up, she aimed her gun at him. He couldn't see the lifeless gun, but he recognized the shape of her hand around its grip.

He didn't stop running, because moving targets were harder to hit, even for the best sharpshooters. Instead, he shook his hands and fire erupted from them, dancing along his fingertips.

On the downside, running ruined his aim, even though his target remained motionless. He pointed his outstretched hand towards the Grey Woman in the trees and the fire burst from him like a flamethrower. He didn't hit his target, but flames wrapped around the tree trunk and the branch where she perched.

The Grey Woman leaped to another tree and then another, getting ahead of him. She screamed something in a language he didn't recognize, but he could tell she was calling to the others, warning them about him.

Their shapes in the forest all shifted, half of them abandoning their loose perimeter around the cabin to converge on him. He counted three in the trees and five more sprinting across the forest floor.

He grinned, because he'd never gotten to cut loose with his powers.

Reaching out to his right and left, he fired long streams of fire, creating walls of flame along the borders of the road. That brought up short the Grey Women on the ground. They fired blindly through the tall flames, bullets hissing around him. Bullets couldn't kill him, not permanently, but that didn't mean the damn things wouldn't hurt if he got hit.

Two leaped down from the trees and into his path near the cabin. The Grey Women shot at him at the same time he directed his fire at them. He narrowed the stream of the flames, targeting the guns in their hands. A bullet whistled past his head, distracting him for a second. He had a limited control of the fire he unleashed, not with the skill Lynna could make water dance, but he wrapped his flames around the guns in the Grey Women's hands. They dropped them before the fire could slip up to their arms.

They each drew a pair of swords and charged at him. He'd never practiced fighting people with swords, but he adopted the same techniques he'd use against people with knives: move fast and get in close enough to grab their knife arm and keep them from stabbing him. The one he got to first screamed as he wrapped his fiery hand around her wrist. She howled in pain as he intensified the fire sending it up her arm. Somehow, she still held onto the sword, but with him holding her by the wrist, she couldn't cut him.

The other rushed at him. Before she could reach him, Raymond slammed the elbow of his free arm into the face of the woman he held to knock the fight out of her. Then he shot a stream of fire at the other woman. She dropped into a roll, ducking beneath his shot and back to her feet right behind him and her partner.

The first woman collapsed to the ground, ripping off her burning jacket.

His clothes never suffered the same fate. Some kind of protective aura saved him from his own fire. Even non-magical fire couldn't harm him.

He unleashed more flames at the woman who'd ducked past him. She leaped away, up into the trees.

"I've got Lynna!" Ava shouted into her radio.

He reached the end of the road as Ava's ray of light blasted from the forest far to his right and across the water behind the cabin.

"Get her out of here, and I'll catch up when I can." He unleashed more fire into the air targeting some of the women in the trees around him. A wide smile parted his lips. "I'm gonna play for a bit."

Someone marched out from behind the cabin. Not a woman, like the rest of Raymond's attackers. The tall man zeroed in on Raymond. He shouted something to the women. His commands—at least, they sounded like commands—sent the women chasing after Lynna and Ava.

Raymond's flames raced across the ground towards the tall man. Before the fire could reach their target, the Grey Man raised his gun, aimed at Raymond, and fired a single shot.

Pain spiked through Raymond's forehead, and everything went dark.

Consciousness returned as it always did for Raymond. He saw a tiny flame flickering with the ebb and flow of his returning awareness, and then it exploded as if latching onto some unseen tinder soaked in lighter fluid.

He screamed as fire dispelled the dark. His body launched from the ground, hovering in midair for a moment, as if a ghost no longer confined by the laws of gravity.

When the flames lessened, he dropped to one knee on the ground.

He grinned up at the Grey Man, retreating from his fiery rebirth.

"Surprise, Gruesome." Raymond stood. "I don't die so easy."

His opponent didn't panic, though. He didn't even look all that shocked. Instead, he smiled back.

"A phoenix..." His deep voice rumbled. "What an unexpected treat."

"Yeah, well I've got plenty more surprises for you."

"Doubtful."

The Grey Man stalked towards Raymond. He took a single shot, but this time, he hit Raymond in the left leg. Pain tore through Raymond's thigh, knocking him off his feet.

The Grey Man came within reach. Raymond blinked, struggling against the pain, trying in vain to get the clarity to unleash his fire at this stranger.

"Have you never wondered why the world isn't overrun with undying fire-birds?" the Grey Man asked as he grabbed a fistful of the front of Raymond's hoodie. Then he dragged Raymond along the ground.

That gave Raymond the time he needed. He forced his thoughts into shape. He grabbed the Grey Man's wrist and the flames alighted from his fingertips to consume his enemy's arm. The Grey Man didn't scream. His grip didn't weaken. He didn't even flinch or slow in his march.

"I am not like my bastard daughters," he said, as if oblivious to the fire consuming the sleeves of his jacket and the shirt beneath it. Nor did his arm's grey flesh blacken or melt. "I've no human mother to weaken my elven blood with mortal frailty."

Blood ran out of Raymond's leg, but it wouldn't kill him fast enough to let him revive and heal his injuries. The Grey Man dragged him towards the river.

Desperation sent Raymond's heart thundering in his ears. Fingernails dug into the Grey Man's arm, but he couldn't cut into his flesh. Instead, he grabbed his attacker's leg, but the Grey Man didn't trip and fall. Instead, he stopped, turned, and punched Raymond in the face. The world blinked again, but not into death as before. Instead, Raymond's head cleared from the dark into pain. Blood spilled from his nostrils while a wild ache throbbed throughout his face.

Raymond unleashed even more fire, covering both him and the Grey Man in flames.

"Immortality is a myth, boy. All things end."

They reached the river, wading in and dousing his fire with a violent hiss of steam. Raymond struggled as they went deeper. Water splashed into his face as he kicked about, trying to get his footing, despite the pain from the gunshot in his leg.

"Even a phoenix can die." The Grey Man took them into deeper waters.

Raymond struggled to find a way to fight back, flailing for anything he might turn into a weapon. He saw the sword strapped to the Grey Man's back, but he couldn't reach the hilt to pull it free.

He bobbed in the water, his head dipping under and then back up into the cold night air.

Then both of the Grey Man's fists yanked Raymond up out of the water. Water ran down Raymond's face and into his eyes. He saw the sword's hilt over the Grey Man's shoulder. He reached for it, but the Grey Man held him at arm's length, keeping the sword out of reach.

"If one wishes to extinguish a bird of fire," the Grey Man said, his eyes narrowing with a look Raymond recognized as the hunger for the kill, "then they need only drown it."

The Grey Man shoved him down. Raymond sucked in a deep breath before the water covered him. He clawed at the Grey Man's arms, but he still couldn't hurt him. He'd not even scratched this man's skin.

He struggled against the water, trying to reignite his flames, driven by the insane notion he might evaporate the river.

The pain beneath his face increased, now from the pressure to hold his breath against the growing need for air. A thin part of his awareness noticed the Grey Man pushing them even deeper into the river. Even though Raymond could get his feet on the ground beneath the water, the Grey Man held him firm. He couldn't force himself back above the water's surface.

Air! He thrashed against that overwhelming need for oxygen, and then he lost the fight.

Water flooded into his throat as the river swallowed his screams. The cold liquid stabbed into his lungs. He gagged, trying to force out the water, but only more water replaced it. An invisible weight pressed on his body, and his arms went limp as he put all his strength into the need to breathe. But it was all wasted, because his world shrank to the dark waters of the river. Then it all went black, without even the promise of that tiny flame that had always called him back from the brink.

Chapter 19: Lynna

Tuesday, 25 January 1983

Lynna's second warning was the silence. The first had been the certainty of the Grey Woman.

Her stomach rumbled with hunger as she caught the scent of burned timber, reminding her of meals over campfires from her childhood during survival exercises. Raymond had left his mark on this place.

Pain where she'd been kicked in her side distracted her with each thrust of her wings, making it difficult to mind her surroundings for attacks. Nothing moved, though. Even the wildlife, what little there had been, had fled at the start of the fight.

She spotted Raymond's prone body on the shore of the river. She followed her training and didn't bite on the potential bait. Her flight path took her out over the river. Each second that passed without a gunshot added to her fears. No ambush revealed itself, not even as she dropped to the ground in a crouch a few feet from her teammate.

"Raymond!" She ran up to him and turned him onto his back. His dead eyes stared at the sky.

She grabbed his throat and felt for a pulse as she watched her surroundings.

The back door to the cabin yawned at her, the shadows inside provided a perfect place for a sniper. No shots came, though.

And Raymond's heart didn't beat. Why wasn't he reanimating? What had they done to him?

She planted her hands in the center of his chest and kept her arms rigid as she started compressions. Pain seared through her side as she pressed in on his chest as fast as she could. "One, two, three, four." She repeated those four numbers under her breath in time with her efforts, and when he didn't improve, she replaced the numbers with all the curses she could recall.

Even in her dragon form, the effort exhausted her, though it took longer to wear her out. When she couldn't keep pressing down on his heart, she collapsed back from his body and struggled to catch her breath.

She didn't know when she remembered to turn her radio back on, not until she was screaming into the transmitter that had somehow stayed attached to her ear all this time.

Everything passed in a daze after that, her mind desperate not to retain any of it. Ava and Vicki drove back to the cabin and helped her load Raymond's body into the back seat of the BMW. Vicki somehow managed to drive the car to get them out of Melzower Forst. Ava sat between her and Vicki in the front seat. Lynna had changed back into her human form before getting into the car, and while the effort didn't cause her to pass out, as she'd feared, she fell asleep almost as soon as they pulled onto the A11, headed back towards East Berlin.

Chapter 20: Lynna

Wednesday, 26 January 1983

Lynna was the last Daemon debriefed once they'd returned to the Greenhouse. The staff had kept them separated from each other as much as possible, but she'd talked to Maria for a minute in passing. She and Pockets had run into some trouble with police while in South Carolina, but before Maria could say more, Agent Mills had ushered Lynna into the conference room.

She managed not to cry through her debrief, not that she hadn't cried plenty in her room as she hugged Chewie while waiting for her turn. Everything in her had gone numb. That the CIA was still trying to figure out a way to get Raymond's body smuggled out of East Germany didn't help matters. His physical absence made it easy to "forget" he died.

She kept expecting to turn a corner and see the boy who couldn't die.

Only he had died.

She avoided looking Agent Mills and Dr. Howard in the eyes as she admitted to going against Vicki's orders and going after Graham. The man debriefing her never bothered to look at her. He asked questions, took notes on a yellow notepad, and occasionally reached across the conference room table to reposition the tripod-mounted microphone recording her answers on the tape recorder between them.

Much as she wanted to lie about some of the details, she didn't dare do it. Bad enough if she got caught in a lie, but worse if she caused the CIA to doubt Ava or Vicki's accounts and pressured them because of it. She omitted one thing, because it was the only thing Ava and Vicki didn't know.

"Is there anything else you'd like to add?" The question came from the unnamed man debriefing her. He still didn't bother looking at her. He held his ballpoint pen, the clear plastic tube with the cone-shaped cover resting on the bottom end, as if waiting to stab it down on his notepad.

Lynna hesitated. She'd omitted the Grey Woman's request to meet in D.C. on Friday night. Vicki had been too out of it to overhear their conversation, and Ava had been distracted with taking care of Vicki. The Grey Woman had made it clear that Lynna needed to come alone, but the CIA would never approve her for the op, especially not after what happened in East Germany.

Lynna answered with a shake of her head, and then remembered she needed to say it for the recording device. "No."

The man looked over at Dr. Howard and Agent Mills, giving them a chance to ask any questions they might have. Both of them shook their heads. This was the first she'd looked at them since sitting down. Dr. Howard offered her a sympathetic smile as their eyes met. Agent Mills kept his face stoic, but the red to his eyes betrayed his emotions, that he'd been crying. Certainly, he didn't cry during the debrief, but he must have at some point beforehand.

"Debrief concluded at," the agent conducting the interview paused to check his watch, "19:17 hours." Then he pressed the stop button on the tape recorder with a loud, plastic click.

Other than a promise to have a copy of the transcripts sent to Agent Mills for the Greenhouse's files before the end of the next week, the interviewer left without a goodbye. Agent Mills walked out with him, closing the door behind them.

Dr. Howard walked around the table to sit next to Lynna.

"You're going to be excused from all training between now and Monday. If you need more time, let me know."

Lynna sat up, surprised that the offer angered her. She wanted to break something with her hands. "I don't need that."

Dr. Howard reached over and placed her hand on Lynna's. When she spoke, her voice was soft but resolute. "It's not a choice."

"What about school?"

"We'll leave that up to you, but if you'd prefer to take off the rest of the week, that's fine. More time, if needed."

"I want to go." The notion of sitting around and doing nothing during the next few days constricted her throat.

Dr. Howard opened her mouth, as if she meant to protest, but then she nodded. Her grip on Lynna's hand tightened. Lynna responded in kind.

"We've made the school aware of Raymond's death." Dr. Howard must have seen the shock in Lynna's eyes, because she added, "We've only told them it was a drowning accident and that we're unable to share any details while it's being investigated. You won't be allowed to talk about it with anyone. Do you understand?"

Lynna nodded.

An odd silence fell between them. Something contorted Dr. Howard's features. She looked confused, as if debating on whether to say something. Lynna felt her breath catch. Did Dr. Howard know she'd left out something, that she'd l ied?

She hated lying to Dr. Howard. Of all the people here, Lynna trusted her most. She'd always been an ally and a friend, even during the bad years, shielding her from the worst of Dr. DeWare's tests.

Right before Lynna was about to confess all of it, Dr. Howard's features relaxed. She smiled and brushed a strand of Lynna's hair behind her ear.

"If you need to talk at any point," Dr. Howard said, "I'll be here for you, no matter the hour."

"Thank you." The words came out quieter than Lynna intended, too ashamed of her lies.

"You should eat. We told the kitchen staff you'd miss dinner, so they've put aside something for you."

They stood together, and Dr. Howard pulled her into a hug, letting Lynna rest her head against her shoulder.

Chapter 21: Lynna

Wednesday, 26 January 1983

The children at the Greenhouse lived in the barracks near the mansion. In the early days, they'd been housed in one large building like a warehouse filled with bunks and equipped with two bathrooms. Even before removing Dr. DeWare from the operation, the CIA had planned to construct new barracks because of concerns about puberty. Odds favored DeWare's "new" barracks wouldn't have been much better than the original, but the Carter Administration bent over backwards for Dr. Howard and built four two-story buildings. One belonged to the security team, but the other three barracks contained more than enough living space and even allowed a small, if cramped, degree of privacy.

Lynna lived in the second floor of Barracks Bravo, and as one of the senior Daemons, she oversaw the girls on her floor as their resident advisor.

When she reached her floor, she heard the shouts but focused on the sharp barks from her silky terrier, Chewie. The brown fluff nugget scrambled down the hallway to her, letting her pick him up and hold him like a baby as she rubbed his tummy. That stopped his barks for the moment. The girls had taken good care of him while she was gone, but he always preferred his mommy.

"Athena, shut up!" one of the girls near the end of the hall shouted from her room. "No one wants to hear you sing!"

"Fine!" Athena's head and her long curly brown hair leaned out of her door. "I'm sorry for being such an awful person!"

Lynna rolled her eyes. Athena could sing, but she never knew when to stop. Every month, she wanted to be a different singer. Her latest infatuation was Stevie Nicks, whose music didn't work with Athena's soprano range. Even worse, Athena thrived on melodrama.

"Athena!" Lynna bit out the name so hard that not only did the 12-year-old go silent, several other girls leaned out of their rooms to see what was about to happen. Lynna hadn't intended to sound that angry. She just—dammit. "Athena," Lynna said the name more gently this time, "at least close your door. As for all of you, it's already after 20:00 hours. Get your showers. I want everyone finished in time for lights out at 21:00."

No chance of that happening, but she could dream.

"Cass, you're supposed to be first this week. Get to it."

Lynna set Chewie on the floor and ignored the stares of the girls as she walked down the hallway to her room with her tiny furry shadow padding after her. Everyone here knew about Raymond and what happened in Germany. No doubt they'd heard how Lynna had put him in that situation by disobeying orders.

Chewie beat her into her room and hopped onto their bed. He fought with a blanket bunched up at the foot of the bed to get it into the shape he wanted.

Lynna closed her door behind her while Chewie worked on his "nest." She dropped onto her bunk next to her pillow. As her floor's R.A., Lynna got the largest room on her floor, but that also put her right next to the bathroom. That meant she heard every flush and each time someone turned on the shower or the sink

Pulling her guitar from its stand next to her bed, she strummed a few chords, but she couldn't find a song in her. She didn't realize she'd stopped plucking at the strings until the knock on her door.

Chewie barked and growled a complaint at the knock, but he didn't stir from his improvised nest. Lynna wanted to tell whoever it was to go away, but she resisted that urge.

"Come in."

The door opened as Lynna placed her guitar back on its stand.

"Is it safe?" Ava asked as she walked into the room and shut the door behind her.

"Barely." She wasn't sure if Ava understood her answer, because she'd mumbled it.

"How'd your debrief go?"

Reaching over to the flat alarm clock radio on her bedside table, Lynna turned it to one of the local rock stations. She didn't plan to say anything she wouldn't want the CIA to know, but she preferred to play it safe. Pat Benatar's *Shadows of the Night* filled the room.

Lynna lowered her voice as she answered. "It went." She shrugged and then curled up her legs to make room for Ava to sit between her and Chewie. "How was yours?"

"Super awkward." Ava sat hunched over with her hands pressed between her knees. "I've never seen Agent Mills and Doc Howard so…"

When it became clear Ava was at a loss for words, Lynna put her arm around the girl, pulling her close.

"It's okay." It wasn't, but saying otherwise felt better than dwelling on the reality.

The wall they leaned against vibrated as the shower cranked on.

"They asked a lot of questions about the Grey Women," Ava said, "especially the one who shot our target."

Lynna stiffened at the mention of the one who killed Graham. "Did you hear anything she said?"

"No, why?"

Lynna shook her head. "It's nothing."

"Do you think we're in trouble?"

"Were you truthful?" The response was automatic, almost a conditioned thing. The staff valued truth above all else, and that thought only added to her guilt about leaving Dr. Howard in the dark about the meeting for Friday night in D.C. Lynna still needed to figure out a way to get there.

Lynna's mind was busy running through possible scenarios for getting off campus unnoticed when Ava's answer pulled her back into the moment.

"Sort of," Ava said, and it took Lynna a moment to connect it to her earlier question.

Lynna tried to look Ava in the eyes, but her little sister focused on Chewie who'd shamelessly placed his head on her leg in a silent demand for Ava to pet him.

"What do you mean 'sort of'?" Lynna asked.

"When I saved you from that one woman, shot her with my energy beam, one of the others shouted something."

"What was it?" She remembered one of the Grey Women shouting, but she didn't understand her and assumed it might have been the name of the one Ava hit.

"Sounded like 'lo-sol-far' to me." Ava shrugged.

"Do you know what that means?"

"No, and Doc Howard says she doesn't recognize it either."

"Wait, so you did tell them about it? I thought—"

"I left out something." Ava's tone darkened, and she stared off into space as she continued to stroke Chewie's back. "I've heard that before. It was the night my mom and stepdad died."

Ava never talked about that. Even when she'd opened up to Lynna years ago after coming to the Greenhouse, she'd refused to talk about what had happened.

"There were two of them." Ava hesitated before the rest spilled out. "They were both women, and they had guns. They shot Mom and Dad in the den. Mom didn't die right away. She yelled for me to run, and then they shot her again, and she wasn't yelling anymore. I tried to open my windows, but they were painted shut. They came in the door. One of them said that strange word, lo-sol-far. They raised their guns, and then I burned them down with my power. My light destroyed most of the house. Took out some trees. The beam didn't get all of them. The lower halves of their legs were left burning on the floor of my room. I don't like thinking about the smell. Until that night, I'd only ever used my power to light a candle to read at night. Until then, I didn't know I could—I could do something like that."

She went silent except for her breathing. Her lips pressed tight as she rocked in Lynna's grip and continued to give Chewie attention. Lynna kissed the top of her hair. She whispered reassurances to her. She could tell her little sister was close to throwing up, but she managed not to.

Only once Lynna was sure Ava was ready for it did she ask the question.

"Did you get a good look at them?"

Ava looked up at her and shook her head. "The lights were off in the hallway and in my room, but…"

"But?"

"There was moonlight coming in my window. The way they looked so dark, I assumed it was because they were in the shadows, but…" She looked down, staring off into memory again. "They could've been. Grey, I mean."

Chapter 22: Lynna

Thursday, 27 January 1983

As soon as Lynna climbed out of the van at the student drop-off at school, she knew she'd made a mistake coming back.

"Surprised you came, too," she said as Nevada crawled out of the van behind her. She was the only other Daemon who'd opted not to take the out offered by Dr. Howard.

Nevada shrugged. She'd also been silent for most of the ride here. She'd never taken off her sunglasses, and based on the wrinkles in her red dress shirt, she'd excavated it from the floor of her room after a month-long stay there.

"You all right?" Lynna asked.

"Headache."

That made it seem even less likely Nevada would have come to school, but Nevada walked off to her first class before Lynna could ask about it.

Lynna headed for the nearest set of stairs to get out of the cold. People tried not to let her see they were looking. Among her watchers were other students, teachers, and even a pair of assistant principals. Thanks to her field training, Lynna couldn't miss their poor attempts to conceal their interest, especially as they muttered to each other about the "drowning."

Only one of her teachers openly checked on her, her well-meaning English teacher Mr. Roof. The one teacher who didn't so much as give her a second glance (or even really a first) was Mrs. Black. While she didn't normally care for her chemistry teacher, she appreciated this little taste of normalcy.

The only attention she welcomed came from Patrick. He came to chemistry class straight from gym, so they rarely got to talk before class started. Instead, he always sprinted into his seat in front of her desk seconds before the tardy bell went off. They never got to trade any notes, because Mrs. Black spent the entire class lecturing. This lady couldn't make her class any less practical. Lynna had learned the best household products for creating improvised bombs and toxic gasses before the age of ten. The only useful thing about today's lecture was how it annoyed her enough to distract her from everything else going to hell in her li fe.

At least, she thought it had distracted her, but when the entire class scrambled to get up and leave for lunch, she realized she'd zoned out and somehow missed that klaxon of a bell that meant class had ended.

Patrick turned in his chair and smiled at her. "Hey, you wanna have lunch in the band room?"

She nodded.

Not surprisingly, he'd reserved practice room number three, his favorite, and already had his drums set up. He usually had to race to assemble them so they had enough time left to play together during lunch. "Mrs. Calladore let me reserve the room for the whole week." Seemed he'd noticed her surprise.

She didn't have her guitar, so they weren't going to jam like they'd planned to on Tuesday. The thought of bringing her guitar today had occurred to her, but she didn't have it in her to play.

He swiveled on his stool from behind the drum set as he spun one of his plain, pale wooden drum sticks in his hand. She took the light brown, metal folding chair, moving it behind the drum set to sit close to him.

"If you'd rather not talk," he said, "that's okay."

She nodded in relief, because talking was the last thing she wanted. "Play something."

He pivoted in his seat, spun both of his drum sticks and went to work. She recognized the drum portion of Jimi Hendrix's *Fire*. As much as she enjoyed jamming with Patrick, she also loved watching his hands when he played. Any other time, he moved with all the awkwardness of a one-legged ostrich, but once he sat behind these drums, his body flowed. She leaned back, resting her head against the dark grey foam soundproofing shaped like rows of waveforms.

When Patrick finished with *Fire*, he moved into something improvised. The steady beat of the percussion hammered into her, and her breathing caught as her throat clenched.

"Stop." Lynna grabbed his arms to keep him from playing. She'd been counting the beats in her head—*one, two, three, four*—same as with the chest compressions on Raymond.

The scent of the damp leaves around the lake still haunted her olfactory senses. Her eyelids clenched tight as she fought against the memory.

Patrick pulled her into a hug, and she rested her head against his shoulder. He smelled like mint. It helped push away the memory.

He stayed silent, and she couldn't be more grateful. She leaned into him.

The worst part of all this was that she did want to talk about it. She wanted to explain why she'd wanted him to stop, but she didn't dare. If she let even one secret out, she knew the rest would spill out of her: the CIA, the Greenhouse, and her being half-dragon.

She didn't realize how long they'd stayed like that until Patrick whispered to her, "The bell is going to ring in three minutes."

In spite of everything, that made her smile. Knowing him, he'd been watching the seconds hand on his watch ticking by until exactly three minutes before the bell.

"Thanks for this." She tightened their hug for a moment before they released each other. She pulled back. Thank goodness she hadn't cried on him.

"I was going to ask you something." He took a quick look at his watch. "I've been meaning to for a while now. It's just that Journey is coming to Richmond on Saturday night, and I got two tickets. I know you say your academy—place—whatever it is—won't let you go out on dates, but I was wondering if you could go? With me?"

A concert.

She'd always wanted to see a real, live rock concert. She'd heard live performances on the radio, but that didn't count, not even close. He'd been insane to ever buy her a ticket. No way Dr. Howard and Agent Mills would let her go. Bad enough if it would have her off campus at night, but it would also be on a date. The only answer she could give Patrick was the one he feared.

Except, what she said was, "I'll go."

Chapter 23: Nevada

Thursday, 27 January 1983

Guilt nagged at Nevada for blowing off Lynna when they were dropped off at school, but her head was killing her. The migraine attacked her Tuesday evening. She'd gone to the nurse and gotten some hydrocodone and washed it down with pig's blood.

She'd come to school, seeking solitude. No one here, beyond Lynna and Maria talked to her. The girls on her hallway in the barracks were good, but the way they kept knocking on her door to check on her throughout the day was likely to get somebody killed. Not literally, but her temper was set to maximum burn.

Also, she wanted to avoid the nurse at the Greenhouse, because the jerk had cut her off of the hydrocodone last night. Said Nevada had already taken too much in the past twenty-four hours. That sounded impossible when her head still felt like someone had set off a nuclear missile in her skull and hit pause on the most painful moment. She'd broken into the infirmary last night and stolen enough to get her through the day. She'd chewed up five pills this morning, most of them before she got to school. By lunch, her misery index had skipped past ten and up to thirteen.

Nevada went to their usual bench, but Lynna never showed. From there, Nevada retreated to the library to find a dark corner among the bookshelves.

That had worked for all of five minutes until a small group of idiots had showed up acting like the space had their names on it. She'd glared at them, but they failed to pick up on the hint to buzz off.

Retreat led Nevada to the upstairs girls' bathroom in the E building, where the math department was located. Most students avoided this part of the campus during lunch, because really, who wanted to get cornered by one of the math teachers, especially when most of them seemed like a bunch of militant, uptight assholes?

In the bathroom, she swallowed three more hydrocodone and washed them down with some of the pig's blood she'd brought with her in her thermos. Damn, it was a good thermos, keeping her drink warm even hours after she'd put it in there. Unfortunately, no matter how fresh the pig's blood was, that didn't change the fact it didn't taste as good to her anymore.

She managed not to make a mess of herself drinking the blood, which wasn't the easiest thing to do. Blood didn't pour from a mug or wipe off a person's upper lip as cleanly as water. Those movies where the vampire fed on someone and then strolled off were utter crap.

Nevada clung to one of the sinks, silently begging whatever higher being was out there to make her migraine go away. She only really entertained the belief in a deity during the worst of her headaches, mainly out of desperation.

Someone walked into the bathroom. Nevada considered moving on, but she didn't want to go back into the brightly lit hall, much less outside in the sun. Instead, she clung to the sink with her eyes closed, willing the pills and the blood to make her head feel better.

"You all right?"

Nevada jerked her head up, startled by the girl's voice.

The girl was a junior, like Nevada. She couldn't remember her name. Might be Allison, Alice, or Ally. For all she really knew, it might be Donna or Margaret. She looked forgettable with the kind of dull colored hair that looks dark blonde in one light and brown in the other, as if her body refused to let her belong to either category.

"Your name's Nevada, right?" she asked. "I'm Emily. You're in my English class."

Okay, so she'd been way off on the name.

"What?" Nevada blinked, trying to figure out why Emily was talking to her. While they did attend Mrs. Markham's third period class, they sat on opposite sides of the room.

Emily repeated her question, but Nevada didn't really hear it. The girl wore a brown v-neck top that exposed part of her throat. All Nevada's attention went to that artery in her neck, enraptured by the way it pulsed. The idea of walking up to her, pinning her to the wall, brushing her hair back, and burying her fangs in her neck left Nevada's head spinning worse than the migraine. She couldn't remember ever seeing Emily with anyone else, and that idea that she could vanish from school and no one would notice...

Emily shrank in on herself as she stepped back. Nevada snapped out of her distraction.

"Sorry." Her voice croaked. "I'm—yeah, not doing so great today. I should probably go."

Nevada ran from the bathroom. Her hands shook, and she couldn't catch her breath. The pulse in the girl's neck haunted her the rest of the day, that and the fantasy of biting her throat and tasting her blood.

She ditched her last two classes and hung out in the woods near the bus lot.

Her biggest worry had been Lynna noticing it, but neither of them said a thing on the ride home. Lynna stared off into space the entire ride.

After they got back to the Greenhouse campus, Nevada went straight to her room, chewed up the few hydrocodone she had left, and crawled into bed.

She waited there until dinnertime. Everyone, including the staff, would be in the dining hall by that point. That's when she slipped into the mansion, snuck past the dining hall, and ran to the end of the hallway where she raced down the stairs to the basement.

Unlike the aboveground floors, this area had abandoned all efforts at hiding the CIA's ownership of this building. The white walls and inexpensive, puke-green floor tiles screamed government-on-a-budget. Long, rectangular fluorescent lights were attached to the ceiling. She sighed in relief, because no one was down here to see her enter the infirmary, exactly as she'd hoped.

Her headache refused to go away, and it started after she came down from the high of that human blood. The only way to make it go away required more. She was simply treating her condition with the right medicine.

That was all.

She picked the lock on the infirmary's door in record time, and then the lock on the cooler. Looking over her options, she opted for the old adage that you are what you eat and grabbed a blood bag of B positive.

She bit back a yelp as she slipped the cold blood bag underneath her shirt and into the back of her pants. If anyone stopped her on the way back to her room, then she didn't want them to see this. Besides, knowing her luck, one of the doctors or nurses might decide to skip dessert and come down here.

A few of the younger kids, including Ava, were outside, walking back towards the barracks. She kept her distance and avoided any eye contact. Once she reached Barracks Charlie, she went in the back door to the first floor, the closest entrance to her room. That let her avoid running into any of the girls who might have already returned to her hall. She needn't have worried, because no one else was there yet.

After she locked the door to her room, Nevada turned on her desk lamp. The light revealed the poster of Big Ben and the rest of the London skyline on the wall above her desk. Her swivel chair creaked as she dropped into it. She studied the blood bag, figuring out the best way to get the blood out. The temptation to simply bite into the bag nearly bested her, but then she thought better of it. A short, thin tube stuck out the bottom of the bag, which probably connected to the IV when it fed into someone the normal way. She took some scissors out of her desk drawer and cut that off.

Blood spilled out onto her desk. She cursed and pinched off the thin tube to keep the rest of the blood in the bag. The smell, though. Even cold, the scent of it filled her room. Her head lolled back with her eyes shut.

"Please let this work," she whispered.

She brought the tube to her lips and sucked in her first taste. It didn't taste half as delightful as what she'd gotten from Vale and Taggart, but it went light-years beyond the disappointing pig sludge from this morning. She sucked in more of it, forcing herself not to stop. Maybe the cold delayed the effect, but when it hit her...

"Oh, fuck." The words came out slow and with a smile of perfect bliss. Not only did her headache vanish, but she felt as if she was floating. Was this what it was like for Lynna when she flew through a cloud? She laughed at that thought.

She finished off the rest of the blood. The dizziness made her giggle, but after the initial euphoria passed, she noticed an even more immediate change. Her room was brighter. No, everything had come into sharper focus. She held up her hand, turning it back to front. Holy crap! Everything looked like she'd traded in some fifties black and white TV for a 3-D Technicolor movie theater.

That was only the start of it, though.

"No. Way." She remembered every detail from Taggart's files and the dates. One of those dates listed. "August 27, 1971."

How had she missed that?

Nevada grabbed a spiral notebook and a pen. She had to get all of this down on paper as fast as possible.

Chapter 24: Lynna

Thursday, 27 January 1983

Ever since the incident in East Germany, Lynna had troubled over how to pull off meeting with the Grey Woman in D.C. Now, she'd added sneaking out on a date with Patrick for Saturday. By the time dinner ended, she'd made up her mind.

After she got the girls on her floor to start on their showers, Lynna went out the back with Chewie on his leash and headed straight for the first floor of Barracks Charlie. Well, as straight as a fifteen-pound silky terrier would allow. He stretched out her one minute walk to Nevada's barracks into five by sniffing at random spots, kicking up his leg a couple of times, and chewing on a few long blades of grass.

Thanks to Chewie taking care of his business, Lynna ended up going in the front of Barracks Charlie instead of the back near Nevada's room. Something flew at her, striking her on the forehead. Whatever hit her, it wasn't hard and dropped to the floor with a soft flopping sound.

"Sorry!" The voice belonged to one of the youngest hybrids a ten-year-old named Misty who had only recently developed her powers, the ability to transform into a snake. She used to have a beautiful afro, but every time she changed, it shed all of her hair. The bald girl picked up the hacky sack. "We were just playing."

Misty and the other three girls stood in the small gathering area that each floor had in the barracks. The chairs were folded up against the wall along with three bean bags shoved up in front of them to make room for the hacky sack game.

"I'm looking for—" She stopped when Nevada stepped out of a room about halfway down the hall.

The girls up front abandoned their game of hacky sack to shower attention on Chewie. He ran from girl to girl, too excited to settle on one person. Lynna left him there, for the moment, and walked down the hall to her friend.

Nevada was decked out in all black with a red fedora she'd nicked while on an op in Paris. Why had she changed clothes this close to lights out? The spiral notebook on a brown clipboard and the yellow pencil in her hand ran counter to her artsy style.

Lynna stopped next to Nevada. "You got a minute?"

"Yeah." Nevada didn't look up from her notebook. "What was your 'gotcha day'?"

"What?"

"You know, the day they abducted you." Nevada shrugged as if that should have been obvious.

"I know what it is, but why are you asking?" She leaned closer to get a look at what Nevada had written in her notebook. Names and dates covered the page.

"I need to check something." Nevada sounded like she was running at super speed. Her headache must have finally abated.

"It was 1969. Why?"

Nevada glared up from her notebook. "But what date?"

"Come here." Lynna grabbed her by the arm and dragged her outside onto the back.

"I need the date."

"It was April 13th." Lynna went to pull the door shut but had to wait for Chewie to race out behind them. Much as he loved to get attention from people, he never liked for his "momma" to go anywhere without him. She snagged his leash as he stopped to sniff at Nevada's feet and then ran behind Lynna's legs as if to hide.

As Lynna pulled the door shut, Nevada started to walk towards the other barracks. "Hey!" Lynna grabbed her by the arm. "Hold on!"

"What? I'm busy."

"And I need to ask you something. It's important."

Nevada growled—actually, growled!— and stepped back towards Lynna. "What?"

Lynna lowered her voice to a whisper. "I need you to help Ava cover for me tomorrow night, make it seem like I'm in my room asleep, in case anyone comes to check on me."

"Are you kidding me?"

"I need someone to make sure my girls get into bed on time and don't do anything to draw any attention while I'm gone. They won't listen to Ava if they get fussy."

"I'm already covering for Pockets. It's their date night." She gave "date night" a special edge of sarcasm.

Pockets and Maria always snuck out of their rooms on Friday nights after lights out to go on a "date," which really meant they found a private spot in the woods, tossed down a blanket, and had sex. Lynna usually covered for Maria, which was why she hadn't asked her, even though Maria was the first floor R.A. in her building.

"Wait, why are you covering for Pockets? He's not even in your barracks." As soon as Lynna got the words out, realization hit her in the gut with an icy fist.

Raymond usually covered for Pockets.

Neither of them spoke. Nevada's features smoothed as her determined focus and irritation faded. She slipped her clipboard under her left arm to keep it out of the way and hugged Lynna with her other arm.

Lynna had forgotten—actually forgotten that Raymond was dead. It had only been for a minute, but it felt like a betrayal.

"You should ask Maria. You've covered plenty for her. Past time she returned the favor. Date night be damned." Nevada patted Lynna's back to comfort her, but then she abruptly stopped and pulled back with her features twisted in surprise. Her lips parted in a wide smile that revealed her sharp canines. "Wait. Are you sneaking off campus for a date?"

"No! I mean, I'm not—uh, not tomorrow night."

Suspicious didn't cover the look on Nevada's face, complete with an eyebrow arched so high that it disappeared beneath the brim of her hat.

Lynna felt her face blush.

Nevada pointed at Lynna with a corner of her clipboard. "I need to finish what I'm doing, but this little story you're hiding is 'to be continued.' We clear?"

Lynna groaned and then muttered, "Fine."

She tugged on Chewie's leash and dragged him straight to the back door of Barracks Bravo, Maria's floor.

When she entered, most of the girls were gathered at the far end in the common area and singing along with the radio to *Sweet Dreams*. Lynna had heard that one earlier this month and instantly fallen in love with it, but what those girls were doing to that song was criminal. Moments like this, she decided dealing with her hall's songbird Athena might not be so bad after all.

She knocked on the door to Maria's room

"What!" Maria shouted.

"It's Lynna."

The door swung open. "Hey, girl! Take your coat off and stay a while."

"Actually, I was thinking we could take a walk."

Maria had picked up a cassette with a pencil sticking through it on her nightstand, but at Lynna's suggestion to go out into the cold, she looked up. The look on her face called Lynna nuts.

Before Maria could protest, Lynna brought her finger to her lips and then pointed towards the back door. The kids had figured out a long time ago that the inside of their barracks weren't safe for talking—not about anything private. Pockets had tested the theory by pretending to plan a breakout with Raymond. When the night came for the supposed breakout, the two boys had pinned a note to a tree with a dart. The message had been a simple "Looking for someone?" The guards had burst into both boys' rooms expecting to find them gone. Instead, both boys were sitting in Pockets' room munching on popcorn and laughing their butts off at the panicked guards.

Maria nodded that she understood Lynna's signal. She glared in protest as she put on her coat. She picked up Chewie, who eagerly accepted Maria hugging him. He licked her face until they went outside on the stairs, where Maria set him back down. He went about sniffing things while they talked.

"Girl, this better be good." Maria sat on the stairs.

"I need you to cover for me tomorrow night."

"You mean Friday night?" she asked, giving "Friday" the kind of emphasis that added an unspoken demand that Lynna had better not keep her from her horizontal time with Pockets.

"Look, I know, but this is important." Her throat went dry now that she was about to share this secret. She sat next to Maria on the stairs and explained in a lowered voice about the arranged meet with the Grey Woman.

After she finished, her best friend let out a long breath that misted in the cold air.

"Okay." Maria paused with her hand held out in front of her as if to arrange the thoughts in her head like notes pinned to a cork board. "So, first thing. How do you know this isn't some sort of trap?"

Lynna had already considered that one. "If she'd wanted to kill me or capture me, why didn't she take her shot at me then?"

"Well, that time you had little Miss Lite-Bright with you, who'd just baked one of Grey Girl's friends. I definitely wouldn't have tried to kick your ass then either."

Okay, so she hadn't considered that.

"That's true." She held up a hand to stop Maria from claiming victory. "But! She killed Graham to make sure that Erlking guy couldn't get him. She's clearly not on his side in all of this."

"Certainly doesn't mean she's on your side." Maria crossed her arms. "She even said as much, didn't she?"

She had. The Grey Woman had insisted Lynna was on the "wrong side" of that fight.

"It's a public place," Lynna said. "It's not even a neutral location. Meeting there actually favors me. It's an open area, making it easier for me to fly out of there, not to mention all the water in the reflection pool."

"I still don't like it." Maria shook her head as she hugged herself more tightly against the cold.

"If I don't go, then we lose any chance at getting some answers. Besides, my gut says I can trust her."

That got Maria to her feet. "Answers! Who gives a damn? We owe the CIA exactly nada. If anything, they owe us. You and Pockets seriously kill me with this nonsense. You are so deep into this 'God and country' crap, it's almost as if you're grateful they abducted you."

Maria's tirade stunned Lynna to the point where she couldn't even find her voice until her friend's body relaxed enough to lean against the side of the barracks.

"The Soviets are trying to find us," Lynna said. "That's not good for us either. Agreed?"

Maria answered with a disgusted groan, which as good as admitted her agreement. "I still don't like you going alone."

"Does that mean you'll cover for me?" Lynna couldn't restrain her grin.

Maria straightened and tightened her coat around her. "I suppose I better let Pockets know. I'll tell him we'll have to wait until Saturday night this week."

"Yeah," Lynna said, drawing out the word. "About Saturday night..."

Chapter 25: Lynna

Friday, 28 January 1983

Lynna waited until an hour after sunset, about 6:30 p.m., before making her escape. She couldn't deny a slight thrill at sneaking off campus. She'd never risked flying any farther than the fence line.

She changed into her dragon form, climbed a tree, and leaped. She risked a dive over the lake to get her momentum and then launched up high to clear the treetops.

Once clear, she whooped and performed a loop-de-loop. Her flight path took her northeast, until she reached I-95. While the interstate didn't provide a perfectly straight path towards D.C., following it made her less likely to get lost.

Using a map, she'd determined the distance from the Greenhouse to the Lincoln Memorial was a little more than a hundred miles. Her maximum sustained speed while in flight reached roughly thirty miles per hour. She could fly faster than that, but not for very long. If she averaged twenty-five miles per hour, she'd still reach her destination with plenty of time to spare.

Her excitement ebbed shortly after she reached the interstate. She'd flown for this long plenty of times, but normally when tracking someone on the ground. A small part of her wondered if she could have talked Patrick into meeting her somewhere and then driving her the rest of the way, but she knew that idea was borderline disastrous for so many reasons. The longer she considered Patrick's invitation, the more she realized he never technically called it a date. She forced that line of thinking away, because it distracted her too much and caused her to slow her flight.

A couple times, she risked flying low enough to read the green signs on the side of the road that showed the distance to D.C. Despite her hopes of making the flight in four hours, she didn't reach the capital until a little after eleven. She slowed down during the last hour of flight to conserve her energy. Not only did she need something left in the tank for the return flight, but she needed to be ready for a fight, if things went the way Maria feared.

She'd expected to be able to land right at the memorial, given the late hour, but plenty of people still strolled around it. Most looked like couples, huddled close for warmth, stealing kisses, and paying little attention to the monument. Making out in view of a giant, dead man's statue sounded creepy as hell to her, but it made it a bit easier for her to land in the shadows of the trees clustered to the left of the monument about 11:30 p.m. The other side included a pond that seemed to draw more of the romantics compared to the grassy field.

Once on the ground, she changed back to her human form and pulled on her trench coat. The wind cut through her thin layer of protection. She couldn't afford anything heavier. Her wings made it impossible to wear a coat in her dragon form, so she stored it in a small, custom-designed backpack that rested above the spot where her wings emerged. Back when the CIA issued her the trench coat, she spent two weeks practicing to fold it just right to fit it in that tiny backpack.

She watched for anyone paying too much attention to her as she emerged from the shadows and walked along the edge of the reflection pool leading up to the memorial. She expected the building to be smaller, but the opposite proved true. Twelve pillars lined up along the front of the tall, Greek-style structure.

Climbing the front steps, Lynna stopped at the top. She took a single glance at the nineteen-foot tall statue of Lincoln before returning her attention to the people around her. She assumed the Grey Woman chose this time to better hide her appearance, but given all the lights at the memorial, she'd still stand out.

One of the things Agent Mills had warned them about when he prepped Lynna and her friends for their first missions was that most assignments involved more waiting than anything else. Waiting to meet, waiting to intercept, waiting to attack, waiting to wait. Staying alert challenged even the best agents. Lynna could appreciate that from her previous assignments, but she'd never been in a situation on the ground quite like this where a possible enemy anticipated her being there. After tonight, she'd never take the element of surprise for granted.

Ten minutes before midnight, Lynna noticed a woman standing near the corner pillar to her left. Unlike the other tourists, this stranger didn't move, even though she'd been there for several minutes. She was decidedly not grey-skinned, though. Her pale-skin and long, blonde hair gave her a Scandinavian appearance.

Lynna drew on her power, that half-touch that caused the world around her to waver in a shade of yellow. The long reflecting pool stretching out between the Lincoln Memorial and the Washington Monument offered another advantage: more than six million gallons of water all at her disposal. Considering the way Lynna had demonstrated her power with water in East Berlin, the Grey Woman might consider this an olive branch.

No matter how this went, Lynna needed to avoid a dramatic display of her powers here. No way would that go undocumented, not with all these tourists around. It would get back to the CIA eventually, and she'd be busted.

Keeping her hold on the water sent a ripple of pain through her body, especially given the amount of it involved. That didn't stop her from maintaining her control as she walked towards the stranger staring her way.

With her powers sharpening her eyesight, Lynna saw details of the stranger come into focus. The sharp cheekbones matched the woman she'd met in the East German forest. The hair style matched, despite the black hair having changed to blonde. If she'd been able to place two identically framed pictures of each look next to one another, it would have resembled that Andy Warhol painting of Marilyn Monroe. Seeing the Grey Woman like this, Lynna realized they must be about the same age.

"That's close enough, dragon." Oh, no doubt about it. Lynna recognized that voice, even with the Grey Woman taming her accent. "How very *Spies 'r Us*. Were you trying to stand out?"

"I don't have a lot of clothing options when I travel."

The Grey Woman had dressed to the nines with a white blouse beneath a dark blue velvet coat that came down to her knees and a long, pink silk scarf hanging loose. "I'm surprised you actually came alone."

Lynna answered with as much snark as she could pour into her words. "And I'm surprised you're pale."

The Grey Woman appeared to enjoy the joke, her expression shifting into a grin.

If all of the Grey Women could change their appearance this drastically, then any of these tourists could be more of them. For the moment, no one seemed to be paying attention to them, save for the men pretending not to ogle the blonde. Having to divide her attention this much made it easier for this Grey Woman to catch her unprepared, if she attacked.

"You said before that I'm on the wrong side of this fight," Lynna said. "Exactly which fight are you referring to?"

"The one between everyone else and our kind, of course. Like you, I'm half human."

"And the other half?"

"Dark Elf." The admission that Lynna didn't already know got an unimpressed grunt out of the Grey Woman. "You and I, we're outcasts in two worlds. I'm not the only one among the Erlking's daughters who recognize we're nothing but a useful army beholden to him, because no other dark elf would take us in anymore than the humans would."

"If that's true, then why are you the only one here?"

The Grey Woman didn't answer right away. They both stayed silent until a couple with their arms linked walked by them.

"Because," the Grey Woman continued, "the others would rather stay with the devil they know than the ones they don't."

"And you wouldn't?"

"I would rather not have a devil."

The way this Grey Woman spoke reminded Lynna of Maria, especially the way she'd gotten yesterday when she'd accused Lynna of believing she owed the CIA anything.

"So why this meeting?" Lynna asked. "I'm not clear what you hope to gain from this."

"An ally." The answer came without any hesitation. "Until you, I've never encountered anyone in the mortal world who could stand up against the Erlking's daughters."

"Wait." Something the Grey Woman had said set off an alarm in Lynna's mind. "You keep calling you and the others his daughters. You don't mean that figuratively, do you?"

The Grey Woman looked away from her. "No, he fathered all of us. He finds women in different parts of your world and impregnates them so that we may blend in." She gestured to herself, perhaps meaning the way she now looked white-skinned with blond hair. "The Elven Council gave him permission to spawn an army to infiltrate your world. He told them that being bound to him by blood would ensure our loyalty."

Lynna decided she didn't want more details about that. Better to get back to why she'd come in the first place. "Why exactly is he after my unit? I mean, he's obviously not working with the Soviets."

The Grey Woman laughed at that. "The Soviets. As if the squabbles between these humans set them apart in any way that matters." She shook her head. "Human is human. The only reason mortal borders and countries matter to us is that we can steal their gathered intelligence. Their divisions do the Erlking's work for him."

"And what exactly is he working towards? You still haven't said that."

The Grey Woman's eyebrows pinched in together, either deciding how to answer or maybe having doubts about sharing anything with Lynna at all. No way to tell for sure, which only added to Lynna's growing frustration. She didn't like standing here exposed. If this girl was being honest with her about working against the Erlking, then being in the open like this endangered her, too. Would she be able to tell any better than Lynna if one of the Erlking's other daughters was here? Lynna kept checking the people around them for any sign of someone taking too much interest in them, but no one appeared to be trying to eavesdrop.

"He's recently adopted his own agenda, but he used to serve the governing council of the Elves. They tasked him with searching for our kind—those beings of mixed breeding and abducting them lest they fall into human hands."

"Why?"

No missing her look of disappointment. "Humans have progressed at a much slower rate. Their development of nuclear arms is insignificant compared to the power the Elves and the Aesir wield."

Lynna didn't recognize the term "Aesir," but the Grey Woman's tongue was loosened. Best not to interrupt any more than necessary.

"A special few among their kind can manipulate the ley lines of reality, the connective tissue between all worlds that permits them to exist parallel to one another. This ability that only the Elves and Aesir possess has allowed for a détente, not unlike the one that exists between the nuclear powers in this world. Compared to the Elves and the Aesir, humans are nothing but a third world equivalent in their conflict. The Erlking's duty was to make sure that never changes by abducting or killing any children who are half-breeds."

"Quit calling me a half-breed." The anger to her own words even surprised Lynna.

"Sorry."

Even though the Grey Woman offered the apology, it didn't come across as though she really understood why it offended Lynna so much. Perhaps she didn't appreciate how much Lynna lived with being treated like some "other" even among the students at her school because of her Chinese ancestry. She and the rest of the children in the Greenhouse had spent their entire lives treated like inhuman outsiders by members of the human staff. Finding the same reception from someone like her was a bitter pill to swallow.

"The point I'm getting at," the Grey Woman said, "is that in humans—specifically, you Americans—hunting and gathering those among them who are more than human is an open declaration of war in a conflict you fools don't even know exists."

Her words turned Lynna's insides to ice, causing her to shiver in a way that had nothing to do with the wintery night air.

"Your little friend who killed one of my sisters in East Germany," the Grey Woman continued. "She is what the Erlking has been hoping to find for decades."

Ava? "Why?"

"Her powers. She is tapping into the ley lines. That little girl could destroy your world."

"Or the Elves'?" Lynna asked.

The Grey Woman nodded and walked a little closer, as if Lynna's sudden understanding somehow made her safer to approach.

"The Erlking has become disenchanted with the Elven Council. He wants to end the détente with the Aesir, but to do that, he needs someone with the power to manipulate the ley lines. You might liken him to a terrorist in this world, many of whom are scheming for a nuclear weapon to destabilize your so-called superpowers." There was no missing the mocking humor she gave that last word.

"And you and I," Lynna said, starting to realize how much danger her little sister was in, "we're what in this game?"

"Ants." The Grey Woman chuckled, wiggling her fingers as if crawling along. "On tiny hills."

Lynna considered that a moment and then remembered Ava's story about the night her parents were killed. "One of your sisters said something when Ava appeared." Lynna winced as she realized she'd given up Ava's name and lost her hold on the water in the reflection pool for a few seconds. If the Grey Woman sensed that moment of weakness, she didn't pounce. "Something that sounded like 'lo-sol-far'?"

The Grey Woman nodded. "Ljósálfr. That is an elf who can manipulate the ley lines—a Light Elf."

"Wait." Lynna's mind struggled to add all of these new dots and connect them. "You said the Erlking was looking for my unit to find her. How did he even know we have a Light Elf?"

The Grey Woman nodded with a hint of pity in her expression.

"Because you, my dragon friend, have a traitor within your unit."

For a split second, Lynna assumed the Grey Woman meant Graham, but then she realized the truth. Ava didn't come into the Greenhouse until after Graham and Dr. DeWare were both gone. Neither of them would have known about her.

That meant this traitor was someone else—a traitor still inside the Greenhouse.

Chapter 26: Lynna

Saturday, 29 January 1983

"Do you know who this traitor is?" Lynna asked, but she already suspected the answer.

The Grey Woman shrugged. "All I know is that they established a line of contact with the Elven Council, but their negotiations must have fallen apart. The council then tasked the Erlking with finding your unit."

"I didn't think he was still working for them."

"They assume he is still their warrior. They do not know he has his own agenda, his own reasons to find your little friend."

"So why don't you want the Erlking to find her? What's in it for you?"

She tilted her head, as if taking Lynna's measure. "Détente is not perfect, but it has created the most lasting peace the Elves and Aesir have known. What is it your nuclear powers call their own cold war?" She paused, her eyes shifting to the side in contemplation and then she nodded. "Yes, mutually-assured destruction."

Lynna considered pointing out that the acronym for that was MAD, something that all too well described the concept of the U.S. and U.S.S.R. preserving peace with the nuclear equivalent of loaded guns held to each others' heads. There were nights she couldn't sleep, caught up in waking nightmares of the Soviets launching their missiles and creating a nuclear holocaust. She couldn't do anything by herself to end the Cold War, but she and her friends could certainly suffer from it.

Trying to convince this Grey Woman of the folly of détente worked against Lynna's interests at the moment, so she decided against engaging in that philosophical debate. After all, if she was going to keep Ava and the rest of the Greenhouse safe, she needed this girl as her ally.

Of course, that's when Lynna realized they themselves were engaged in their own small-scale détente. She relaxed her hold on the reflection pool, lifting the yellow haze to her vision. Once she did, she realized the Grey Woman's hair was more of a strawberry blond.

She held out her hand, offering it to the Grey Woman. "My name is Lynna."

The Grey Woman took her hand and shook. "Olivia."

"So, is this what you really look like?" Lynna asked as they released their hands.

Olivia scowled at her. "Do you really believe the dragon is any less what you look like? Do not be so narrow-minded. We are both. This," she pointed to herself, "this is my glamour. It is still part of me. I cannot make my appearance anything I like. Nor can the Erlking do this. He is not half-human, as we are. He can only ever appear as all dark elf, which is why he has bred his half-human daughters to act as his foot soldiers within this mortal world."

"So what about these Aesir? Who or what are they?"

That amused Olivia. "You would probably think of them as Norse Gods."

"Like Thor and Odin? As in Ragnarök and all that?"

She scowled as she waved off the question. "That's all made up cow dung, but yes."

Lynna lost herself in her thoughts for a moment as she processed all of this. Olivia had handed her a whole new world of complications. The only way she managed to bring herself back in to focus was with the simple question of what came next.

"I need to figure out who it is inside my unit that contacted the elves and why they did it."

"I have given you all I know regarding that, but if I learn more, I will let you know." Olivia reached up slowly, probably to make it clear the gesture was not meant as an attack, and grabbed her by the arm. "Understand, you cannot share any of this that I have told you with anyone, not even this Ava you care so much about. The Erlking has spies within your CIA and the KGB, as well as the Stasi and many other intelligence networks. If any of this knowledge were to leak, it would alert the Erlking that he has a traitor of his own and would endanger me. I have risked much tonight, more than you realize."

Lynna nodded, if only because she had already assumed as much. "We need a way to communicate."

Olivia shrugged. "Chalk marks work well."

CIA operatives often marked mailboxes or other things in public view with chalk marks to send signals for a meet or to warn a double agent to run. That required someplace Lynna would pass on a daily basis, and if the Erlking discovered Olivia doing that, then the landmark would place him that much closer to where the Greenhouse was. Also, if this dragged on for months, school did go on summer break, and Lynna would barely go off campus until the start of the next school year.

Lynna shook her head. "Not an option for me. What about a wrong number ploy?"

"Phone calls are possible. I use an answering service in New York for contacts I've cultivated during the past few years. None of them know I'm a dark elf."

"Aw, I feel so special." Lynna couldn't resist teasing her, but she suspected it was dangerous letting her guard down with Olivia. They didn't really know each other that well. Even though her training included the art of developing informants, the CIA had never given Lynna a chance to put it into practice.

"Oh, shut up." Olivia smiled, but then her expression sobered. "So how do I call you?"

"We have a phone on the floor of my barracks. Every few weeks we get calls from debt collectors trying to reach some Albert Iniango. I guess he used to have our number. Call and act like you're a debt collector for him. All the girls on the floor have to report any wrong numbers to me, so even if I don't answer, I'll know about it."

"Not bad, but how will you know it's me calling and not one of these debt collectors?"

"Oh, good point." Lynna snapped her fingers as she thought of a solution. "We change the first name. Ask for Dorothy Iniango instead. It'll make it seem like they're trying to reach Albert through some relative, using his old number. Shouldn't be likely to tip off whoever monitors the calls into my barracks."

Olivia gave Lynna the number to her answering service. "This is a big risk for us both. If my father discovers I've betrayed him, he will kill me."

"I doubt the CIA would kill me," Lynna said, not wanting to admit out loud that the CIA saw her more as property than a person, "but that doesn't mean they wouldn't shove me into a cell. Although, technically, treason is punishable by execution, so maybe they would kill me."

They worked out a few more logistics before they parted ways. By the time Lynna launched back into the sky to head home, it was almost one in the morning. Thankfully, Ava knew to let her sleep in. She prayed Maria and Ava had kept anyone from realizing she'd gone off-campus.

The entire flight home, she troubled over who the traitor might be. She didn't know any of the current guards well enough to gauge their trustworthiness, but the traitor might be someone closer to her. Her mind kept twisting little things people said and did into something more. The way Dr. Howard had acted like she might have been about to say something more after her debrief came to mind. There was also the way Agent Mills had obviously been crying prior to the debrief. Nevada creating that list of everyone's "gotcha days" smacked of intelligence gathering. Even the venom to Maria's anti-CIA rant made it difficult not to suspect her a little.

It could be anyone.

Chapter 27: Lynna

D ate night.

The phrase tasted strange, but the night was almost here.

Her jaunt to D.C. had gone unnoticed. She'd slipped back into her barracks shortly before five, making better time on her return flight. Her fears of being caught had motivated her to fly as fast as possible. She'd been off-campus for almost twelve hours last night. With the exception of her wilderness survival training and missions, she'd never been away that long, not even for school. Even better, no one had disturbed her as she slept until noon. Truthfully, she could have slept later, but she decided not to risk it. Would be her luck for Dr. Howard to get worried if she missed both breakfast and lunch and then checked on her later in the evening while she was at the concert.

Her exhaustion provided an easy excuse to avoid her friends. Maria and Ava both asked how the meet had gone, and Lynna lied to them, claiming the Grey Woman had never shown. Lying to Ava hurt more, especially when it was her life at risk. Lynna would have to come clean eventually, but not until she figured out who in the Greenhouse had contacted the elves.

Elves.

Aesir.

Ljósálfr.

Ley lines.

After lunch, she took a walk through the woods to clear her head, and it made last night's meeting seem more like a dream. She wished it had been, because then she wouldn't be puzzling over who the traitor was.

That she would be going to a Journey concert with Patrick in a few hours didn't seem real either. She also felt uncomfortable with the idea of going off-campus and leaving Ava unprotected, because after last night, she had no way of knowing who she could trust to keep an eye on her little sister.

At least she wasn't as stressed about the actual act of sneaking away from here to go on her date. Not only would she be able to leave here a little later than the previous night, meaning it would be even darker to conceal her departure, but she'd also be back much earlier this time.

Maria caught her as she ran out the back door of her barracks and down the stairs.

"Girl, I expect some spicy details, so you'd better come back here with more to tell me about than the concert."

Lynna laughed and hugged her.

Before Lynna ran off, Nevada raced over to them. "Hold up!"

Both Lynna and Maria shushed her. "Seriously, girl?" Maria said. "What part of stealthy escape are you vague about?"

"I'm calling an emergency Daemons meeting," Nevada said, meaning just them, Pockets, and Ava, and no adults. "Tonight."

Lynna exchanged a look with Maria, silently asking her if the third member of their trio was out of her damn mind.

"Midnight in the clearing." Nevada said it as an order, pointing at Lynna and Maria, her hand shaking. Was she pissed off? About what? "I'm guessing you'll be back by then anyway. You can't tell me dork boy doesn't have a curfew."

"Did you just call my date a dork?"

"Hey, he's cute, but he's still a dork." Nevada had never flinched from making her opinions known, but usually tempered them with a joking tone. Not this time. She sounded spiteful.

The urge to punch Nevada in the face caught Lynna completely by surprise, but thankfully, she didn't follow through with it. Lynna knew how to throw down, but everyone in the Greenhouse recognized Nevada as the best at hand-to-hand combat.

"I gotta side with my girl here." Maria pointed to Lynna. "I saw that boy getting on the bus in his track shorts during cross country season. His legs are definitely not dorky."

And now Lynna wanted to punch Maria for looking at her guy's legs.

"Relax." Maria laughed at her. "His legs really haven't got anything on my man's."

Nevada groaned. "Gross. Make sure both of you are at the clearing at midnight." She pushed past the two of them to climb upstairs. "I'm gonna let Ava know. Oh, and Maria, I already told Pockets. He's hoping you'll stick around afterwards for the two of you to do that thing you do."

Maria crossed her arms and glared up after her. "*That thing we do?* For real? What crawled up her ass pipe?" Then Maria turned her scowl towards Lynna. "What are you still doing here? Get flying. You got a cute boy waiting for you."

Lynna hugged her again and then ran into the woods.

In her excitement, she forgot for a minute about her suspicions about Maria and Nevada from the previous night.

After a quick flight—oh, so much quicker than last night!—Lynna reached downtown Richmond. She landed in an alley near the Coliseum before seven. She'd ended up a lot farther away than she'd expected, though. She sprinted to make it to the Coliseum on time. The cold barely touched her, and she was sweating like crazy by the time she got there.

"Lynna!" Patrick flagged her down from the corner of Leigh and 7th Streets. He wore that grey windbreaker of his over a yellow, button-down shirt.

They both laughed as she sprinted across the street to him. There was an awkward moment where they seemed about to hug but then chickened out at the last second.

"I worried you wouldn't make it." He had the dopiest grin, but it was cute, too.

Lynna leaned over with her hands on her knees as she caught her breath. "Wasn't sure I'd get here in time." She paused twice saying that.

He held out his arm for her. After a second's hesitation because of how sweaty she must be, she hooked her arm into his. Thank goodness she'd showered and put on some deodorant before leaving her barracks.

She wondered if they looked like the couples she'd seen at the Lincoln Memorial last night. For a moment, she almost mentioned it, but then realized she'd have to explain why she'd been in D.C.

"You look great," he said.

"Thanks." She appreciated the compliment, but she doubted she looked all that good. One disadvantage to flying here for her date was that she had to stick with a black t-shirt and a light, old blue jacket that would fit in her backpack. As such, they were wrinkled as hell.

She'd never actually seen the Richmond Coliseum until now. It was both impressive and hideous. The round building, made of brown brick and glass, reminded her of a giant, bargain-basement flying saucer with zero chance of ever getting off the ground.

Once they got inside, he led them to their seats, far up and on the opposite end of the Coliseum from the stage.

"I know they aren't very close," he said. "Sorry."

"Are you kidding? It's still a lot closer than on the radio." She took his hand in hers to reassure him. His hand felt cold but still felt nice.

Yes, she told herself, this was most definitely a date. No way he'd be holding her hand like this, if it wasn't, would he?

"Thanks," she said.

"For what?"

"For getting me to come." She leaned over and kissed him on the cheek without thinking, and then as soon as she pulled back, panic hit. She'd kissed him! If this wasn't a date, then she'd ruined everything!

He smiled at her, though.

Instead of pulling back, he leaned towards her.

"I'm really glad you came. I know being able to get away for this wasn't easy, and that means a lot."

The sincerity to his words caught her off guard. He seemed to understand how much she'd risked to make it here. There was no way he could, but that didn't matter. What mattered was that he'd worried about her and wanted to be with her this much.

She wasn't sure if she'd leaned back towards him or if he'd pulled in closer to her, but then they kissed. It started as his lips to hers, and they lingered like that, feeling out one another as the kiss deepened. His body's warmth invited her to pull closer, and she didn't resist as his arms held her tight. She'd never kissed anyone, not like this, and her inexperience both terrified and thrilled her.

They reluctantly pulled apart as cheers went up through the auditorium. The opening act was taking the stage.

Patrick held onto her a moment longer. He looked like he wanted to say something, but he only smiled.

She gave him another quick kiss.

The lead singer, a blond-haired rocker in a black leather jacket, took the stage carrying his guitar. His raw and raspy voice infected the crowd, singing back the "na na na na" part of the chorus to one of his songs. Even with all its rough edges, his music contained a romantic quality that hungered for a connection. Lynna itched for her own guitar, wanting to play along. Instead, she held onto Patrick's hand. They didn't let go until the opening act finished, so they could applaud.

"Felt like a modern take on rockabilly to me," Patrick said as the band left the stage.

"Definitely an old school rocker, but not in that campy Stray Cats way."

Patrick laughed. "Don't speak ill of the Stray Cats. You know I love their music."

"I learned to play the guitar portion of *Rock This Town* for you." She'd recorded the song off of the radio and ruined the cassette playing it repeatedly until she figured out the chords.

The Coliseum filled up in the break between the opening act and Journey taking the stage. About four rows in front of them a tall man worked his way past the people already seated who struggled to make room. As soon as Lynna saw him, she jerked down into her seat as low as she could go.

No, no, no... This is not happening.

The tall man sitting down four rows ahead of her was Agent Mills.

Chapter 28: Lynna

Saturday, 29 January 1983

This couldn't be coincidence, could it?

To her relief, Agent Mills didn't look her way as he reached his seat.

Patrick didn't miss her sudden slouch. He leaned in close and whispered into her ear, "What's wrong?"

As stupid as it was, the sensation of him that close, his breath brushing against her ear and the back of her neck gave her an unexpected thrill. Any other moment, and she'd have reveled in it. Only, this couldn't be a much worse situation.

"That tall dude who sat down," she whispered back to him, wondering if Patrick was enjoying the feel of her lips brushing against his ear as much as she had.

She shifted for him to whisper back. "The big, Black guy in the brown leather jacket?"

Lynna nodded. "He's the," she hesitated, "I mean, he's an instructor on my campus."

Oh, good grief, she'd nearly called him the CIA liaison, like a glorified rookie.

Even sitting down, Agent Mills was so tall that he'd have an unobstructed view of Lynna, if he turned around for any reason.

"Do we need to go?" Patrick asked.

Lynna leaned back to look him in the eye. He couldn't be serious. This boy, who'd spent Lord knows how much money on these tickets, was willing to walk away before the concert even started, just for her. He really was too good to be true.

Then the lights dimmed, and the crowd jumped to their feet when Journey took the stage.

"Looks like we're staying!" Lynna shouted to him, laughing as she stood with the crowd. This once, she took comfort in being short, because the people standing in front of her would hide her from view, assuming they stayed on their feet.

As it turned out, the crowd stood for the entire concert.

Her jaw dropped at Steve Perry's voice. She didn't think it possible he could sound as good as he did on the radio, but he nailed every note with a humble confidence. The lyrics flowed out of him and possessed every person in the coliseum.

Lynna swooned when they performed *Faithfully*. The entire crowd lost it at that point. People waved their lighters to the music and sang along.

She and Patrick cheered and danced in place as the concert continued, and when the whole thing closed out with *Separate Ways...* Listening to that on her cassette player was never gonna compare with this. Never again. Not that it would stop her from playing it for the rest of her life, even if she had to break out a pencil to rewind the tape to start it over.

But then it all ended and the lights in the Coliseum went back up. That's when reality hit.

Agent Mills looked as if he might turn to look in their direction.

Lynna did the first and only thing she could think to do, not something she'd been trained to do but something she'd seen in a film. She grabbed Patrick and kissed him, turning his back to Agent Mills to hide her from view. This wasn't the nip of lips kiss again. No, the way he kissed her, it was as if the universe had carved him to be her perfect fit. She didn't want it to end, but then the guy next to them laughed.

"Get a room, kids!"

She risked opening an eye to look around Patrick to see if Agent Mills was still there. Relief flooded her as she saw him exit his row and go down the stairs.

They stole more kisses as they followed the crowd outside the Coliseum. These embraces were fast, frantic, and hungry. She didn't question as he pulled her along, holding her hand in his as they ran for several blocks. They didn't stop until they reached his car, a blue Buick Skylark. She didn't protest that she should be heading back to the Greenhouse. Patrick held open the passenger door for her, and she climbed inside. As soon as he got in the driver's seat, he locked the car and they kissed again. She'd wanted this for so long, and now that it was here, she felt dizzy. Her body ached as his teeth raked lightly against her throat, and when she returned the favor, he groaned.

She lost track of time, but when they stopped, she knew it still wasn't near enough. Maria had tried to describe having sex with Pockets, how it made her feel, but somehow it never really translated. Lynna didn't think she could find the words for this either, but she finally understood.

When Patrick spoke, his voice came out winded and amused. "Would it be safe now to say this is our first date?"

Apparently, she wasn't the only one who'd been unsure about that. She laughed, resting her head against his shoulder and held him tight.

"Definitely."

"So where are you parked?" he asked.

Lynna's mind blanked. "What?"

"I can drive you to your car," he said.

"My car." Oh, heaven help her. She hadn't considered this. She'd planned to fly home after the concert. No way she could do that now, not without him asking a million questions she couldn't answer. Not a chance, and she was still too high from making out with him to think of any other clever outs. "I..."

"Do you need me to drive you home?" he asked.

"Oh! Yes! That would be fantastic. Yes, please."

She glanced at her watch. It was already a quarter until midnight. How long had they been making out? So much for that eleven o'clock curfew.

Nevada was going to kill her.

Chapter 29: Lynna

Sunday, 30 January 1983

Lynna told Patrick to head for their school to get her bearings. From there, she directed him towards the Greenhouse campus.

"Your place is really close to Powhatan." Patrick leaned over the steering wheel to peer down the poorly lighted road. "Don't see how you're zoned for West Chester High School."

"I suspect money was involved." She said it as a joke, but she knew for a fact that a lot of money traded hands. The CIA, using a corporate shell company, had donated almost the entire cost of the school's construction. About the only thing they hadn't covered was the price tag for a theater. The school district had said they'd cover that. The map in the school's orientation handbook even had a dotted square where the theater should go and would eventually be built. Yeah, r ight.

"Wouldn't shock me." He grinned as he said it.

Damn, he really was cute. They'd held hands for most of the drive here. She forced herself to focus on the road.

"Stop here," she said as soon as she spotted the turn.

"Ouch!"

"Sorry!" She'd squeezed his hand too hard. "But seriously, do a u-turn here and pull onto the shoulder. Don't go any further."

He let go of her hand to turn the car around. The right turn signal continued to blink as he pulled onto the side of the road. He leaned towards her, but no kissing ensued. He looked out her passenger door window. Then his eyes slid over to her.

"You can't be serious."

"It's fine. Honest."

"Are you kidding?" His voice went up a couple octaves. "There are horror movies that start like this."

"Name one."

"Okay, I can't, but that's not the point. This is the middle of nowhere. I can't drop you off here."

"It's not the middle of nowhere. It's the Powhatan County border."

The look he answered her with made it blatantly clear she'd proved his point.

"I promise that on the other side of those trees is where I live. You knew I had to sneak out for this date. Well, that means I have to sneak back inside, too."

He didn't argue, but the look on his face was near panic.

"It's fine. Trust me." She leaned into him and pulled him into another kiss. How she pulled back before it could turn into another full-blown makeout session, she wasn't sure, but she managed it. "You do trust me, don't you?" she said as she caught her breath.

"Of course I trust you." No, he wasn't convinced, but judging from his frustrated groan, he'd finally accepted defeat. "I don't suppose there's any way you could call me in a half hour, once I'm home."

"No, but I'll call you in the morning."

"You better call, because if you don't, I'm gonna be driving up to the front gates like what's-his-name shouting for Stella."

"You mean Marlon Brando?" She laughed.

"Okay." He sighed, his head hanging in defeat. "Call me in the morning."

She reached over to cup his chin in her hand. "I promise."

After one last kiss, she got out of the car and ran into the woods. A fence appeared about ten feet from the road, but by that point, she was well out of his view. She heard the car pull away a minute later. By that point, she'd already slipped off her jacket and t-shirt to change into a dragon. She stuffed the clothing into her backpack and then climbed the trees. She hopped from tree to tree instead of taking flight. She didn't want to take a chance of diving out towards the road with a car coming.

She scrambled to where she needed to go. The time was close to 12:30. She wondered what the odds were that the others were still waiting for her in the clearing.

When she dropped down into the spot, she discovered the answer was a most definite "no."

She sighed. Nevada would give her hell for this, but at least Maria would let her off the hook. Once she heard about the epic kissing in the car, Maria would forgive all.

"Freeze!"

Lights mounted on rifles surrounded her on the right and at her back. Crap. She was beyond busted.

One of the rifles lowered, and with the light no longer blinding her, Lynna recognized Agent Mills. "Dammit, Lynna! I was really hoping you weren't in on this, too."

What was he talking about? In on what? The meeting with her friends? Why was he so upset?

"Human form," he said. "Now."

She glanced towards the other rifles still aimed at her. He raised a hand to cue them to lower their rifles. Once they did, she changed back to her human appearance.

"Sorry, but what is going on?" Had he seen her at the concert, after all?

"Lynna, with me." He snapped out the words. "The rest of you, this is all of them. You can head back to your posts."

She followed him down the path towards the mansion and didn't speak until the guards had gotten out of earshot.

"I'm sorry. I didn't..." Her words trailed off, not really sure what to say.

"You didn't what? Think perhaps?" He stopped, and she stopped with him. "Do you have any idea what the CIA might do if they got even a hint that we don't have you and the other kids under control? Dr. Howard and I are trying to protect you, because Director Brand is itching to militarize this whole damn operation."

His free hand was clenched as if to squeeze Brand by the throat. "We don't want what happened to Raymond to happen to the rest of you. Don't you get it? Elyce—I mean, Dr. Howard would die if you got hurt."

She couldn't meet his eyes. The only thing she managed to say was "I'm sorry."

"I hope whatever you were doing was worth it." He marched past her and waved for her to follow. "Your friends didn't give you up. Only reason we knew you were gone was because we immediately did a roll call of all the barracks."

In spite of herself, Lynna couldn't help but smile. They'd stuck by her, even though she'd been late.

Chapter 30: Lynna

Sunday, 30 January 1983

Agent Mills didn't lead Lynna inside the mansion. Instead, he took her to the back patio, where Dr. Howard and her friends waited.

The patio was made of large grey tiles, each with an engraved image of a tobacco leaf. A short, stone railing separated them from the low cliff that overlooked the lake. Ten-foot-tall lampposts spaced out along the railing provided enough light to see. Everyone gathered here sat in black, wrought iron chairs next to two of the matching, round tables that had been pushed together. Water spilled down a sculpture of a flower as big as a boulder resting in the middle of a round fountain. Life-sized statues of starlings sat on the north, east, south, and west points of the pool's edge.

What Agent Mills had told Lynna about Brand looking for an excuse to oust him and Dr. Howard offered all the explanation she needed for why they were gathered here in the cold instead of the warm conference room. Even if the CIA had planted bugs out here, the running water would muffle anything they said, as long as they didn't get too loud.

The first face Lynna focused on was Ava's. Her little sister didn't wave but stared at her with a wide-eyed and tight-lipped expression. The message fell somewhere between panic and laughter as if to say, *"You wouldn't believe the night we've had."*

Lynna took the seat next to Ava and patted her on the shoulder as she sat down with the fountain at her back. She kept thinking about Olivia's warnings. The Erlking didn't want all of the Daemons, just Ava.

Maria, Pockets, and Nevada all stared straight ahead at nothing. Nevada tapped a finger on her spiral notebook, sitting on the table in front of her. One of her fangs was sticking out over her bottom lip as she chewed on it. Lynna never understood how Nevada could do that without drawing her own blood, and had her fangs gotten longer at some point?

Dr. Howard sat at the "head" of the conjoined tables. Her pale blue eyes had watched Lynna walk from the door to the chair, even when Agent Mills sat down next to her and whispered, "She's fine." A hint of a smile that went right back into annoyance followed that. Dr. Howard whispered a "thank you" to him that Lynna only made out by the movement of her lips.

Sitting up and pulling her black winter coat tight, Dr. Howard said, "Now that we're all here, I believe Nevada has something important to share."

Lynna had expected Dr. Howard to jump straight into the grandmother of lectures. Were they really getting off this easy? Was she?

Nevada cupped her hands and blew into them to warm them up, her breath misting in the air. Then she flipped open her notebook. The paper thwapped back and forth until she found the page she wanted. Judging from the pages Nevada skipped past, she'd been using this as a journal or maybe to write stories. If they didn't get locked into their rooms after all this, Lynna would have to ask her about that. Then Nevada reached a page with a grid filled with dates and multiple columns of initials and dollar amounts.

"When I broke into Dr. Taggart's computer in his office, there was a disk hidden on his bookshelves. It contained dates going back more than two decades. Agent Vale took the disk with him, but I remembered the contents long enough to write them down as soon as I got back to the Greenhouse."

Pockets, who was sitting next to Nevada, pointed to the page sitting open in front of her. "You memorized all that?"

Nevada didn't look at him. Instead, her eyes retreated to the notebook. "There's four pages of it."

Lynna leaned forward to get a better look at the page, across the table from her. There were also multiple columns of dates. Nevada had arranged it by the first column of dates, though. How did she remember all that? Sure, they'd trained in memorization techniques for years, but this went well past anything the rest of them could do, and even Nevada had never demonstrated this much skill.

Agent Mills got the conversation moving again. "What exactly is it?"

"I wasn't sure, at first." Nevada shrugged. "The next to last column is a set of dates, and once I noticed the one for August 27, 1971, I started to realize what I was looking at."

Dr. Howard leaned forward, her eyes widening. "That's the day DeWare brought you to the Greenhouse."

Nevada nodded. "One of the columns on that same row has two letters in it: NB."

Pockets let out a low whistle, obviously getting what it meant. Lynna was the first to say it, though. "NB... Nevada Brandle."

"I'll come back to the other columns in a moment." She cleared her throat. Nevada never liked to be the focus of a crowd, even if she often drew attention her way. "But once I realized that, I got curious. Pockets, what's your gotcha day?"

He answered without missing a beat. "January 3, 1971."

She flipped to the next page and pointed at a line near the top. "RB.... Rowan Beltrami."

Pockets brought his hand up to his face, hiding his mouth, but his eyes suggested he was fascinated and repulsed.

"I checked with all of the Daemons who could remember their gotcha day. Not all the dates show up and some are off by a few days, but most of us are here."

"Me?" Ava's voice squeaked.

Nevada shook her head. "No, you're one of the few who are missing from this list, and I'll come back to that in a moment, too."

"How does this civilian have all this information?" Agent Mills asked in a hushed voice.

"That's where the dollar amounts and two of the other columns come into it." She didn't focus on the money column, though. She ran her finger down one that only had one letter in each row. "There's a designation next to each dollar amount: C, F, or K. Given all the rows with F don't include a dollar amount or, if they do, it's substantially less than the others, I suspect the 'F' stands for failure."

"Failure to do exactly what?" Maria was looking past Pockets at the page Nevada had sitting open. Probably looking for the row with her gotcha date.

"Based on all of the dates that match up with the gotcha dates I gathered from everyone, I'm pretty sure 'C' stands for capture or caught. The 'K' is most likely for kill." She punctuated this by planting both of her hands flat on top of the notebook. "My guess is that Taggart, our English professor, is really a mercenary who specializes in abductions and assassinations."

Agent Mills rubbed his hands together to warm them. "You said there was another column that tied into those two."

Nevada nodded. "There's something else all of our gotcha dates have in common. There's a column with another set of initials. The initials vary in that column throughout the ledger, but the ones for everyone brought to the Greenhouse all have 'RD' listed there."

Dr. Howard had been hugging herself to keep warm, but at those initials, she placed her hands on the table and leaned forward. When she spoke, she said the name with all the deserved venom. "Rudolph DeWare." She shook her head. "I always wondered how he managed to get all of you here."

"Wait," Lynna said as she resisted the urge to turn into her dragon form to fight back the cold, "this doesn't track. If the CIA and DeWare hired Taggart to gather all of us, then why did they let us go investigate him? Wouldn't they have immediately recognized who he was on that list I took from the contact in East Berlin?"

"No." Dr. Howard smiled softly to Agent Mills, who looked as surprised by her response as Lynna felt. "Watergate," she said, as if that explained it all.

"When Nixon got caught in the Watergate scandal, the CIA went into a panic. They purged all of their most sensitive documents. Most of you were abducted during Nixon's administration, so it's little surprise they wanted to dump all of that. That's also why the abductions stopped. The CIA never even let President Ford know the Greenhouse existed. They also kept President Carter in the dark, at least until Zach died. The ADD prior to Brand had a conscience and refused to sweep all of this under the rug. I suspect even some of the most senio r officials in the CIA had been left in the dark up until that point, and they only brought Carter into it, because none of them wanted to take the responsibility for cleaning up a previous administration's mess."

"So any paperwork on Taggart regarding the Greenhouse wouldn't exist." Nevada sounded as if that settled some unresolved piece of the puzzle for her.

Agent Mills only looked more troubled, though. After a moment, he stood. "You all keep going, I'm going to make a quick call."

Nevada stood as if to protest, but before she could say anything, Agent Mills added. "Don't worry. I'll be keeping this close to the vest."

He marched inside the mansion's dining hall and into the heat Lynna was coveting because of her thin jacket.

Dr. Howard broke the silence that had fallen over the group. "What else have you got, Nevada?"

"Yeah, what about me?" Ava's wrought iron chair scraped along the stone tiles as she hopped with excitement.

"What Dr. Howard says about Watergate fits with what I'm seeing here. After 1973, the steady flow of abductions for DeWare ends. It makes sense that Ava doesn't show up, because DeWare was gone by the time she came into the Greenhouse. He'd only been gone for about a month at that point, but you also didn't get picked out by the genetic testing the way the rest of us were."

Dr. Howard filled in the blank on that one. "Ava was unique, sent to us because of the unusual circumstances around the attack on her family. President Carter had hoped the Greenhouse could become a home for children like her, whose powers were too dangerous and likely to make them targets for other nations or terrorist organizations hoping to follow DeWare's lead. I'm afraid that never really developed beyond Ava, though. Didn't help that when the current administration took over, they went back to seeing all of you as weapons instead of children."

A cloud fell over Nevada's face as she flipped through the pages to the last one of the copy she'd made of Taggart's list.

"Yeah, that's what has me worried."

The door to the mansion opened, and Agent Mills stormed out onto the patio.

"Lucas?" Dr. Howard was the only one, including the staff, who ever called Agent Mills by his first name.

He pulled out his chair with a loud scrape. "I just got off the phone with Agent Vale."

"Punk-ass bitch," Pockets muttered and then looked up to realize everyone was staring at him. "That was out loud, wasn't it?"

"Accurate, though." Nevada said. She and Pockets exchanged a fist-bump.

Agent Mills snorted. "Fortunately, he's a useful punk-ass bitch."

"What did the punk-ass bitch say?" Ava asked, hopping in her chair again. When both Dr. Howard and Agent Mills scowled at her, she sulked and grumbled to herself. "Everyone else got to say it."

"Lucas, can we...?"

Agent Mills nodded. "Anyway, Vale says the higher ups came to him a couple days after your op," he pointed to Nevada. "They confiscated the disk you took from Taggart and told him to drop it. Which, of course, explains why none of us have gotten any sort of follow-up on this investigation since then."

Lynna waved a hand to interrupt. "But if that's the case, then that means they realized who Taggart is and how he connects to the Greenhouse. How would they have done that if all the paperwork is ash or stuck in some box inside an off-site warehouse?"

"That's what I was about to get to." Nevada tapped on the last page of her hand-written copy. "The lines for DeWare stopped in 1973, but unless the initials are a coincidence, they start up again a little less than two years ago, in the spring of '81, shortly after the start of the current administration."

Dr. Howard turned almost white, mouth hanging open as her breath escaped in a trail of steam. She didn't speak, didn't seem capable of it, and she didn't need to say anything, because Nevada spelled it out for anyone who hadn't pieced it together.

"I think the administration has DeWare running a second Greenhouse."

Chapter 31: Lynna

Sunday, 30 January 1983

The conversation fell into a free-for-all, starting with Lynna. "But how did the CIA still not realize this before sending us to investigate Taggart?"

"They probably aren't running the new one out of the CIA," Pockets said.

"My guess?" Nevada jumped in. "It's operating under the Pentagon's supervision."

"Or the NSA," Maria added.

"Jesus!" Agent Mills grabbed Dr. Howard's forearm. "They did it. They've militarized it."

Dr. Howard slammed her fist on the table. "No wonder they've never sent anyone new to us since Ava."

"There's no telling how many kids they've sent his way," Agent Mills said.

"That's not true," Nevada said as she held up her notebook, "I can safely say he's at least got ten, so far."

That silenced everyone.

All Lynna could think of was Zach. That son of a bitch was going to do it again. He would torture and kill more kids. If Nevada had guessed right, the military would run it in an even less humane fashion than the first time.

"We have to find him," Lynna said, pausing in surprise at how much anger she heard in her own words, "and we have to stop him."

"Whoa!" Agent Mills reached past Ava to plant his hand near Lynna.

"No!" Lynna jumped to her feet and kicked her chair behind her. "No, dammit! He doesn't get to do this again!"

"I agree." Mills kept his voice slow and even, looking over each of them so they could see he was serious. "But we've got to play this smart. Are we all clear on that?"

Nevada flipped her notebook shut. "I vote we find him and kill him."

"No." Agent Mills got to his feet. Damn he was tall.

"That's enough," Dr. Howard said, "all of you." She hadn't raised her voice, but the command in her tone did the job.

Once Dr. Howard appeared satisfied she'd gotten everyone to stop talking, she looked back at Nevada. "I'm assuming that's all the information you have?"

Nevada nodded, but Lynna struggled about whether to say something. She knew something none of them did. They had a traitor in their unit. Maybe? What if the information was bleeding out of the second Greenhouse? Someone might be feeding all of Dr. Howard's files to DeWare's new unit. She couldn't be sure. As long as any chance existed someone here was working with the elves, she couldn't risk—

"Lynna?" Dr. Howard said her name as if it wasn't the first time she'd tried to get her attention. Everyone else had started to leave.

"I'm sorry?" Lynna said.

"I said I'd like you to stay a moment longer."

Ava smiled up to her before following the others into the mansion. Even Agent Mills left, closing the door to the dining hall once they were all inside.

Dr. Howard tapped on the table near where Agent Mills had been sitting. "Come here, and don't worry about the statue."

"The statue?" Lynna looked over her shoulder. Her chair was on its side, next to a stone carving of a bird that had been on the edge of the fountain. "Sorry!"

"I said don't worry about it." Dr. Howard tapped on the table again, directing Lynna to sit next to her.

The chair scraped along the stones as Lynna sat. Didn't take long to realize what this was about.

"Where were you tonight?"

Lynna slouched in her chair. Moments like this, she still felt like she was five.

Dr. Howard placed her hand on Lynna's. "It's all right, but I need you to be honest with me."

"If it helps any, I was with Agent Mills most of the evening." When Dr. Howard's face contorted with both surprise and concern, Lynna quickly continued. "He didn't know I was there. I went on a date at the Journey concert."

Dr. Howard smiled, the look on her face both beautiful and reassuring. "Patrick?"

Lynna felt herself blushing. "Yeah."

"How did you know Agent Mills was there, too?"

Lynna groaned. "He sat down a few rows in front of us."

Dr. Howard snorted, and then quickly covered her mouth as she regained her composure. Even when she removed her hand, she was fighting the urge to laugh. "Well, that must have been awkward."

Lynna nodded. She still couldn't believe Agent Mills didn't catch her. The guy had eyes in the back of his head.

"However, Agent Mills came home shortly after eleven. You didn't get back until more than an hour later."

Lynna couldn't even look her in the eyes. She felt her cheeks getting even warmer as she remembered making out in Patrick's car.

"Well then," Dr. Howard said in a voice that at least reassured Lynna she was smiling, "I do hope you at least used protection."

"We didn't do that!"

"It's okay. I wanted to make sure you were safe."

Lynna risked looking up. "So does this mean I'm not in trouble?"

The swift change in Dr. Howard's expression answered that. "You went off campus without permission. No one knew where to find you. At least none of the adults here did. I'm pretty sure Maria knew, judging from the insipid way she grinned at you."

Lynna cleared her throat. "I'd prefer not to confirm or deny that."

"Oh, I'm sure. But yes, there will be consequences. You should have told me."

That mustered up Lynna's courage. "Really? If I'd asked for permission—"

"No, you're right. I'd have denied it. It's not fair, but Brand would lose his mind if he had any idea what you did, even if I had given you permission. Ever since being given control of the Greenhouse, my intention was to ease all of you into civilian life, but they keep tightening the leash." She pointed to herself as she added, "On all of us."

"I know, and after Raymond, I just..."

Dr. Howard didn't say anything. She nodded with tears rimming her eyes. Lynna leaned over to hug her.

When they broke the hug, Dr. Howard had pulled herself back together.

"For now, you're restricted to your barracks except for school and meals for all of next week. Are we clear?"

"Yes, ma'am."

At least she hadn't taken away her phone privileges. That would have been disastrous. She wouldn't have been able to call Patrick in the morning or get any signals from Olivia. She made sure to sound and look bummed by Dr. Howard's orders. Rule one of getting punished: never act relieved, or the adult will assume you need more punishment.

Dr. Howard trusted her to walk to the barracks on her own. She ran into Agent Mills as he headed back to the mansion. Apparently, he'd escorted everyone else to their rooms.

"Don't be going downstairs to see Maria," he said. Seemed he'd also noticed the way Maria looked at her. "The guards are on the stairs for the rest of the night, and if one of them has to wake me, someone is getting a boot up their ass."

After he continued walking back towards the mansion, Lynna called after him. "You shouldn't have missed the opening act. He was pretty good. Not as good as Steve Perry, though."

He stopped in his tracks, turned and stared at her with his jaw hanging open as what she'd said sunk in.

She turned and danced her way towards the barracks, singing the opening lines to Journey's *Don't Stop Believin'*.

The look on Agent Mills' face was totally worth it.

Chapter 32: Lynna

Tuesday, 1 February 1983

Despite being grounded, Lynna enjoyed the next couple of days, especially at school.

She and Patrick reveled in officially being an item. The best part of the change was the physical contact. Knowing how they both felt about each other lifted the taboo preventing them from touching one another. They held hands whenever they walked together. They stole quick kisses between classes. For the first time, she enjoyed when people seeing them together pointed and whispered.

At lunch on Tuesday, she brought her guitar to school, and they jammed together. It was fortunate the doors to the practice rooms were mostly glass, because otherwise they wouldn't have played their instruments at all. Of course, that's also why the windows in the doors sucked, because she would have really loved what they would have done with the privacy.

"I guess we'll have to figure out a way to have a second date," Patrick said as he scrambled to pack up his drum set near the end of lunch. "We could try to go to another concert or maybe go somewhere for dinner. What I'd really love to do is take you to New World to go dancing. That would be fun as hell!"

"Well, it's not happening this week." She zipped up her guitar case. Dr. Howard would probably let her go on a real date after the punishment ended...

maybe. Lynna suspected Dr. Howard was right about ADD Brand having a conniption fit if he ever learned of it. "I really did have fun."

He grinned over to her. "Me, too."

After school, he walked her to the student pickup, staying with her while she and the other Daemons waited for the van to take them home. He'd done this on Monday, too. His kiss goodbye held a promise that this was going to be the new norm from now on. She loved it.

Nevada grumbled as she slouched in the front seat of the van and tilted her fedora down to cover her eyes. "All you face suckers are grossing me out."

Pockets laughed, apparently approving of the description.

"I think they're cute." Ava elbowed Lynna. "I like him."

Lynna couldn't stop grinning. "I'm glad he's got the Little Sister Seal of Approval."

When they walked in the front door of their barracks, the on-campus hybrids were already back from their own classes. Most were in their rooms with a couple in the common area watching TV.

Athena was on the phone down at the other end of the hallway across from the door to Lynna's room. She beckoned to Lynna and pointed to the phone. "Hold on, ma'am," Athena said into the receiver. "She just walked in the door."

"Who is it?" Lynna asked as she set down her guitar, letting it lean against her door.

"It's an agent lady." She handed the phone to Lynna. "Oh! And we got another one of those Iniango calls."

Lynna froze for a second, holding the handset. "Really? For Albert Iniango?"

"No," she said, with a confused look on her face. "Now that you mention it, they asked for a lady's name this time. D-something. Diane, maybe. Oh! No, it was Dorothy, but I told them they had the wrong number. Wish these jerks would pay their bills."

Lynna stood there and looked at her watch. Of all the days for Olivia to call for a meeting. How could she pull this off? She was so distracted that she forgot about the phone in her hand until she heard a woman's voice on the other end going, "Hello?"

"Sorry!" She brought the handset up to her mouth. "This is Lynna."

"Hey, this is Vicki." Lynna was so distracted that she spaced for a few seconds until the name and voice finally clicked, Agent Morgan from West Berlin.

"Hey! How are you?"

"Tired, but that's par for the course these days. Was worried about you and Ava. Wanted to check on you."

Speaking of Ava, she barreled out of her room. "Bathroom!"

Lynna lifted the cord of the phone for Ava to duck under it. Once Ava ran past and the bathroom door slammed shut, Lynna moved to stand next to the phone so she wouldn't block the hallway.

"Thanks. We're doing all right." She wished she could have told Vicki about her date, but the CIA recorded all of their calls. She couldn't risk it getting back to Brand. "School has been busy. My English teacher announced we have to pick a topic for a term paper before the end of the week. No idea what I'm going to do yet."

"I do not miss those days." Vicki laughed. An uncomfortable silence followed before Vicki continued. "I'm really sorry I can't be there for Raymond's burial. Tried to get approval for the leave, but we've got an ambassador flying into West Berlin tomorrow for a series of meetings during the next two weeks, and they need me to babysit. If they haven't already had the funeral, I'd like to send some flowers."

"Wait, what do mean about a burial? Last we'd heard from the CIA, they weren't able to get Raymond across the border."

Another uncomfortable pause followed, and it was again Vicki who ended it. "We smuggled him out on Friday and got him on a plane that evening. I personally handed him over to the escort waiting on the plane at Tempelhof."

Lynna twisted her fingers in the phone cord. "Vicki, I need you to tell me everything you can about this escort."

Minutes later, Lynna sprinted out the door and down the stairs. The guard standing watch tried to grab her, but she ducked past him.

"I've got to see Dr. Howard now!"

She ran across the field and to the driveway and up to the front door. The whole thing reminded her of the night Zach had died, when she'd run past the guards, changing into her dragon form for the first time and flinging that bastard Graham to the ground when he got in her way. That had been the middle of the night, but even the sun's glare didn't remove the sense of déjà vu.

Lynna shouted as soon as she entered the mansion. "Dr. Howard! Agent Mills!"

They didn't answer right away, so she did the same thing she did that other night and ran past the pool table, heading towards Dr. Howard's bedroom.

"Dr. Howard!"

She wasn't in her bedroom. Lynna berated herself, realizing Dr. Howard was probably in her office upstairs.

Sure enough, she found her in there. Lynna stormed into the room, sweating and out of breath. Agent Mills was in the office with her, sitting on the edge of her desk, chatting with her. They both stood, startled by Lynna's entrance.

"Lynna, what's wrong?" Dr. Howard asked.

"I think DeWare has Raymond's body."

Chapter 33: Lynna

Tuesday, 1 February 1983

Agent Mills led them down to the fountain so they could speak more openly. With each detail Lynna shared about her call with Vicki, the more horror-stricken Dr. Howard looked. She sat on the edge of the fountain once Lynna mentioned the slight Scottish accent and the bruises that were on the face of the supposed CIA escort at Tempelhof.

"Does that match the injuries Nevada gave Taggart?" Lynna asked.

Dr. Howard and Agent Mills exchanged glances. They'd both sat in on Nevada's debrief. Agent Mills answered for both of them, though.

"Yeah, that sounds like our guy. There's something else that locks it. Agent Vale called me this morning." He glanced at Dr. Howard apologetically and then got this sheepish smile on his face. "Sorry, I meant to tell you when I stopped by your office, but I got distracted. Vale realized he'd forgotten to mention something he'd learned before the higher ups told him to stop investigating Taggart. The last bit of traffic he received on Taggart had him flying out of JFK Wednesday night for West Berlin. I didn't think it had anything to do with Raymond, because for someone on the run from the U.S, getting behind the wall into East Berlin makes sense. I mean, personally, I'd make a run for Cuba, but some guys don't mind the cold."

"There was one other thing Vicki mentioned," Lynna said. "The CIA apparently sent strict instructions not to cremate Raymond's body in order to get him out of East Berlin."

Dr. Howard turned a shade of green.

"Elyce?"

She stared straight ahead at nothing as she answered. "There are two things that come to mind and neither is good. First, it's the only chance anyone has had to perform a full autopsy on Raymond. Typically, when he's died, he's reanimated too quickly to attempt anything like that. Who knows what DeWare might learn from that? Second, when he's reanimated, it's always resulted in a burst of fire. There's a chance that cremating him could force him to reanimate. I haven't said anything to any of you, because I didn't want to give you false hope."

"God in Heaven," Agent Mills whispered. "Which do you think DeWare is more likely to do?"

"No, Lucas, you misunderstand." Dr. Howard stood and placed her hand on his arm. "He's going to do both. And worse, if he can revive Raymond, he'll try to repeat killing him in the same way the Grey Women did it. He'll do it repeatedly until it's no longer a benefit to his research."

Lynna hugged herself to make sure she didn't shake. This was even worse than she'd thought when she ran to the mansion. "We've got to find them now, but how do we do it?"

"We can't call Brand." Agent Mills clenched his fists. "The second he realizes we've figured out what's going on, he'll cut us off at the knees, order us to stand down. After that, any action we take would be considered treason. We're already on borrowed time, because the details of your phone call will reach him soon enough.

"Worst case scenario, if DeWare pulls off what you're suggesting, the CIA and the administration would see that as a huge success. Imagine the implications if DeWare can figure out how the whole process works, find a way to duplicate it in other people. Seeing he's close to solving that riddle? The administration will think they're better off taking the kids away and handing them back over to DeWare."

"We'd sooner all run away or fight," Lynna said. "Maybe both."

"I respect the sentiment," Agent Mills said, "but we both know that's easier said than done. For all we know, these Grey Women are a product of this new Greenhouse."

"They're not."

Both Dr. Howard and Agent Mills looked at Lynna with the same question on their faces. Crap! She'd slipped up, given up that fact too quickly and with too much certainty.

"I mean..." Lynna screamed at herself to think fast. "I mean, there's no way he found all of these women and got them to work with him. Most of them looked like they're adults, and if he's only been up and running again for two years, I don't think he'd have figured out a way to mass produce their abilities."

Agent Mills shrugged in agreement. "It's already after four. I'm gonna drive to the nearest payphone and call in some favors. I don't dare make those calls from here."

Dr. Howard touched him on the arm again. "Be careful, but get back here as fast as you can. Okay?"

"I will, but it'll probably be a few hours."

They exchanged smiles and then he marched into the mansion.

Lynna's mind started to rewind things. The way Dr. Howard and Agent Mills had been positioned near each other behind the desk when she ran into the office. The way Agent Mills had started calling her "Elyce" instead of "Dr. Howard." Dr. Howard also called him by his first name, too. And there was the way Dr. Howard had touched his arm—twice. Lynna wouldn't have given it a second thought until this week, but it was like her and Patrick, now that they were free to touch one another. And had Dr. Howard been checking out his ass when he walked away?

"What?" Dr. Howard drew out the word, obviously seeing the way Lynna was looking at her.

Lynna's grin widened as the details clicked into place. "Are you and Agent Mills—um, you know?"

Dr. Howard's eyes went wide. "Let me be very clear about this. There is nothing happening between me and Agent Mills, because," she gave that word added emphasis, "if there was, it would be a serious conflict of interest that the CIA would never brook. Do you understand me?"

"Yes, ma'am."

Dr. Howard mouthed a silent "Thank you."

Lynna couldn't help but smile back at her. She loved the idea that Dr. Howard might have someone like Agent Mills to make her happy the same way Patrick did for her.

Even though no one was on the patio with them, Lynna whispered, "How long?"

Dr. Howard didn't look pleased by that, but she caved. "A month."

Lynna spun around in place, dancing as she pretended to scream and mouthed, "That's awesome!"

Dr. Howard cleared her throat and then said out loud, "You should get back to your barracks."

"Sorr—I mean, yes, ma'am." She gave Dr. Howard two excited thumbs up before she left.

She was really happy for Dr. Howard and Agent Mills. She liked them a lot, which made what she needed to do next that much harder.

Chapter 34: Lynna

Tuesday, 1 February 1983

Lynna didn't return to the barracks. She'd realized before leaving Dr. Howard at the fountain that coming up to the mansion had given her an honest excuse to get past the guards. She couldn't waste that opportunity.

The sun felt glorious against her scales as she launched into the sky. She couldn't remember the last time she'd gotten to fly in daylight. Night skies were wonderful, too, but something about bathing in the sunlight made her feel free.

The only bad thing was that while she always wore one of her specially designed tank tops, in case she had to change into her dragon form, she didn't have her small backpack to shove her shirt and jacket into, forcing her to ball them up and hold them to her chest in a death grip. More than once, she came close to losing them to the wind.

She circled downtown until after sunset. Then she landed in an alley in the Shockoe Bottom area. As soon as she returned to her human form, the cold hit her hard. She scrambled back into her shirt and jacket, glad she hadn't lost them.

From there, she walked down towards the train station on Main Street. She knew from what Patrick had said that the New World dance club was located somewhere near there on East Franklin.

She couldn't miss the place once she found the street. The brick building had a large window in the front with a neon sign hanging on the inside. The words

"New World" were stacked with "New" in bright blue and "World" in brilliant pink.

Going by the particulars they'd figured out at the Lincoln Memorial, Olivia's signal meant she wanted to meet here at 21:00 hours. It wasn't even 19:00 yet. When her stomach grumbled about missing dinner, she considered going into the club early. The food there probably sucked, though. Plus, she didn't have a lot of money in her pants pocket.

She spotted a business across from the club. The store's bright yellow sign with black letters had drawn her attention. "Southern Sun" looked like a small café. The inside was sparsely furnished with a small bake case next to a counter with a cashier sitting on a stool behind it and in front of an espresso machine. The old man on the stool looked Hispanic and was reading that morning's copy of the Times Dispatch. He looked at Lynna over the top of his newspaper. "What can I get you?"

Lynna glanced at the drinks menu written in chalk on a blackboard hanging next to the espresso machine. "I'll get a medium café mocha." Then she looked back at the bake case. "Oh, and one of the honey butter croissants."

"You want the croissant warmed up?" He folded up his paper and set it on his stool as he pulled a mug from the shelf along the back wall.

"Yes, please."

A few minutes later, Lynna parked herself in a cozy chair next to the window. From there, she watched the foot traffic passing by. Things picked up across the street at New World around seven. Even though she took her time savoring her drink and croissant, she'd polished off the pastry and reached the bottom of her mug a little before eight p.m.

She considered getting another pastry until she saw a familiar blonde go inside New World. The girl wore a purple, zebra striped shirt beneath a black leather jacket. Even though her outfit didn't look nearly as expensive this time and her hair was pulled back into a ponytail, it was definitely Olivia. Thank goodness! Maybe Lynna could get her meeting over with early and get back to the Greenhouse before anyone noticed she was gone.

Lynna slipped her jacket back on and dashed across the street.

Despite watching all the comings and goings, Lynna hadn't realized how crowded New World had gotten. An inconspicuous sign near the entrance declared this place shouldn't by occupied by more than fifty people, but she'd wager the crowd had grown well past that. The inside turned out bigger than she'd expected, too. The front of the club was narrow, but the inside stretched into the shadows. A light-up dance floor near the back provided most of the illumination, with the pattern of the lights matched to the beat of the music. *She Blinded Me With Science* started playing.

A bar—an actual wooden bar—ran along most of the right wall. Surely a teen dance club wasn't serving alcohol, but they'd stocked the back wall of the bar. Only, as she got closer, she realized these were recycled liquor bottles with the labels replaced in an effort that was one part clever and five parts lame. They'd taken a boxy bottle with a round cork stopper and relabeled it "Tequila Mockingbird." A stout bottle contained a bright green liquid, almost certainly water with food coloring, and was labeled in a fancy old English font as "For Class" and then beneath it in plain text "Absent."

Much as she adored Patrick and knew he liked this place, it was cheesy. She kept moving before the bartender could ask her if she wanted anything. Were they even technically a bartender, if they didn't serve alcohol? A faux-tender, perhaps? She wanted to find Olivia and get out of here.

Someone in a zebra print shirt shouldn't be that difficult to find, but with the crowd and poor lighting, Lynna could see little better than four people beyond herself in any direction. Being short didn't help.

"Lynna?"

She spun around as the person who called out her name pushed their way through the crowd to her. The smile that greeted her melted her heart, even as it sent her into a panic.

"Patrick."

Lynna's questions paused as he kissed her. The first kiss was a quick one, a simple "hello," but when they realized they were really here together, the next kiss lasted longer as they embraced.

Once they came up for air, Lynna grinned at him. He smiled back, but his eyes narrowed in confusion.

"What are you doing here? Thought you were trapped in timeout for the week?"

For the second time today, her thoughts screamed for her to think up an explanation as the DJ switched the music to the Steve Miller Band's *Abracadabra*. She loved that song and hadn't heard it in a while. The distraction didn't help her brain as it scrambled for a way to explain how and why she was here.

"I snuck out." She flashed her best grin. "I'm meeting—I mean, I hoped I might find you here."

Sure he was grinning now, thrilled that she'd risked getting into trouble for the chance to see him again, but how would he react once Olivia showed?

"Am I interrupting?"

Oh, perfect timing. Standing there in her Technicolor zebra print, Olivia's eyes shifted from Lynna to Patrick. Her gaze looked him down and then back up in a show of disdain.

Lynna tried to respond to Olivia, but her tongue stumbled all over itself. Yes, she was very much interrupting, but then again, she'd come here to see Olivia.

"I'm Patrick." He held out his hand to Olivia.

She stared at the hand. Her eyes slid over to Lynna appearing to ask if she really had to go along with this. Lynna did her best pleading, nervous smile to beg Olivia to be nice.

Olivia shrugged and then took his hand. "Olivia."

"Do you two know each other from the private school?" he asked.

Olivia answered before Lynna. "No." She scanned the crowd, clearly done taking his measure.

Something shifted in Patrick's expression. Lynna had never seen him turn so serious. The way he looked at Olivia bordered on suspicion. What was going on here?

"She, uh," Lynna scrambled to cover for Olivia's answer. "Her parents took her out of my academy a few years ago. So we used to be there together." She said that last part extra loud to make sure Olivia heard it.

"Oh, so where do you go to school now?" Patrick's hard stare suggested he knew this was all a lie. How could he know? Why would he suspect anything of anyone? His home life resembled something straight out of a *Leave it to Beaver* rerun. She'd have laid odds his mom even baked cookies for him when he got home from school.

Olivia returned her attention to him, and she mirrored the look on his face. She needed to separate these two fast.

"Can you give me and Patrick a minute?"

"Of course." She sounded less than happy about it, but based on the little they'd interacted, a smile wasn't Olivia's most natural expression. The Grey Woman headed towards the bar. "I'll get something to drink."

Patrick leaned closer to talk directly into Lynna's ear, so she could hear him over the music and crowd.

"So is she a good friend of yours?"

"Yes. Well, no. More like an acquaintance."

"That's a relief." He didn't look relieved. "Because she seems like a bit of a snot."

"Yeah. She comes from—um, money."

Oh, good grief. This was turning into a bigger mess by the second.

"Are you okay?" The hard edge to his words and in his brown eyes made it clear he wasn't asking to be polite. Sure, he acted intense at school sometimes, but she'd never seen it directed at someone instead of a task.

Then some 70's disco music started. It sounded familiar, but it didn't click until about a half minute into it. "Is that the *Star Wars Theme*?"

Patrick was grinning again. "Oh, man! They haven't played this in ages! Isn't it awesome?"

"Yeah—nooooooo." Much as she wanted to pretend otherwise for him, this song achieved a level of cheese whiz she didn't think possible.

"But..." Patrick stared back in wide-eyed horror. "...it's *Star Wars!*"

She placed her hand against his chest. "I'm sorry, but they really should leave the original alone. Some things aren't meant to be disco. I mean, I love you, but I —"

Oh no! What did she just say? No, no, no... she did NOT do that. And the look on his face. His eyes went as wide as hers felt.

She was going to scare off her first boyfriend after one date!

But then, he smiled. He placed his hand on top of hers, which was still pressed against his chest. "I love you, too."

Well, now she definitely wasn't going to rush home. No way she'd ditch the boy who just said he loved her.

She leaned in to give him a quick kiss. Thinking of Saturday night made it difficult to restrain herself and pull back before things got out of hand again.

"Let me go talk to Olivia real quick. After that, I'm all yours."

"I'll wait here, if you need me." There was that edge again. Did he really dislike Olivia that much after meeting her? Was that all? It had to be. Patrick never acted like this with anyone.

She peeled her hand away from his chest and went over to the bar as fast as she could manage through the crowd. The disco version of the *Star Wars Theme* kept pounding away with all sorts of R2-D2 beeps. For all that was good and pure in this galaxy, that remix was blasphemy. She really must be in love to forgive Patrick for liking this song.

Lynna slid into the open space at the bar to Olivia's right. Lynna wondered if she'd scared off whoever had been there.

"My heart aches over the asshole who thought adding a beat to classical music was acceptable." Olivia glowered as she picked up a curved glass bottle of Coca-Cola sitting on the bar in front of her and shook her head.

"I think you're referring to *Hooked on Classics*." Lynna waved it off. "You know what? Never mind."

Olivia sipped her Coca-Cola, but it failed to make her smile. "I do not like your boyfriend."

"Yeah, I'm pretty sure he noticed."

"And this place..." Olivia paused to point at their surroundings with the bottle in her hand. "...sucks. We are not meeting here again."

"Yeah, it's a little cheesy. There's a café across the street called Southern Sun. We can use that next time."

Olivia perked up at that. "Does it have alcohol?"

"This is Virginia."

"What?" Olivia stood ramrod straight, as if Lynna had told her Mars was about to collide with Earth. "Virginia does not have vodka?"

"Not if you're under 21."

Whatever Olivia said next wasn't in English, but a good, solid curse never really needed translation.

"Look," Lynna said, "can we get to why you wanted meet?"

"Father has figured out where your base is. He and my eldest sister are planning an attack for Friday night to abduct your little friend, the ljósálfr."

"What!"

The "faux-tender" came over at that moment.

"You want something?"

"Not now!" Lynna glared him away. He cursed in English, but at least he left. Lynna refocused on Olivia. "Are you certain? They've got the location figured out?"

"Said it's off some road called Midlothian near Po-white-tan."

The neighboring county was actually pronounced "Pow-uh-tan," but correcting Olivia's pronunciation didn't really matter at the moment.

"I don't know if you two have noticed," Patrick said as he walked up behind them, "but you're being shadowed."

"Yes." Olivia glared straight ahead at the back wall of the bar. "I'm noticing him right now."

"Her." Patrick ignored Olivia's shot at him. "Three hers, at least."

Olivia looked over her shoulder. She managed to make it casual, more so than Lynna did. Lynna didn't see anyone, because of the poor lighting. She winced as she drew on her powers, letting her see better with her dragon eyes. As soon as she did, she found exactly who Patrick was talking about. The closest to them stood at the edge of the dance floor and resembled Olivia the most, with long blond hair. The rest were brunettes, including one of Asian descent.

"There's four," Lynna said.

"Fick mich seitwärts!" That curse was in German, and Lynna certainly understood that one. "They set a trap to see what I'd do."

"If that's the case"— Lynna stopped, choking on the rest of the thought.

"They aren't waiting to go after your little friend. They must be attacking now."

"Ava."

"I'll try to draw them after me." Olivia didn't give Lynna a chance to argue, she slipped away, heading for the back of the club.

Patrick leaned back against the bar beside Lynna. He smiled, but Lynna could see it was forced. Lynna's mind drowned in questions about him. How did he know these people were watching them? Why wasn't he panicking or acting confused? Why would he not think it strange for people to be tracking her or Olivia? What didn't she know about him?

"Only two of them are following her," he said.

Her questions about Patrick would have to wait, because he was right. Two of the pale-skinned brunettes were heading straight at them and ten feet away. She'd hoped all four would go after Olivia, so she could use the phone behind the bar to call the Greenhouse and warn them, if it wasn't already too late.

"Front door," Lynna said. "Run!"

Thankfully, he did as he was told.

The Grey Women, maintaining their glamours, shoved their way through the crowd. Lynna glanced up as they were halfway to the door. She needed to slow them down and create some cover. Fortunately, this club used a sprinkler system. Embracing her powers, she grabbed hold of the water in the pipes and directed enough pressure to force the sprinkler heads to activate.

"Grab hold of my jacket!" she shouted to Patrick as the water rained on the crowd.

Shrieks and screams drowned out the music from the speakers, which had started playing the Human League's *Don't You Want Me?*

"Where are you parked?" she shouted.

"What?" he shouted back.

She'd have to ask him again once they were outside. The confusion in the club made it impossible to see how close the two Grey Women were.

Once outside, the cold hit that much harder, thanks to the sprinkler system drenching them.

Lynna made a gut call, and went to the left since most of the crowd had gone straight into the street or to the right.

"Where's your car?" she shouted as they ran up the sidewalk.

"I'm parked in front of Fountain Bookstore."

She hoped that was close. "Where is that?"

"The opposite way."

Of course it was. She glanced over her shoulder as she yanked him across the cobblestone street.

"Where are you parked?" he asked.

As they ran onto the red brick sidewalk, Lynna glanced back towards the club. Both Grey Women stood on the edge of the crowd, searching for them. One of them spotted her and Patrick before they could get out of view around the corner.

"Where is your car?" He didn't sound the least bit out of breath, but that wasn't surprising since he ran on the cross country and track teams, part of why he had such nice legs. Good grief! Was she really thinking about that now?

"I didn't drive a car!" she snapped back, realizing she hadn't answered his question.

"So you can fly!" She heard the smile in his voice.

"If we live through this, you and I are about to have our first fight."

He wisely didn't attempt to defend himself to her. "Right at the next corner!" he shouted.

Only one of the Grey Women was chasing after them. No, that didn't make sense. Why would the other?—

"Across the street!" Lynna grabbed him by the arm, darting into the traffic. Even at this hour, Main Street was crowded. Cars slammed onto their brakes, honking horns at the two idiots.

Once they made it across the road, they were under the cover of several trees for a moment, dropping them into shadows. Lynna gripped her powers again. She needed to see if she was right. The second Grey Woman ran along the rooftops on the side of the street and then stopped to aim her gun.

"On my left!" She grabbed his arm and yanked him over to place herself between him and the Grey Woman on the roof.

No time to worry about being seen by the public. She forced her transformation. Her wings appeared and ripped apart the shirt and jacket she was wearing. As the wings formed, a bullet bounced off them.

A heavily intoxicated, homeless man stumbled towards them. He went all bug-eyed as he got a look at Lynna.

"Cool costume, girl!" he slurred as they ran around him.

"Thanks!" she shouted back.

Another gunshot bounced off the bricks of the sidewalk in their path. Lynna grabbed Patrick by the arm, making sure he stayed in the cover of her wings.

The elevated train tracks and I-95 overpass were ahead of them, across from the old, abandoned gothic Main Street train station. Once they got under the tracks, the Grey Woman on the rooftops would have to drop to street level to continue the pursuit.

"How much further?" She glanced over her shoulder. The one who stayed on the ground was still on the opposite side of Main Street. She'd abandoned her glamour, though.

"Let's cut across to Cary Street here!" He led them beneath the train tracks and overpass into a thinly occupied parking lot.

Lynna dropped back a step behind him to throw open her wings. It slowed her down, but the wings provided protection for Patrick from any gunshots.

As she glanced over her shoulder, one of the Grey Women tackled her from behind. They went down, skidding to a halt along the asphalt in the shadows of the overpass.

"Keep running!" Lynna shouted to Patrick. Thankfully, he didn't try to stay and fight.

The Grey Woman who tackled her didn't bother to get up. She yanked out her handgun and pointed it. Lynna threw a wing in front of her as the Grey Woman fired a shot that deflected off her improvised shield.

The other woman who'd been on the rooftops sprinted into view, coming straight at Lynna. This one drew a sword.

Lynna crouched and launched at the one with the sword as the first Grey Woman fired at her again. She stopped shooting as soon as Lynna got near her sister.

The back of Lynna's arms were more heavily armored than most of her body. She couldn't take a direct strike from the sword's edge without it cutting her, but she swatted aside the Grey Woman's swings by hitting along the flat of the blade. The Grey Woman cursed at her, growing more exasperated with her inability to cut her.

The Grey Woman swung too hard, putting herself off-balance. Lynna took advantage of it, seeing the attack as it was coming. She dropped beneath the swing, and swept the Grey Woman's legs with her wings. Her attacker dropped face-first to the ground. Lynna hammered the back of her head, as she tried to get back up, smacking her face against the ground with a painful crack.

"Good luck in your next life, dragon!" the one with the handgun had come up right behind her, gun barrel pressed against Lynna's back.

Headlights blinded both of them as a car screamed into the parking lot, heading straight at them. Lynna jumped as high as she could and the Grey Woman leaped backwards, firing her gun at the car. The front passenger side caught her on the leg, sending her spinning away and shattering the headlight.

The car screeched to a halt as Lynna dropped to the ground right behind it. Patrick leaned out of the driver side window. "Get in!"

She ran for the nearest door, the rear, driver side changing back to human in order to dive in. More gunshots went off, slamming into the passenger side of the car. Two bullets went through the passenger seat and into the back seat, barely missing Lynna. She yanked the door shut as Patrick hit the accelerator. The Buick bounced over the curb, across the sidewalk and onto Main Street.

Lynna climbed into the front seat to sit next to him. A bullet hole had shattered the center of the windshield, creating a spider-web of cracks from that spot.

"Are you all right?" She looked to make sure he wasn't hurt.

"She missed me." He pointed towards the shattered portion of his windshield. "Dad's gonna kill me."

"I need to get to a phone right now." She had to warn Ava and Dr. Howard.

Patrick ran a traffic light to get them onto the Downtown Expressway heading westbound. "Probably best we get out of downtown first." While it wasn't exactly a question, he looked over to her for her approval.

"Yes, but don't go too far." She glanced over at the shadow of the city's skyline racing past them on her right. "Slow down. You've got a busted headlight. You keep going like this, and you'll get pulled."

If that happened, she'd be hard-pressed not to subdue the unfortunate cop. She had to get home now.

"You look so beautiful in your dragon form." He grinned at her. "I always wondered what you'd looked like."

He stopped when he saw her glare.

"You have a lot of explaining to do," she said.

"And you don't?"

"Apparently not!" How had he known? She felt betrayed, even though she knew she had no high ground on this. It was as if he'd stolen the one normal thing in her life.

"My mom's an elf." He dug into his jeans pocket for some change to use at the approaching toll booths. "I didn't get any cool abilities, at least nothing like yours, but I'm able to see when someone is more than human."

"So you've known all along about me?"

"That you're half-dragon? Yes." He winced as he got another glance at her glare when he slowed for the toll plaza. He sped away as soon as their toll lane's striped arm went up to clear their path. "Sorry, but I wasn't sure when we first met if you even knew about yourself. Lots of people have no idea they're carrying around something amazing in their ancestry. It was only after I saw the others from your academy or whatever that place really is that I assumed you probably knew. I wasn't sure if it was safe to tell you about me. My parents made me swear to never tell anyone."

"So can you change how you look?" she asked as he pulled away from the toll. Was it possible she'd never even seen what he really looked like? "I mean, is this a glamour like those dark elves can do?"

"Like I said, I don't have any cool abilities." He shrugged. "I just see my surroundings a little more clearly than most." He pointed at the approaching exit. "We can probably find a payphone at the Carytown Ukrop's. I've got a dime you can use, if you need one."

A minute later, they pulled off the interstate and into the grocery store's parking lot. Patrick kept the car running as she ran to a payphone mounted on the outside of the store.

She dialed her barracks first, but all she got was a busy signal. Then she tried calling Dr. Howard's office line. The line rang without any answer. After that, she went for the phone at the guard post. Busy signal again. She tried at least three other numbers she knew, including the phone in Maria's barracks and Nevada's. No one answered.

She was too late.

Chapter 35: Nevada

Tuesday, 1 February 1983 [Ninety Minutes Earlier]

The Greenhouse's mansion included two ball rooms, which Nevada had always considered beyond absurd. Had the idiot who originally owned this place expected to host dueling parties at the same time? As far as she was concerned, too much money drove people insane.

When the CIA took it over, they converted the east wing's ball room into a mess hall. The three rows of tables must have come with the building, because they were made of red oak and polished to a shine that even more than a decade of abuse from Nevada and her peers hadn't dulled.

After Nevada picked up her dinner tray, she made her way toward Maria and Pockets, in their usual spot in the far corner. Most of the other groups self-sorted by their barracks. They weren't required to sit with their dorm mates, but after Dr. Howard established the current barracks, cliques naturally followed.

Nevada's tray clattered onto the table. She sat facing the large wall of windows because Pockets always wanted it at his back, even though this time of year the sun set early and didn't cause an issue for his eyes.

She had her knife and fork in hand to attack her rare steak even before her butt hit the chair. The time was a few minutes past 18:00 hours. Most people here, especially the staff, didn't tend to disperse until 18:30 at the earliest. She wanted to get out of here well ahead of that.

Halfway through her steak, Pockets snapped his fingers almost right over her plate. "Yo, Fangs, you hearing anything we've said?"

She glared up at him as her tongue loosened a piece of steak that had gotten stuck in her teeth. Both Pockets and Maria stared at her as if expecting her to say something.

"What?" she asked.

Maria answered. "I asked if you knew where Lynna was?"

She glanced to her left at the vacancy where Lynna usually sat. Leaning to look past Maria and Pockets, she confirmed their friend's absence. "Not here, I guess." She sawed off another large bite of steak and shoved it into her mouth.

"Little hungry?" Pockets asked with an amused lilt to his voice.

Despite the pain aching beneath her forehead, Nevada managed to answer with a cold smirk. "You have no idea." He really didn't, because the only reason she was shoving this steak down her throat so fast was to get to the real treat, same way a regular kid ate their vegetables to earn their dessert.

Maria leaned in closer from across the table. "I got a seriously bad feeling about this. Worried she's gone AWOL again."

Pocket's laughed. "I'm telling you, she's got it bad for Patrick. Ten bucks says she's at his place making out."

Nevada did not need this melodrama. She glanced at her watch. 18:10 hours. "Not my problem."

Maria threw her hands in the air. "It definitely will be if she gets caught and they end up cracking down on all of us."

"Spare me." Nevada cut off a bit of fat. "You two are scared you won't get to go boink in the woods. It's not like the rest of us are going to suffer any more than we normally do." She waved her left hand, still holding her fork, in the air as if to ward off a ghost. "Oooo... We'll get stuck in our barracks instead of behind a stupid fenceline patrolled by sharpshooters."

Pockets looked pissed. Good.

Maria didn't go that way, though. She reached over as if to place her hand on Nevada's. "Are you all right?"

The show of sympathy disturbed Nevada more than if Maria had snapped at her. She jerked back.

Pockets snort-laughed. "Seems like her black cloud is in its usual place."

She was done playing this game. "Fuck you, Pockets." She snatched her tray as she stood and marched it over to the trash can, upending her plate to spill her leftovers in the trash and then slapping down the tray, plate, and utensils on the counter at the window opening up into the kitchen. Most of the kitchen staff was sitting in the hall to eat with everyone else, which spared her any questions about her dinner.

Out the corner of her eye, she saw Maria stand. Did she plan to follow her out? The last thing Nevada needed was for good intentions to stop her short of what she needed. At best, she had fifteen minutes before anyone else finished eating and left the dining hall. That gave her barely enough time to get into the basement, break into the infirmary again, grab some blood, and get back to her room.

She ran to the end of the hall and took the stairs to the basement three steps at a time. Same as the other night, no one on the staff was down here.

She didn't hear any footsteps behind her, so Maria hadn't followed her. Of course, that assumed Maria hadn't gone intangible and invisible to catch up to her. Maria moved more than ten times faster than most people in her intangible state. That girl's heart was too big for her own good. If she got one whiff of what Nevada was doing, she'd probably say something to Doc Howard.

The storm brewed in Nevada's head again. She refused to let it get anywhere near as bad as the last time. She knew the human blood would do the trick, so she didn't see any point in delaying the right "meds" for the job. She wasn't going feral or some nonsense like that. Hell, the Greenhouse had already reaped the benefits of her hitting the human blood supply, because that's how she'd recalled all that information from Taggart's records. No way she would've remembered all that otherwise, but they probably wouldn't hear that part around the whole "I need some human blood to make my headache go away."

This time, she decided to try what she figured was the vanilla of blood types, grabbing a bag of O negative. She sucked in a sharp breath as she slipped the cold bag into the back of her pants. She really needed to find a way to hide this stuff without freezing her ass off.

She made a bee-line for the front door and fought the urge to sprint for her barracks. Even better, no sign of Maria. Perhaps her friend had given up and gone back to her boy toy.

Halfway to the barracks, a series of angry yapping barks rushed towards her from out of the woods. The glow of the driveway's light posts reflected off of Chewie's black eyes as he barreled towards her.

"What are you doing out?" She reached down to pat the small dog's head as his muddy paws paddled on her jeans as if to climb her like a cat going up a tree. Maybe this was why Lynna had been a no-show at dinner. If Chewie had gotten loose, she might've been out looking for him.

As she was about to pick up the dog and carry him back to his home, the smell hit her. That scent on the wind almost knocked her to the ground, as if she'd stumbled into a kitchen right as someone pulled a batch of chocolate chip cookies out of the oven. Only, she wasn't smelling melted chocolate.

She knew that scent all too well now. Human blood—a lot of it, and it was fresh.

Before she knew it, she'd forgotten about the "cold but sure thing" stuffed into the back of her pants and the yapping dog at her feet. She walked towards the source of her distraction, going between her barracks and Lynna's. Only after she'd entered the shadows of the trees did she realize Chewie was following her, sniffing excitedly around the woods at everything.

The smell of the blood clouded her brain with the mental equivalent of her stomach growling.

She snapped free of the fog when she found the body. He'd been one of the compound's guards, and his head stared up at her about five feet from the neck it was supposed to be connected to.

Chapter 36: Nevada

Tuesday, 1 February 1983

Nevada's training kicked in once the shock of the guard's body focused her thoughts. She grabbed the handheld radio from his belt and pressed the transmit button.

"Any guards, respond." No one answered, so she tried something more specific. "Gate house, do you copy?"

More silence.

"Anyone on this channel, respond!"

She reached for the guard's gun, still in its holster, but then she stopped. The blood from the guard's neck was still fresh. She ran her tongue over her left canine as she considered it. Catching her breath grew more difficult. When she pulled her hand back, she wasn't holding the gun. Her fingers drenched in dark red. She licked them clean and the rush hit her hard enough to knock her to her knees.

Her mind sharpened. The night turned brighter, as easy for her to see now as if she was in daylight. All of her senses leveled up, including her sense of smell. That's when she noticed them.

At least four distinct scents, all similar, led from here and straight back towards the barracks. She couldn't explain how she knew it, but she did.

"Sit tight, pal." She ran her fingers through the silky fluff of fur on top of Chewie's head. "I'll be right back."

She took off through the woods, heading straight for Lynna's barracks. If Chewie had gotten loose, then that suggested someone had let him out. Lynna might not have been at dinner because she was in danger.

Chewie didn't sit tight, though. The silky terrier chased after her. Thankfully, he didn't bark while he ran.

When she reached the back of the barracks, he didn't follow. He was busy sniffing at the corner of the building and then kicked up a leg.

Nevada took the stairs as quietly as she could. The rear door had a slender rectangular window. She crouched and pressed her ear against the door's metal surface. Eyes closed, she put all her focus into listening. That's when she heard the thumps. They were faint, but once she noticed them, she couldn't miss them. Heartbeats. She'd never been able to hear this well, and the novelty distracted her for a moment.

The heartbeats overlapped, making it impossible for her to tell how many she was listening to. Four or more? Was Lynna one of them? Too many odors overwhelmed her, too. Most of them belonged to the girls who lived in here, not that she could place names to all of their scents. The freshest scents in the mix belonged to the ones she'd first detected in the woods.

She could tell they were on the opposite end of the barracks, probably by the front door. The girls might come back here at any moment. She considered running for the mansion to get the others, but if these strangers had Lynna captured, Nevada had no guarantee she and the others would make it back before they killed Lynna or abducted her.

Nevada hid to the side of the rear door, turned the door handle, and pushed it open. The door squeaked, which she hoped would draw the strangers in there to this end of the barracks. She leaped onto the handrail and then grabbed the edge of the roof, flipping onto it.

She waited for the intruders to appear. If there were four, they'd probably split up to check the rear door. Assuming they were smart, at least two.

These people were good. She struggled to hear their movements. Their footsteps were light, but whatever they wore made enough noise for her to tell there were two of them approaching the rear door.

In her mind, she ran through her plan. As soon as they stepped out the door, she'd attack. She'd take out one with a kick as she dropped and then she'd work over the second. She had surprise on her side. The same thing that had stirred in her at the sight of the decapitated guard's blood was hungry for more.

The door squeaked as they opened it wide.

Step out. She repeated the thought as if to will them outside.

A hand reached out and gripped the side of the door frame.

That's it! Come on…

"Come on!" The whining voice in the distance belonged to Athena, the girl always singing in Lynna's barracks. "I wanna watch the second part of *Shogun* tonight."

"Are you kidding? You're the only one who wasn't bored out of their minds watching that thing last night."

"Let her watch it," Ava said. "Not like there's anything else on TV tonight."

The girls were already heading back from dinner.

The hand that had been on the door slipped back inside the barracks. She couldn't hear the movements of the people waiting below her, not over the chattering of the girls approaching from the mansion.

Nevada hesitated. Did she go in the back that was already open, or did she shout to stop the girls from coming any closer? She had a perfect opportunity to surprise these people from behind, but the girls were too close.

Dammit!

Nevada ran across the slanted rooftop. There was no way the people inside wouldn't hear her.

"Get back to the mansion now!" Nevada shouted as soon as she reached the front end of the barracks. Five girls stopped and stared up at Nevada, but Ava recovered first.

"Move!" Ava grabbed Athena's arm and pulled hard on her.

The door below Nevada slammed open. As Nevada looked over the edge of the roof, a shadow slipped up onto the slanted roof with her.

Moonlight glinted against something metallic as the shadow swung at her. Nevada jumped back, and a short sword hissed short of her stomach. More swings followed, forcing Nevada into a retreat. She got enough of a look at this shadow in front of her to realize she must be one of the Grey Women Lynna had fought in East Germany.

The angle of the roof made for treacherous footing, and as soon as the Grey Woman swung too hard, Nevada took the opening. She grabbed her sword arm by the wrist and twisted as hard as she could. The crushing pressure didn't break any bones. Whatever these Grey Women were, they weren't delicate.

Nevada instantly followed her grab with a punch to the face, but the Grey Woman swept the swing aside with her free left forearm and punched Nevada in the chest. The hit crushed the air out of Nevada and sent her tumbling down the rooftop. She realized as she reached the edge that it was too late to stop her fall.

Other shouts from the girls on the lawn and a flash of light, probably from Ava, distracted her as she tried to twist in midair. Something cracked in her left arm as she hit the ground, failing to get her body into a roll that would redistribute the force of her landing.

The Grey Woman landed on her feet as if the drop hadn't meant the equivalent of a three-story fall. Nevada rolled away before her enemy could stab her. Damn, this lady was fast! Nevada's heart raced with her growing anger, even as something cold in her thrilled at the challenge.

Heat filled her left forearm as something shifted within her. Whatever bone had broken in that drop, it was healed. Human blood. Yes, that's the stuff. She vaguely remembered the blood bag stuck in the back of her pants, wishing she had time to drink more for the extra kick. She'd have to work with what she got from the murdered guard.

Nevada rolled away from another sword attack and up onto all fours. A growl curled around the back of her throat.

"Schmutziger mischling," the Grey Woman said in German.

Nevada launched at her, like the "dirty mongrel" this foreign invader had dared to call her. No longer on a slanted surface, Nevada moved much faster. Her tackle knocked the sword out of the Grey Woman's hand.

They struggled, well past fancy fighting techniques. Instincts kicked in as the combat on the ground grew more frantic. Elbows jabbed. Fingernails clawed. Feet dug in for better leverage.

When the teeth joined the fight, that's when it all went Nevada's way. The rush of blood pouring out of the Grey Woman's neck and down her throat had her cresting a wave of bliss that left her dizzy. She heard the shouts of the others from across the lawn, but the euphoria of feasting on that blood reduced it to the static of a vacant TV channel.

Chapter 37: Maria

Tuesday, 1 February 1983

When Maria couldn't find Nevada outside the mansion, she'd given up and gone back to sit with Pockets in the dining hall.

"I don't see what the big deal is," he said between bites of a roll drowning in butter.

"I'm worried about her." Maria loved Pockets, and while she wasn't surprised he hadn't noticed Nevada growing more distant ever since South Carolina, his dismissal of her concerns righteously ticked her off. "She's been off for a while now. It's like she's holding onto something too tightly and it's got her ripping apart at the seams."

"Nevada is always pissed off about something."

The way he tossed that out there only angered her more. The glare she gave him should have bored a hole through his thick skull, and the fact he wasn't picking up on that made her want to grab him by the throat and throttle him.

A bright light flashed, but it didn't come from the wall of windows. Instead it came in through the door to the foyer.

Pockets and Maria jumped to their feet at the same time.

"No way that was lightning." Pockets ran for the front of the mansion.

The flash hadn't included any thunder, but the thrum of energy behind it vibrated through the walls.

"That's definitely Ava." Maria was a step behind him with Dr. Howard chasing after them.

"Everyone stay in the dining hall," Dr. Howard ordered as she followed them to the front of the building.

The front door flew open as three of the girls from Lynna's barracks fled back into the mansion.

"Are any of you hurt?" Dr. Howard asked as Maria and Pockets kept going for the open door. Ava sprinted across the lawn from the barracks. A path of scorched earth reached out behind her and into the forest.

Two women in dark clothing descended on Ava, like wraiths pursuing a nymph.

One of them pulled out a gun and even though there wasn't the crack of a gunshot, Ava dropped face down in the driveway.

Pockets launched out of the mansion faster than Maria.

"Ava!" He pulled ahead as they both sprinted to reach Ava before the two Grey Women. One of his black holes erupted in the air to the left of the Grey Women. A volley of machine gun fire spilled out of the hole, but as soon as he'd formed his hole, another opened beside the Grey Woman and another next to Pockets. The bullets he'd released came back at him and Maria.

Maria shifted into her intangible state. She couldn't reach Pockets to grab him and make him intangible, too. Even as the world melted into a fog with slow-moving shadows, she saw Pockets' silhouette dive to his left. She hoped he was diving, because otherwise, he was falling. She couldn't tell if the bullets had hit him. She ran for the Grey Woman who mimicked Pockets' powers.

She raised her fists and aimed for the center of the Grey Woman's chest. Before she would have passed through her, Maria shifted out of her intangible state and rejoined the normal flow of time. For that split second, she moved superhuman fast. When her fists nailed the Grey Woman, she knocked her back twenty feet and onto her back. Maria shifted back to intangible before the Grey Woman could hit her. She shifted in an out, landing punches on the other woman's head and stomach. On the third strike, the Grey Woman grabbed hold of Maria's shirt. When Maria shifted, the contact turned the Grey Woman intangible, too. Before she could do anything to break the contact, something smashed into her temple. Only after the fact, knocked to the ground and shifted back into a tangible state, did Maria realize it was the gun the woman had shot Ava with.

Maria looked up as the barrel aimed at her. She struggled to focus and shift, but she wasn't able to. Nevada tackled the Grey Woman as she pulled the trigger. The dart whistled past Maria's left shoulder, missing her.

Nevada and the Grey Woman wrestled on the ground. Maria tried to stand, but as soon as she put her weight on both feet, she fell. The blow to her head still had her spinning. Her next attempt to stand hit her with a wave of nausea.

Nevada screamed and then went silent.

One of the Grey Women shouted something. Was that German?

"Pockets!" Out the corner of her eye, she saw the Grey Women running into the woods. She didn't see him. He'd hit the ground, but she never saw him stand. Where was he? She screamed his name again, but no answer came.

She crawled over to Nevada. Her friend pawed at the air as if still trying to reach up at the Grey Woman who was no longer there.

"Nevada?" Maria placed her hand on her shoulder. "Are you—?"

Hands like iron latched onto Maria's shoulders. In an instant, they'd switched positions with Nevada on top and pinning Maria to the ground. Nevada hissed, a slow and drowsy noise, as her glassy eyes seemed to stare at Maria without recognition. Maria screamed her friend's name, which made Nevada blink in confusion. The hesitation gave Maria a moment to see three darts buried in Nevada's torso. She assumed the darts were what the Grey Women used to knock out Ava, but even with three of them flooding her system, Nevada was still awake and moving.

Despite her slow movements, Nevada had Maria pinned. Something sticky dripped from her lips onto Maria's face. The stench of blood was all over Nevada like too much perfume.

"Let me go!" Maria didn't see a hint of acknowledgement. "Nevada!"

Her friend growled like some dog, a shiver running through her.

Maria fought against her grip, but she couldn't break free.

Nevada's fangs lunged at Maria's throat. They missed as someone grabbed Nevada from behind and lifted her off the ground.

"Stop fighting me!" Agent Mills held onto Nevada and finally pinned her face down on the ground. Once he seemed confident he had Nevada trapped, he looked back at Maria. "The guards at the entrance were killed. Please tell me Nevada didn't do that."

Maria shook her head and then quickly stopped, because the movement made her dizzy and nauseous. "I think it was Lynna's Grey Women."

"Anyone else get hurt?"

"I think Pockets got shot."

"Where is he?" Agent Mills grunted as he pushed down harder on the still struggling Nevada.

Maria forced herself to sit up, despite her dinner's attempts to lurch out of her stomach. Other than Agent Mills and Nevada, Maria didn't see anyone else. "I think the Grey Women took him and Ava."

Chapter 38: Lynna

Tuesday, 1 February 1983

Lynna's fears that she'd make it back too late were confirmed as soon as the campus came into view beneath her. A distinctive scorch mark from Ava's blast, ran from the lawn all the way into the woods with at least a dozen trees knocked down.

She'd flown straight here from the grocery store rather than letting Patrick drive her back and having to follow the roads.

A black vehicle similar to an RV was parked in the driveway with people milling around it. Lynna spotted Dr. Howard and Agent Mills near the front of the vehicle talking to someone in a cheap black suit and tie that screamed government agent.

Lynna's landing drew everyone's attention. She shifted back into her human form as soon as she was on the ground.

Dr. Howard ran up to her first.

"Where is Ava?" Lynna asked.

Dr. Howard grabbed Lynna by the shoulders and shook her. "Where have you been? I thought you were dead!"

Lynna stumbled in Dr. Howard's grip.

"I was meeting a contact."

"A contact?" Dr. Howard shouted. "We've had people combing the woods looking for your body!"

Agent Mills walked up beside them and placed a hand on Dr. Howard's arm. He whispered to her, his eyes focused on the other agents on the property. "Not here. Let's get her to the patio."

Once they were behind the mansion and beside the fountain, Dr. Howard rounded on Lynna. "Where were you?"

"Lynna!" Maria shouted as she ran out of the dining hall. Chewie ran out with her, yapping as he circled his momma's feet.

Maria looked awful, her hair in disarray and her mascara smeared from tears. She grabbed Lynna in a tight hug. "They got Pockets and Ava."

"They took Pockets, too? Why?"

Agent Mills crossed his arms. "You're not surprised they took Ava." The same anger that had Dr. Howard ready to throttle Lynna was taking hold with him, too. Maria must have sensed it, because she let go of Lynna and stepped away from her to get clear of the emotional crossfire.

"What the hell haven't you been telling us?" he asked.

Lynna picked up Chewie when he pawed at her leg to hold him.

"One of the Grey Women I encountered in East Berlin." Lynna hesitated after she said that, not sure for a moment what to say, but then she forced herself to continue. "She's been sharing information with me and arranged a meet with me tonight. She'd learned her father and sisters had figured out where the Greenhouse is and wanted to warn me that they were planning to abduct Ava. They told her they were going to attack on Friday, but it was a setup. They wanted to see what she'd do with the information. Last I saw her, two of her sisters were chasing after her. I got away, but by the time I reached a payphone, no one was answering."

"Sounds like pretty damn convenient timing to draw you away." Even though Agent Mills didn't voice it, there was no missing the way his body quivered with restrained anger and disappointment. "They killed five guards and carried off Pockets and Ava."

"Lynna," Dr. Howard spoke the name in a way that threatened something worse than a simple punishment, "why in heaven's name didn't you share this information sooner?"

"Because we have a traitor in the Greenhouse feeding information to the Grey Women." She summed up what she knew, which came out in a jumbled mess.

"Well, now they have Ava and Pockets," Agent Mills turned away, flinging his hands up in the air. "You should have told us!"

"I couldn't!" Lynna was shaking and couldn't stop it. "I still don't know who fed the elves the information on us. For all I know, it could be anyone here, including you."

"Oh, Lynna." Dr. Howard held her hand to her head as if it hurt.

"How could you think either of us would ever betray any of you like that?" Agent Mills hesitated, gesturing almost as if having a conversation with himself on what to say or do next and unable to reach a conclusion.

Then his radio squawked. "Agent Mills, we've got two people at the front gates to see Dr. Howard."

He snatched up the radio from his belt. "Who are they?"

There was a pause. "The driver is Kyla Rogers. Says she's here to see Dr. Howard, but her name isn't on the approved visitors list. She's also got a kid with her. You want us to turn them away?"

Dr. Howard sighed. "Tell the guard to let them in."

Lynna held onto Chewie as they all waited on the front steps of the mansion. Patrick's mother parked her silver Toyota Corolla. Kyla Rogers got out first. She had long, curly black hair and beautiful brown skin with an unnatural glow to it. Any other time, Lynna would have written off her beauty as good genes, which was probably accurate, but now that she knew she was an elf, she wondered whether this might be a glamour.

When the passenger door opened, it wasn't Patrick who got out, though. Olivia, in her pale-skinned, strawberry-blonde-hair appearance, stumbled out of the Corolla and held onto the top of the car and the edge of the door to stay upright.

Before Lynna could say anything or ask for an explanation, Dr. Howard spoke.

"Kyla, this really isn't a good time."

"I'd have preferred to stay home with my family, but this young lady insisted I bring her to you."

Lynna looked from Patrick's mother to Dr. Howard as the realization settled in that these two knew each other.

"Well, technically, she asked to be taken to her." Mrs. Rogers pointed at Lynna.

Lynna decided against outing Patrick's mom as an elf, not sure if Dr. Howard or Agent Mills already knew. Perhaps the Grey Women kept tabs on elves living among humans, which would explain how Olivia had known to contact her.

"This is Olivia," Lynna said as she realized all eyes had turned to her. "She's my contact in the dark elves."

"Was." Olivia winced as she shoved the car door shut and walked around to the mansion's front steps.

Maria clenched her fists as she moved to meet Olivia. "She doesn't really look like the other Grey Women."

Olivia's form faded, like a color image dissolving into black and white. Her strawberry blonde hair shifted to a dark black.

Agent Mills drew his handgun, but Dr. Howard gestured for him to lower it. "Kyla wouldn't have brought her if she was a threat."

"What are you doing here?" Agent Mills scowled at Olivia as he holstered his gun. "Your friends have already gotten what they wanted and more. I'm not convinced your warning wasn't intended to remove Lynna from the campus while the others attacked, to keep her out of their way."

Lynna had considered that, but the way things had gone down at the club made it clear to her that Olivia wasn't tricking her. If keeping Lynna out of the way or killing her had been the Grey Women's only goal at New World, they'd have all come after her instead of splitting up to chase both of them.

"I trust her," Lynna said.

"So what is it you want?" Agent Mills asked.

Olivia looked from him to Dr. Howard. "You are the one in charge here, yes?"

Dr. Howard nodded.

Olivia looked down a moment as if engaged in a silent debate. Then she took a deep breath and looked back up to meet Dr. Howard's eyes. "I am requesting asylum, and in return, I will help you recover your people from the Erlking."

Chapter 39: Lynna

Tuesday, 1 February 1983

Dr. Howard didn't immediately agree to Olivia's request, but given her obvious injuries, they took her down to the infirmary. They didn't say much of anything and avoided using any names while Dr. Howard stitched the knife wounds to Olivia's arms and back.

Lynna's attention went to the bed at the far end of the room. Nevada was passed out and strapped down.

Maria joined Lynna and kept her voice to a whisper. "She got completely out of control when the Grey Women—dark elves—whatever—attacked the compound."

"Maria?" Nevada didn't open her eyes, but her voice croaked out of her.

"You okay, girl?" Maria hesitated before she placed her hand on Nevada's shoulder.

"Sorry about earlier." She tried to open her eyes but immediately shut them. "Was trying not to pass out from those darts, and then it all went red."

"You killed one of the Grey Women." Maria paused with a nervous sideways glance towards Lynna. "You bit open her throat."

Nevada moaned slightly, but not in a way that suggested something unpleasant, even though she winced. "Yeah, I remember that. Couldn't possibly forget.

Was better than…" At that point, Nevada partially opened her eyes. "You okay, Lynna? Worried they got you."

"They tried, but I got away."

"I found Chewie wandering around outside. Guess they let him out by accident when they broke into your barracks."

Lynna had taken him back to her room, because he started getting restless with his nightly routine shot to hell. His grumbles had made it clear he considered it bedtime, dark elf attacks be damned.

That's when Nevada turned her head to glance towards Dr. Howard and the others with Olivia. "What the fuck!" She struggled against her restraints, and for a moment, Lynna thought the girl would break loose.

"It's okay!" Lynna went to the other side of the bed to hold her down on her right side as Maria kept her still on the left. "She's on our side."

"Are you kidding me? How long was I out?"

"Only a few hours," Maria said.

Agent Mills came over. "You got your head sorted?"

She stared at him as if looking through a fog. Then she lightly hit the back of her head on her pillow as if to pound it against a wall. "Sorry."

"Thought I was going to have to break your arm to restrain you earlier." The way he said that made it sound as if he was asking whether he'd need to do it again, if they let her up.

"Those Grey Women aren't human." She closed her eyes again. "Wasn't ready for the kick their blood would have."

Lynna decided against pointing out that the Grey Women were half human. This didn't seem like the time. Agent Mills crossed his arms and sucked in the side of his mouth before he responded.

"How would you know their blood is different from human blood?"

Nevada didn't answer. She looked as if she might cry.

"How long?" His voice was firm but not threatening. "How long have you been drinking human blood?"

Nevada still held her silence, but Maria answered for her. "I'm guessing since we went down to South Carolina to investigate Taggart." She patted Nevada's shoulder to comfort her.

"Yeah." The rest spilled out of Nevada in a desperate confession: the headaches, the pain meds, and the stolen blood.

"You know they'd have noticed the blood missing from the infirmary, right?" Agent Mills said, but not without some sympathy.

"Figured by that point I might have proven I could handle it."

"Jesus, kid. You gotta tell us these things. We're no good to you if you don't."

Nevada—looking more like her usual sarcastic self—rolled her eyes at him. "Really? And if I'd told you and the Doc? What would you have done?"

The only answer he offered was a nod in which he avoided meeting her eyes. "We undo these straps, you going to be able to keep it together?"

"Sure."

He unbuckled the strap keeping her legs down. "Good, because we need all of you ready to go. Head to the patio. We've got to make some plans, and we don't have much time."

Only then did Lynna remember why he'd been away from the campus. She wondered what he'd learned about Raymond's remains and the other Greenhouse.

Chapter 40: Lynna

Tuesday, 1 February 1983

After Dr. Howard stitched up Olivia, everyone but Agent Mills went straight from the infirmary to the patio. Olivia shared most of the information she'd already told Lynna at the Lincoln Memorial regarding the "cold war" between the Elves and the Aesir.

Lynna and Maria stood on opposite sides of Nevada, an unspoken show of support if the adults tried to come at her for what she'd done. They also wanted to keep her in check, if need be.

Olivia stood across from them with the moon at her back and Patrick's mother beside her. Since the cat was out of the bag about Olivia being a dark elf, she hadn't bothered restoring her glamour. Seeing how Olivia flaunted her grey appearance made Lynna wonder if she could ever walk around in her dragon form as easily. Somehow, she doubted it, and the realization produced a strange sense of guilt.

Agent Mills joined them shortly after Olivia finished her "AP Dark Elf History" lecture.

"I just got off the phone with Brand. Let's simply say it didn't go well, but I was able to maneuver the conversation so that he didn't realize Lynna went off-campus. He's locked us down until they can assemble additional guards to place here. At best, we have until 12:00 hours before those reinforcements arrive."

"You can bet they'll all be Brand's personal boot lickers, too," Nevada said.

Maria pointed at Olivia and at Patrick's mom. "Are we going to finally address the elephants in the room?"

"Elves," Olivia said the word in her accent as if she'd chewed it out. "We are elves, not elephants."

"Wait," Maria looked past Nevada at Lynna and whispered in a way that everyone could hear. "Your boyfriend is an elf?"

Patrick's mom scowled when Maria referred to Patrick as Lynna's boyfriend. Could this night get any worse? "Half-elven. His father is human."

"Can we get back to the part about being 'locked down?'" Nevada said. "You're delusional if you expect us to sit on our asses while these bastards have Pockets and Ava."

"That's what we're here to figure out," Agent Mills said.

"You can't act against the Erlking without first eliminating your traitor," Olivia said.

Dr. Howard sighed as she cradled her forehead in her hand. "There is no traitor in our unit."

"Then how did they find out about Ava?" Lynna asked, but she didn't have to wait for an answer. The way Dr. Howard's shoulders drooped gave it away. "You?"

Dr. Howard looked up and made a visible effort to stand straighter.

"Shortly after Carter left office, I could see the government's intentions towards the Greenhouse would undo everything he'd promised. I refused to stand by and let the CIA steal your lives for a second time and turn you into weapons. If I couldn't put my trust in human allies, then I needed to find mythical beings willing to help."

Patrick's mom pointed at Dr. Howard. "I confronted Elyce at the high school when my son told me about all of you. The first time he noticed Lynna, it didn't seem odd. There are always people who have a bit of something otherworldly in their DNA, but when it became clear that your special campus was populated with such people…" She shook her head. "Wasn't difficult to figure out that this facility belongs to the government or some corporate endeavor."

"Kyla put me in touch with the elves. Things looked promising at first"—Dr. Howard paused as she shook her head in disgust—"but when they focused on Ava, I realized the elves also wanted to weaponize her. I thought I'd found refuge for all of you. Instead, it turned out to be another cage."

"It's worse than you know," Olivia said. "The Erlking intends to use her as a weapon to end the détente between the Elves and the Aesir."

"The 'ah-what'?" Maria asked.

"Norse gods," Lynna said, a part of her unable to believe they were having this conversation.

"Fine," Maria said, her tone scathing, "but that only explains why they took Ava. Why did they take Pockets?"

The answer didn't come from Olivia, but from Patrick's mother. "To keep you from attempting a rescue. He has abilities unique to certain Dark Elves. Those portals he opens can also be used to travel to where the Elves reside."

Lynna looked back at Olivia. "Can you do the same thing as Pockets? Open portals?"

She shook her head. "It's a rare gift among Dark Elves, but that doesn't mean we don't have other means to get there. I can guide you where we need to go."

"I appreciate your offer," Dr. Howard stepped over to Olivia. "But I feel obligated to point out that I can't guarantee the United States government will agree to your request for asylum."

Olivia snorted. "I am not asking your government for asylum. I am asking you."

"Can we hide her from Brand?" Dr. Howard's question went to Agent Mills.

"Assuming Brand doesn't throw both of us out of here tomorrow?" The way he shook his head made it clear he considered that scenario all too likely. "We could fold her into the staff. There's no way to mix her in with the children, not without drawing unwanted attention."

She nodded as she considered it, pausing to look over at Lynna. There seemed to be a silent question there asking if Lynna believed Olivia was worth the risk. Lynna nodded to her.

"We'll find a way to make this work," Dr. Howard said.

Agent Mills held up a hand and shook his head before looking over at Olivia. "One question: why are you willing to betray your own kind to help us?"

"I am not betraying my kind. I'm betraying the Erlking." She looked over at Lynna and then back to Agent Mills. "I would not think I need to explain to you what it is to have your mother murdered and your life stolen."

"Fair enough," Agent Mills said. "Lynna, Maria, you're going to accompany Olivia to rescue Pockets and Ava."

Nevada stepped forward. "You're sidelining me?"

"No." He crossed his arms. "You and I have our own mission. I've made some calls, and I confirmed Lynna's suspicions. Taggart picked up Raymond's remains from Germany. He's delivering them to Dr. DeWare in the morning."

"So Dr. Asshat gets his hands on a dead body. I don't see the big deal."

Dr. Howard answered. "Given Raymond's specific power and how he was killed, there's a slim chance that cremating his remains might kick-start his powers and revive him. We can't let DeWare get his body."

Nevada let out a low whistle as Maria muttered, "Holy crap."

The corner of Agent Mills' mouth twitched with a hint of a smile as he stepped closer to Nevada and looked down at her. "You up for this?"

"Oh, yeah." There was an edge to Nevada's voice that made Lynna uncomfortable.

Olivia walked over to Lynna and Maria. "We should make plans."

"We can do it on the way. I need to get one of the girls in my barracks to look after my dog while I'm gone."

Maria glared at the dark elf. "I don't care what the doc and Agent Mills say. If we don't get Pockets back, I'll trap you in a cement wall."

Olivia's lips twisted into a smile before looking over at Lynna. "I like her."

Lynna shook her head and then led them to the barracks. "You're so weird."

Chapter 41: Lynna

Tuesday, 1 February 1983

After Lynna checked on Chewie, which mostly involved the small furball cursing her out in a long series of barks for ignoring his needs, Patrick's mother drove Lynna's team to Carytown. Lynna would have preferred to ride in the backseat, but Kyla Rogers insisted on her sitting up front. Neither of them said much for most of the drive. As they took the hill up River Road onto Cary Street, the scenery changed to high-end real estate and ritzy mansions barely visible from the road.

"My son talks about you constantly." Mrs. Rogers didn't say that in a way that made it sound like a complaint, but she wasn't exactly leaping for joy either.

Not sure what to say, Lynna went for what seemed safest. "He's a great drummer."

Mrs. Rogers' irritated groan wasn't the response Lynna had hope for.

She must have read the panic on Lynna's face when she glanced at her. "I do agree," she said as if to defend herself. "But it's not the most pleasant musical instrument to live with. We had to exile his drums to the garage to muffle them."

"He told me that." Lynna bit her lower lip in an effort to restrain her grin.

Mrs. Rogers stole another glance at Lynna. "He let me know what happened downtown. Thank you for protecting him."

"He saved me, too." Lynna didn't hold back her smile this time, remembering the way he'd hit one of the Grey Women with his car.

"Yes, but you could have flown away."

"I would never abandon him like that."

Mrs. Rogers didn't answer. Her hint of a smile looked troubled, though.

Lynna decided to change the subject. "How long have you known Dr. Howard?"

"I approached her when she attended the parent-teacher night at the start of the school year." She shook her head. "I shouldn't have told her how to contact the Elves. I'm grateful I didn't let her go through me directly. I made her promise not to mention me or my son, but I warned her that this might not work out the way she hoped."

"Then why did you help her?"

Mrs. Rogers tightened her grip on the steering wheel. "Elyce was reaching out randomly in hopes of finding otherworldly beings. It was only a matter of time before she succeeded, and odds favored the ones she reached would be far worse than the elves. I'd wager my entire vault her first contact would have been with the vampires, and that would have ended in disaster. It's a miracle I found her before that happened."

"Vampires," Lynna muttered under her breath. Not that the idea of vampires should shock her, given Nevada, but the confirmation still troubled her. The CIA kept them sheltered. Lynna and the others sometimes wondered what contact the Agency had with any mythical beings beyond the Greenhouse. There must have been some to make them invest in DeWare's experiments.

Lynna glanced into the back seat. Olivia rested with her eyes closed and her head back. Maria stared off into space, not out the window, just straight ahead. She was a ball of barbed wire coming apart.

Lynna wondered if the reason Agent Mills hadn't sent Maria with Nevada was because he knew she would insist on going after Pockets. The other reason might be he didn't trust Olivia and wanted Lynna to have Maria for backup.

The mansions fell away, and they crossed over the interstate into Carytown. It was almost midnight. They passed the shopping center with the grocery store where she'd tried to call the Greenhouse on their left, and it was completely dark. Mom-and-pop shops in colorful buildings made up the rest of Carytown.

Mrs. Rogers parked her car a few blocks down from the Ukrop's. Given this was a weeknight, the foot traffic was nonexistent.

"That's where you can get into the elven world." Mrs. Rogers pointed to the space between a brick building on the left painted a bright red and a vet's office on the right in an ugly shade of green.

"Two blocks away." Lynna wanted to scream. She'd been within walking distance of this place. If she'd waited, she might have intercepted them, assuming they'd come this way.

Olivia tapped on the back of Lynna's car seat. "Let's go."

Lynna and Mrs. Rogers climbed out and popped the front seats forward so Maria and Olivia could climb out.

"This is as far as I go, girls." Mrs. Rogers stared into the narrow alley with something that suggested she wished she could go with them. She must have seen Lynna's unspoken question when she looked back to her. "I'm in exile. If I go back, they'll kill me, and if they learn about Patrick, they'd go after him, too."

Then she narrowed her eyes on Olivia and said something that must have been in elvish. Olivia looked as impassive as ever as she responded, but whatever she said, Mrs. Rogers' eyes widened a bit in surprise. She climbed back into her Corolla and nodded to Lynna before she pulled away.

The three of them stood in front of the dark space between the two brick buildings.

"What did she say to you?" Lynna asked.

"To bring you back safe or she'll use my eyes for beads."

Maria's eyes widened. "What on earth did you say to that?"

"That I'll bring her the Erlking's balls instead."

Maria shook her head as if to fling off that mental image. "Wow. Tolkien really missed the mark with you elves."

"So this is where we need to go?" Lynna asked. "Between an art store and a vet's office?"

Olivia pointed into the space. "The shadows of this place expose a tear that links our worlds. There are many places in your world like this. This one goes by many names. Að eilífu Virginíu Göng, Skugga Framhjá þrjú hundruð tuttugu og þrjú, and Purgatory Alley."

Maria leaned forward, as if to get a better look into the space between the buildings. "Well, at least they don't call it the Door to Hell."

"No, that's in Montana."

"Girl, we seriously gotta work on your sense of humor."

Lynna decided not to point out that Olivia didn't sound like she was joking.

Olivia stepped off the sidewalk and into the narrow path of shadows.

Lynna followed, with Maria right behind her. Even though there wasn't that much noise on Cary Street, the small alley muted the rest of the world. The brick walls gave way to something more than black or shadows. The view beyond the alley darkened despite the nearby street lights. Even the scents of exhaust fumes diminished. The walls of the alley created the sensation of a void. Lynna was glad she wasn't in her dragon form, because she couldn't possibly keep her wings from brushing against the boundaries.

"And what exactly are we doing here?" Maria asked and then muttered under breath, "Other than trying to get mugged."

"Some shadows are"— Olivia paused, as if searching for the right word—"more. They have life as varied as animals. This is a shadow nest, and some of the shadows gathered here can take us where we need to go. It is how elves who cannot create or manipulate the shadows travel."

Olivia turned to face the wall to their left and started talking in a language Lynna didn't recognize.

Lynna looked over her shoulder at Maria and shrugged, not wanting to interrupt. The weird part was that Olivia's cadence didn't resemble some witch casting a spell. She sounded like she'd rolled up to a drive thru to order a cheeseburger with fries and a large soda.

When Olivia stopped talking, a few seconds passed in silence. Then whispers came from the walls.

Maria's eyes looked as wide as Lynna's must have been. "You know this is some Stephen King type shit, right?"

Olivia ignored Maria's gripe. "We should hold hands." She grabbed Lynna's right hand and Maria took Lynna's left.

"And neither of you move until I tell you to." Olivia's grip tightened

"This isn't going to hurt, is it?" Lynna asked.

Olivia snorted.

Then three pairs of glowing red eyes opened within the walls. The shadows lunged out at them, and everything went dark and silent.

Chapter 42: Nevada

Wednesday, 2 February 1983

Nevada and Agent Mills left the Greenhouse campus shortly after midnight, and they weren't alone.

"Bet you weren't expecting to see me again so soon, Brandle." Agent Vale leered back at her from the front passenger seat.

"Great." She dragged out the word with all the mock enthusiasm Agent Vale deserved.

"He offered to come along," Agent Mills said as he drove down Route 60, which at this hour was reduced to shadows and paint lines.

Nevada didn't hide her skepticism, even though Vale was still looking at her. "How did you find out about this?"

"Lucas here got me to dig up some of the information on your friend DeWare." Vale pointed his thumb towards the front of the car as if the coastline was already in view. "The mad scientist is running his new side show on some Chinese research vessel the Navy got its hands on a few years back. No clue how. It's traveling under the name *Hylonome*, whatever that means."

"Oh, that asshole." Nevada couldn't hold in the curse at DeWare.

Agent Mills glanced at her in his rear view mirror. "Care to share?"

"*Hylonome* is the name of a centaur in Greek mythology. You know, half-human, half-horse." Of course DeWare would name his ship after a daemon.

"Well, if we're lucky, we won't even need to deal with DeWare or his ship," Agent Mills said in a way that seemed to chide Nevada. "He's scheduled to dock in Norfolk around five in the morning. Our job is to intercept Taggart before he makes the delivery and get Raymond's body."

Agent Mills' declaration sucker punched her in the gut. This wasn't what she'd been expecting. "What about the kids on that ship?"

He didn't move his attention from the road. "We can't interfere with that. We do, and you can be sure ADD Brand will act against the Greenhouse."

"You think he won't notice Raymond back at the campus?" She supposed that was getting ahead of herself. For all they knew, the hopes for reviving him might be more ephemeral than smoke. They had to save him, though. Despite being an epic prick, Raymond was one of them.

Mills didn't answer right away. His expression, what Nevada could see of it in the rearview mirror, didn't change either.

Vale turned away from both of them, staring out of the passenger window, his face hidden from view. It made it impossible to tell what he thought about the matter, which was probably the point.

"One problem at a time." Mills' tone made it clear he was done discussing it.

Much as Nevada liked Mills and Doc, they were trying to stitch a slit throat, playing by the rules. The way things were going, the CIA would eventually hand them over to DeWare again. The memory of the man left her feeling cold and cornered.

Chapter 43: Lynna

Wednesday, 2 February 1983

The dark hid everything. Lynna didn't sense light, sound, or motion. Not even time. The red eyes of the shadows that had reached out and grabbed her had vanished almost as soon as they appeared.

Only two things reassured Lynna she wasn't dead: Maria's hand in her left and Olivia's in her right.

When light returned, it brought back everything else. The sudden sense of motion slammed her skull with a tidal wave of vertigo. Her hold on Olivia and Maria kept her on her feet.

"We should move," Olivia said as she released Lynna's hand. "My car is in a garage near here."

"Well, Toto." Maria didn't bother to finish the line from the *Wizard of Oz*. Instead, she let out a low whistle.

They'd emerged onto a stone, square-shaped platform at least thirty feet on each side. In the middle of the platform stood a ten-foot-tall cube of shadow. Sidewalks stretched out in every direction into a futuristic-looking city. Lynna's fears they would stand out evaporated as she watched people bustle in and out of the cube. Yes, elves made up most of the population, but Olivia's grey skin tone turned out one of many shades. Some elves even looked a pale blue similar to Lynna's dragon scales. The elves weren't the only beings walking these streets, though. Some people looked human. A pair of four-foot-tall anthropomorphic trees walked past them. Lynna's heart sang as a twenty-foot-long, red-scaled dragon flew over them and launched into the sky.

Maria pulled on Lynna's arm to follow.

Artificial light of all colors bathed the city, illuminating the night. Lamps hovered above the street and sidewalks without the benefit of posts. Discs mounted on the side of a cylindrical building flashed with alternating images and texts in what appeared to be ads. Wooden vehicles shaped like octagons with round glass tops in the middle rolled past them on the winding roads.

"I think we've walked into elven *Blade Runner*." Maria's hand clenched more tightly around Lynna's, as if she expected the tide of foot traffic on the sidewalks to force them apart.

Lynna struggled to keep up with Olivia, even though the dark elf would pause to look over her shoulder and confirm they were still behind her.

"I don't trust her." Maria stared up at another building with those circular billboard screens mounted on it. This structure spiraled up like a DNA strand, dotted with what appeared to be apartments or maybe offices.

"The Grey Women want her dead as much as they want to kill us."

Maria pointed at the ad playing on the side of the DNA building. The discs showed elves marching in formation, complete with the clomping of boots and a woman's voice booming across the street with whatever message went along with the ad. The text that followed didn't contain any letters that Lynna recognized, but she got the gist that this was some kind of wartime propaganda piece.

"Elven fascists," Maria said in a lowered voice as she leaned closer to Lynna. "Now I really have seen everything."

Olivia stopped and scowled as they caught up to her. "Would you both like to go ride a Ferris wheel while you're busy acting like you're on a vacation?"

Lynna ignored Olivia's gripe and shifted her eyes towards the nearest street corner. "Should we be worried about the police?" Two pale, pointy-eared men dressed in the same uniforms from the ad held up glass screens that they shifted about as if to frame people in the crowd. Their movements resembled police officers wielding a radar gun, but they obviously weren't hunting for speeders.

Olivia shook her head. "The soldiers aren't looking for you two."

Maria crossed her arms. "What about you?"

Olivia pulled up her left sleeve to reveal a tattoo of twisted lines that reminded Lynna of a Gaelic knot. "Skin craft. It confuses their slides."

"And you're certain they won't recognize we don't belong here?" Lynna asked.

"They're looking for onskadomnen." She must have noticed Lynna and Maria's blank expressions. "Wanted criminals."

"They really won't notice we aren't from here?" Maria sounded less than convinced. "It's not like we have a driver's license here or passports."

"Fyrodden is a truce city." Olivia gestured to the crowd navigating around them. "Half of these people come from other worlds and lack profiles."

They followed Olivia to the corner. Lynna focused her eyes on their guide's back, trying not to look like she was avoiding the soldiers' gaze, even as the closer of the two pointed his glass slide towards her.

She let out a long breath as they crossed the street without the soldiers detaining them. Lynna noticed that despite the congestion of people and vehicles, it lacked the stench of gas or diesel. The collective body odor was there, and so was the occasional whiff of food. They passed places that suggested small restaurants or cafes. One place let people sit on a small patch of grass, like a miniature park, to enjoy their drinks. Every structure, including the walking bridge they'd crossed earlier, was made of wood. Some buildings appeared grown from the ground up somehow. Did these people have access to magic? Did they even consider it magic, or was it the equivalent of picking up a toolbox and supplies from a hardware store to build something?

They reached the parking garage a few blocks later. This wasn't the first they'd seen. They were round with multiple ramps leading out in different directions from the various levels onto the surrounding dirt roads. Lynna wondered how they dealt with the muddy mess when it rained. Maybe they used some kind of magic to keep the dirt from turning to mud.

"You parked a long way from that shadow cube." The tone to Maria's voice made it a question.

"I didn't want the Erlking or my sisters to find my car and realize where I'd gone."

Lynna decided against pointing out how well that hadn't worked.

They climbed a giant spiral staircase at the center of the garage, going up until they reached the sixth level.

"You people don't believe in elevators?" Maria asked.

"No."

They passed the same kinds of cars they'd seen on the dirt roads. It was strange to see a car made entirely of wood, including the wheels. Sure, some people had station wagons with wood paneling on the outside, but the entire car?

Olivia circled the car, looking under it and in the wheel wells. Lynna wondered if the elves also used car bombs. Then Olivia placed her hand on the hood of the car, and the glass top and chassis unfurled like a flower to let them climb inside and sit.

"Okay," Maria said. "I'll admit that was really cool."

The seats in the car were arranged in a diamond formation with the driver seat placed at the front center of the car. Olivia sat and placed her hand on the steering wheel, causing the car to fold back together. The cars on the road hadn't roared or rumbled. They'd hummed, and Lynna wondered what that would sound like from the inside.

The vehicle shivered and jumped. Olivia jerked her hand off the steering wheel.

"Out! Now!" She planted her hand against the glass, but it didn't unfurl the car this time. The wood creaked and popped. The same way the car had unfurled, it now crushed in on itself.

Lynna changed to her dragon form and slammed her fists against the glass, which didn't shatter or crack. "Out how?" she shouted.

Maria grabbed her wrist and turned them both intangible. The creaking instantly slowed to a deep groan as time moved slower for them. "Come on!"

Lynna hoped whatever elven magic or tech was crushing this car wouldn't prevent them from passing through the car's collapsing exterior. They ran out of the car. While they passed through the wood and glass, the sensation resembled what she imagined it felt like for a tub of gelatin to get sucked down a narrow drain. Her breath caught until they stumbled out into the open air.

"Stay put!" Maria said as she let go of Lynna's wrist.

The world rushed back into its normal passage of time for Lynna as Maria vanished.

Lynna turned and saw the car folding in on itself. She screamed as it reduced to half of its size and kept folding into a wooden box no more than three feet long and two feet wide.

She didn't see Olivia or Maria. If they were still inside the car, then they weren't alive.

Then the air popped with a rush of wind as Maria and Olivia appeared. The dark elf stared wide eyed at Maria as she let go of her wrist.

"I did not like that," Olivia said with awe in her voice. "But thank you."

Maria let go of her arm. "I definitely think your sisters found your car."

Olivia spit on the ground as she glared at the box of wood and glass. "We must move quickly. They'll know I'm here now."

Chapter 44: Nevada

Wednesday, 2 February 1983

Nevada pressed the button on her watch to light up the face. The digital display showed it was close to two in the morning. They were outside of Norfolk at a 7-11 where Agent Mills had insisted they stop for the bathroom and to get something to drink.

Agent Vale returned to the car first. He climbed into the passenger seat and handed a can of coke to Nevada.

She hoped Agent Mills wouldn't take long. The idea of being alone with this creep made her want to preemptively break his wrist.

"So you ever actually been to London?" Vale asked as he popped open his can of coke.

"No." She held in a growl. Most of the other Daemons had gone there at least once, but not her. One day, dammit. She wanted to see London and then go to Canterbury to explore the cathedral there. She didn't feel like sharing any of that with Vale, though, so she kept silent.

"Kind of glad I got to join you for this little op." He paused to sip his coke. "Been thinking about our assignment in South Carolina for a while now."

She stiffened, wondering if he'd remembered her feeding on his blood to take down Taggart. "Why is that?"

He glanced over his shoulder at her. "Something you said. That whole bit about being stuck where you are, that there's nowhere you could really go."

Part of her was relieved, but she didn't care to enter some stupid debate she'd already closed the door on. She sipped her soda.

"Given it a lot of thought," he said. "Decided it's bullshit."

"Drop dead, Vale." Sadly, he didn't turn to receive the matching look intended to turn him into dust.

"Listen. I'm serious." His cocky attitude had vanished and when he turned to look at her, his eyes narrowed on her. "You talk like you've been left helpless, because you're a teenager. You're not a normal teenager, though. Can you really tell me that all that training you've received since birth can't let you hack into bank accounts and create fake IDs? And God help the idiots they'd send after you, because from what little I've seen of you and your teammates these past few months, you'd mop the floor with most agents' faces if they were dumb enough to take up the chase."

She was past silent. What he said had frozen her. Was he testing her, some CIA stunt to check her loyalties? Or was this him being honest and calling her out on her self-pity?

"You can say all you want about being trapped in that place, but as far as I'm concerned, where you are is a choice you make every morning you crawl out of bed."

The driver side door pulled open and Agent Mills climbed inside. He hesitated, looking from Vale to Nevada.

"Everything all right?" Even though he left it open for both of them to answer, the way he watched Nevada's reaction made it clear he wanted her response.

"We're good." She smoothed over the edge to her words by raising her soda as if making a toast and then taking a chug of it.

As they pulled back onto I-64 east, Vale piped up again. Fortunately, his focus was back on the mission and directed towards Agent Mills. "Been thinking about something, chief. This car isn't exactly ideal for transporting a body. How are we thinking we'll fit this corpse in the trunk?"

"We aren't." Mills looked in the rear view mirror at Nevada. "Care to answer this one?"

She hadn't considered it until Vale asked, but now that he'd brought it up, the answer came easily enough.

"Which one of us is stealing Taggart's car?" she asked, hoping it would be her. She didn't trust Vale with Raymond's body.

The way Mills chuckled answered that for her. She was starting to like this plan again.

Chapter 45: Ava

Wednesday, 2 February 1983

The inside of Ava's skull felt as if someone had fought a nuclear war. When she opened her eyes, she saw a faint glow obscured by a bag of pale brown fabric covering her head. Each exhale blew back against her face. Sweat rolled down her brow and when she reached to wipe it away, she realized her arms wouldn't move.

She jerked her body upright with a panicked grunt. Chains jingled against her wrists as she struggled to move her arms again, but they were bound against her back.

A large shadow passed in front of the light and then the fabric blocking her view was ripped away.

The hood dangled in a man's hand. Even in the dim light, she saw his smooth, grey skin.

"I've waited a long time to meet you, Ava Lanier." His voice rumbled in a way that made him louder with little effort. "I am the Erlking."

He smelled like a forest and towered over her. Her training told her not to show any fear, not yet, but everything in her body had kicked into fifth gear, especially her heart. He wore a brown, leather jacket with black pants. The clothing looked custom made and fitted to show off all of his muscles.

She forced herself to look away from him to take in her surroundings while she could, since he might throw the bag back over her head.

The light she'd first noticed through the bag came from a small sphere hanging off what resembled a vine running along the wall in the hallway beyond the room's open door. It reminded her of Christmas tree lights, only more practical. One of the Grey Women stood there with all the intimidating demeanor of a guard.

Rays of moonlight also spilled into the room from a window at her back. She glanced over her shoulder and through the bars in her window. Two moons hung in the sky. Well, she certainly wasn't in Virginia anymore. Little chance she'd fit through those bars, but her energy beams could punch a large enough exit in that blue brick wall. At first, she thought they'd painted the walls, but the longer she studied the bricks, the more she suspected blue was their natural color.

Ava tried to stand, but the chains binding her wrists ran through the back of the chair. More chains bound her ankles to the chair's front legs. She jerked on the chains and tried to shake the chair, but it didn't move. They'd attached the chair to the floor.

"Welcome to my home." The Erlking seemed to have concluded she wasn't going to say anything. "You may consider it your home, as well, because you will be living here for the remainder of your life."

Ava tapped her right foot at a furious pace and kept asking herself, "What would Lynna do?" She knew Lynna would go silent, but Ava stunk at that.

"I like Chicken Fried Rice for dinner on Thursdays but no peas or carrots in it. My favorite dessert is chocolate cake with lots of icing. I don't know the recipes, but I'm guessing your people can probably break into a restaurant and steal them. And I like to snack on Peanut M&M's with raisins."

The Erlking's expression cooled, but his lips held the barest hint of a smile. "You have a strong will. That means you'll be all the more devoted and determined once you're broken."

What an ass. "Your people killed my mother." Did he really think she'd ever cooperate?

"One death," he said as he leaned in close, making that scent of a forest that much more pronounced, "compared to my two daughters you killed then and the third in East Germany. My claim for revenge outweighs yours, so be grateful I value you too much to kill you. Understand that won't prevent me from harming you, if you force the matter."

His daughters... "You sent them." She closed her eyes fighting against the memory of her mom dying. This thing had ordered her death.

"You slipped away," he said, "but then we learned your government had taken you into their care. It was only a matter of time before I found you again."

She'd heard enough. She aimed at the wooden floor and attempted to obliterate it with her energy blasts. She might kill herself, but she'd take him with her.

Only, nothing happened.

The Erlking grinned, seeming to recognize her new distress. "This room," he pointed to the narrow space around them and the silver runes etched along the ceiling, "is warded against your gifts."

She could feel her powers, knew they were still there, but it was as if searching for a specific page in a book that someone had glued against another page and no matter whether she approached it from the front or the back, she couldn't get to it.

"You needn't worry, though." He paced in a circle around her. "I plan to let you use your gifts. Together, we are going to change this world and many others."

She glanced over her shoulder, first at him and then at the twin moons. "Which world is that?"

"If it eases your mind, know I have no interest in unleashing your abilities on your home world."

She didn't answer, not sure if she believed him.

He stopped in his pacing behind her and ran his fingers through her hair in a way that made it obvious he considered her his property. She pulled away from him, but the chair and her bindings prevented her from escaping his touch.

"For centuries, I've served the Elven Council, hunting down the half-breeds on your world. They led me to believe I was protecting our world and even yours, but I know better now." His voice rumbled with controlled anger. "They profit from delaying an inevitable conflict with the Aesir. War is the only way to change things, and I will use you to burn away the lies and bring about a true peace."

One look at the Grey Woman in the hallway made it clear she was fine with the Erlking's plans. That same look also made it obvious she considered Ava less than a person and little more than an object.

The Erlking stopped stroking her hair and walked to the door to leave.

"Why even bother to tell me this?"

He stopped short of the door and turned back to look at her. "Because what I'm doing is necessary." He gestured to the Grey Woman in the hall. "We, all of us here, serve a cause to better this world. You will understand that in time, and I hope that will make things easier."

She stayed silent. He wasn't threatening her. All he intended here was to lay the ground rules. One look at the obedience of the Grey Woman guarding her door made it plain.

The Erlking left without another word. As his steps receded down the hall, the guard shut the door to Ava's cell. A metal bar screeched into place.

A person could escape any prison, given enough time. The Greenhouse had taught her that. The question was whether she could do it before the Erlking broke her.

Chapter 46: Lynna

Wednesday, 2 February 1983

The exterior of the car Olivia "borrowed" was polished black wood with interior seats carved out of the same. Thankfully, battered cushions offered some padding, even though bits of golden fur stuffing stuck out at the edges. As with Olivia's obliterated car, the seating arrangement was shaped like a diamond with the driver positioned at the front with two seats in the middle and the fourth in the back.

The only vibrations came from the road, and whatever this thing had for an engine ran silent, except for a subtle clicking that conjured images of hundreds of tiny little feet stomping.

Maria squirmed in her seat, jumping each time the car jolted from some imperfection in the road. "How far away are they?"

"Our turn is ahead," Olivia said. The road she'd taken them onto reminded Lynna of an interstate. The traffic had lightened up a little once they got outside of the city, but not by much. Signs lined the road in that same language she didn't recognize.

"Since they're expecting us now, what kind of welcome can we expect?" Lynna asked. They'd originally anticipated having the element of surprise.

"The Erlking will know I'm here, but that doesn't mean he knows any of you are with me or that I intend to free your people."

"You really think we'll get that lucky?" Maria's tone made her skepticism clear.

"No, if he hasn't already, he'll summon as many of my sisters as he can."

"Better we don't waste time getting in there then," Lynna said. Even though she was strapped in with crisscrossing vines for seat belts, she grabbed the bottom of her seat when Olivia turned the car off-road with a violent jolt.

"You want to go in guns blazing?" Maria glanced over at Lynna as if seeing her for the first time. Lynna did prefer to have a plan for this sort of thing, but nothing of late had played out as planned.

"No, but I don't see any reason to change our plans. The longer we wait, the more opposition we'll face." Lynna leaned forward towards Olivia. "You still think our best chances are to split up, with me going in from up top?"

"You make an excellent distraction." Olivia grinned, her teeth shiny even though it was dark inside the car. She glanced for a second over her shoulder at Maria. "Unless you are sure you can only handle one extra person at a time?"

"One is the limit," Maria said. Lynna didn't see the eyeroll, but she heard it in Maria's voice. The doctors had worked overtime on that one with Maria, hoping to work her up to making more people invisible and intangible. They'd only managed to give Maria some spectacular headaches and nosebleeds. "Are you sure there isn't some way for me to get into Pockets' and Ava's cells?"

Olivia shook her head. "You could get into their cells, but then the wards would pull you out of your shifted state and trap you with them."

Maria surprised Lynna by not asking if they should still start with the dungeon before checking the top floor. Olivia had said both had warded cells and had insisted on starting their search in the dungeon.

Olivia stopped the car where a stream blocked their path. Bits of wood bit out of the land like teeth with nothing to bite down, suggesting there used to be a bridge here.

When Olivia pressed her palm on the steering wheel, the window and chassis unfolded to let them out.

"When we figure out exactly where your friends are," Olivia said, "we can radio you their locations and let you begin the distraction."

"Itsy-bitsy catch with that," Maria said as they climbed out of the car. "I can't actually use my radio while I'm intangible. We'll need to go visible for that, and we can't search that whole castle without me taking a break. I don't take in enough air while I'm intangible. We'll eventually pass out if we stay that way too long, and while we're going through a wall, we won't get any air."

"This explains why I hated it." Olivia walked over to the edge of the stream, looking to her left.

Lynna used her dragon sight to look in the same direction and saw the outlines of the castle's towers. "So is the dungeon still the best place for you two to start?"

"If nothing else, that's not where the Erlking will post my sisters." Olivia had mentioned while they originally planned this attack that the dungeon was impossible to access from outside of the castle. "He'll place my sisters at the dungeon entrances at the base of each tower. They can catch people whether they go up or down at those positions."

Olivia didn't look at them as she spoke. Instead she seemed to stare off at nothing while patting at various places on her body. One of the spots concealed Olivia's handgun, suggesting she was taking inventory of her weapons.

Maria shifted her dagger to her left hip. The grip included four holes to slide her fingers through and use them like brass knuckles. "Are you really sure they'll have kept Pockets alive?"

Olivia shrugged. "Given what you say his abilities are, he's half-dark elf. The Erlking has trained us to capture any elven half-breeds. If he can determine your friend's parent is someone of import, he'll use that knowledge to blackmail them. Such unions are forbidden without permission from the Elven Council. Punishments have been as extreme as loss of title and property, sometimes exile."

Lynna placed a hand on Maria's shoulder to comfort her. "So they at least want him alive."

Olivia shrugged. "Unless his parent is of no import or has no wealth. Then the Erlking would kill him."

Maria looked ready to pass out.

Lynna glared a silent plea at Olivia to limit the dire predictions. "But that takes a while to figure out, right?" She gave that last word some added emphasis.

Judging from Olivia's eye roll, she got the message. "Yes, a few days, at least."

They checked their equipment, including a test for Lynna and Maria to make sure their radios worked.

"Well, Pointy-Ears," Maria said, "let's visit the dungeons first."

"I'll wait for your signal." Lynna pulled her best friend into a hug. "You stay safe."

"Ditto."

Olivia cleared her throat. "We will." She added extra emphasis to the "We."

"I think someone is jealous," Maria whispered with a laugh before releasing Lynna from the hug.

Lynna watched as Maria followed Olivia into the trees and out of her sight.

Chapter 47: Nevada

Wednesday, 2 February 1983

The Algonquian Shipyards turned out to be busier than Nevada expect-ed. Trucks loaded with containers rolled in and out of the main gate. The guards checked their IDs before letting them enter the maze of stacked metal boxes. Vale had brought them fake IDs with fresh identities, so the CIA wouldn't connect the aliases to them. The name on Nevada's was Claudia Rice.

"We're looking for dock C23," Agent Mills said to the guard at the gate.

"Go straight ahead between those two rows of containers. When you get to the end of it, hang a right and go down a ways. That'll take you to the Charlie docks. Those are mostly small boats, so watch for the signposts or you'll blow right past it."

Clouds hung low in the black sky, reflecting some of the city's light. A lot of that included the lights scattered throughout the shipyard. The large bulbs on the utility poles had a bluish-green hue, but orange lights on the cranes and other heavy machinery dominated the darkness.

Agent Mills' car crawled into long shadows as the stacked containers blocked the manmade light and formed nameless streets for them to navigate. Despite the cold and the windows of the Chevy being raised, the scent of oil-tainted ocean air filled their car. Nevada wished this was summer. She'd been to a handful of beaches in her lifetime, but she'd only gotten to enjoy it once during a training exercise when she was ten. The instructor, some old army drill sergeant with a head like a cue-ball and the stench of bourbon and cigars, had insisted on giving the Daemons some break time when Raymond had let it slip they'd never gotten to play on a beach. The happy memory caught her off guard. She held in her laugh to keep it to herself. There was something about Raymond. He'd always been able to charm people.

"You sure you're going the right way, jefe?" Vale asked.

"I'm following the directions the guy at the gate gave us."

Nevada leaned forward as she spotted a pair of headlights coming towards them. She squinted, trying to make out the type of car.

"What time did you say DeWare was supposed to dock?" she asked.

"05:00 hours." Agent Mills said that with a rumble of discomfort to his voice.

Nevada hit the light on her watch. It was about a quarter to three.

Both their car and the one approaching them slowed, because the narrow lane created by the walls of shipping containers wouldn't provide much room for them to travel past one another.

Nevada leaned into the space between the front seats, struggling for a better look at the approaching vehicle. The car heading towards them passed through a narrow line of light slipping through a break in the containers, revealing its long shape.

"That's a hearse."

Mills jerked the steering wheel to the left, blocking the lane. Their inertia flung Nevada against the side of the passenger seat. The driver of the hearse slammed on his brakes, stopping short of running into them.

This close, the lower halves of the passenger side doors blocked the hearse's headlights, allowing them to see through the windshield of the other car. Her eyes met the driver's.

"Taggart."

Wheels squealed as Taggart threw his car in reverse.

Nevada didn't wait for Mills to react. She shoved open the car door and ran after the hearse. The winter air cut into her lungs, which threw off her speed for a split second, but then she hit her stride with all of her senses hyper aware.

The length of the hearse prevented Taggart from turning around until he got to the end of the lane. The plates on the hearse were from North Carolina. She committed them to memory: Golf-alpha-kilo-zero-six-one-three. Beneath the squeal of the hearse's tires, the sound of footfalls chased after her, probably Vale.

A hand popped out of the driver side window and pointed a gun at her. She shifted a few steps to her left as Taggart fired. Her position made it more difficult for him to aim at her, not that he could aim that well while trying to drive in reverse.

Vale cursed from somewhere behind her. He didn't sound hit, just pissed. One of the three bullets pinged as it ricocheted off a container. He missed Nevada, but she doubted he'd expected to hit her. More likely, he'd hoped to slow her down, scare her into ducking for cover. If anything, she ran faster.

The gun deterred her from leaping onto the hood of the hearse, though. At least for now, she was a moving target.

Taggart pulled the gun back into his car. He increased his speed. She saw the silhouette of his head as he turned to look behind him.

She couldn't match his speed, but he couldn't reverse forever. He didn't need to. The lane formed by the containers was near the end. She saw the illuminated hull of a container ship. Gears groaned as a crane lifted a container from the deck of the ship.

If he risked stopping at the end to throw the car in drive, she'd get a couple seconds to act. What she did at that point depended on which way he turned. The same two words repeated in her mind as she struggled to keep as little distance between her and the hearse as possible.

Turn right. Turn right. Turn right.

The hearse cleared the lane in front of the docked cargo ship. No one was moving about. The wheels squealed as the car spun, and it went to her right.

The cumbersome car jerked to a stop.

Taggart didn't throw the car into drive, though. With the gun still in his left hand, he aimed at Nevada.

She was committed, though. No cover to seek. At best, she could dive for the asphalt, but that would turn her into a stationary target. He shot at her twice but missed.

He cursed and he threw the car into drive. Before he could accelerate, Nevada dove at him through the open driver side window.

The car's engine screamed as they collided, and Taggart slammed his foot on the accelerator. With Taggart in the way, she couldn't get all of her body inside. Her torso landed in his lap. The hearse took off blind as they struggled, their limbs engaged in an inelegant battle. They fought over his gun and the steering wheel.

He tried to shove Nevada back out the window, partially succeeding. Her sneakers scraped along the asphalt. The car jerked right and left, as they each tugged the steering wheel in opposite directions.

She gave up on pinning down his left arm and the gun and crushed his throat with her elbow. He lost his grip on the steering wheel, and it jerked hard to the left. His gun went off. The bullet didn't hit her. She grabbed at his gun arm but missed it and almost fell out. Her fingers found the inside door handle as he slammed on the brakes.

Too much of her body was hanging outside of the car, though, and the momentum flung her out the window and onto the ground near one of the dock's abandoned berths.

The impact knocked Nevada dizzy. Her eyes focused in time to see Taggart's shaky right hand aiming his gun at her. A single eye stared down his barrel at her.

He grinned.

Headlights blinded them both. Before either of them could react, Agent Mills' Chevy Impala slammed into the rear passenger corner of the hearse, causing it to spin away from Nevada.

Both cars jerked to a stop.

Nevada leaped up and went straight for Taggart. This time, she had the advantage. She grabbed his gun arm and slammed his wrist hard on the edge of the car window frame. Ripping the gun from his grip, she pistol-whipped the bridge of his nose. Before he could do anything else, she reached inside, turned the car off, and yanked the key out of the ignition.

They had him.

"Damn, you're good." Vale gasped as he jogged up to them.

By this point, Mills was out of the Chevy, which only had a busted headlight. He went straight for the back of the hearse and jerked open the door. Mills didn't speak. He didn't need to, because the look on his face said it all.

Taggart laughed. Even though it came out as a weak rasp, it didn't diminish the sound of victory.

"Looking for someone?" Taggart choked out the words.

Nevada jerked him partway out of the window. Her anger fueled her muscles, and the only reason he didn't fly out onto the ground was his seatbelt.

"Where is he?" She grabbed a fistful of his hair and slammed his head against the window frame when he didn't answer right away. "DeWare wasn't supposed to get here until five! Where is he?"

Mills came around and grabbed Taggart from her and pulled him the rest of the way out of the car and flung him onto the ground.

"Answer her!" He pointed his gun at Taggart.

The mercenary rolled onto his back and stared at the sky. "One of the things I've always liked about DeWare." He paused to cough as he tried to catch his breath. "He always runs ahead of schedule."

Agent Mills didn't say a thing. He closed his eyes as he lowered his gun and hung his head in shame.

Nevada didn't wait. Mills had made it clear from the start that they wouldn't board DeWare's ship. Too much risk.

She hopped into Mills' Chevy, threw it into drive, and took off with Mills and Vale yelling after her. If she reached DeWare's ship before it left, she might save Raymond.

Chapter 48: Maria

Wednesday, 2 February 1983

As Maria followed Olivia through the woods, she remembered why she'd always hated survival training. Her sneakers got stuck in the mud. She tripped once, and the only thing that saved her from a face-plant was the trunk of a tree she grabbed. At least it was winter here, too, meaning next to no insect life. It also tamped down the stink of animal life and rotting plants. Yeah, she was unapologetically a city girl.

Olivia stopped next to a large cluster of bushes and held up a hand for Maria to wait. "This is as close as we can get without being seen."

That meant it was time for Maria to do her thing. "I know you got the crash course earlier, but a few rules about this. No one will hear us when we go intangible and invisible, not exactly. We'll have to talk louder to hear each other. To anyone around us, it'll sound like a fly buzzing around that they can't see."

Olivia stared at her. Maria decided to interpret her silence as understanding and agreement.

"Also, the transition from being shifted into our normal state can be extremely disorienting, because there's a split second where you're still moving ten times faster than normal. You can use it to deliver a hell of a punch, assuming you don't break your hand." Maria slipped her hand out of her pocket, showing the brass knuckles she was wearing. "Only problem is that it's really easy to trip or run into a wall, because you don't realize how quickly you're about to run into it. Probably best if you leave the speed-punches to me and focus on staying on your feet."

They stared at each other. It was Olivia who broke the silence this time, though. "What are you waiting for?"

Maria restrained her desire to slap Olivia and held out her left hand. "Remember that you have to stay in physical contact with me. If you let go of me, I can't keep you shifted."

Olivia took her hand. Her skin felt rough as stone. Maria wondered if it was the product of calluses or the way all these dark elves' skin felt.

"One last thing." Maria glared at her. "I'm here for Pockets. Don't think for a minute we're going to cut and run without him."

Olivia stared at her. "Would you also like to tell me the night sky is black? Or perhaps that dogs bark?"

"I honestly didn't think anyone could be more Nevada than Nevada."

The air cracked like a soft slap as Maria turned them intangible, with the air rushing into the space they no longer occupied.

"Let's go," Maria said.

Olivia led them out from behind the bushes. The Erlking's castle came into view. An elevated bridge went over the stream and led into the front gates of the castle. The gate had an honest-to-God portcullis. Maria couldn't hold in her grin. They were storming an actual castle!

The shape of the place looked as promised with the gate in the center of a long wall that curved outward. The structure had three towers, forming a triangle. The middle tower was the tallest, and even with the curved wall to block her view, Maria could see the top of that corner tower. The two smaller towers were on each end of the curved wall in front of them. Slender trees, at least thirty feet tall, with red leaves sprouted from the top of each tower. Bright, round bulbs hung from the branches and glowed with warm light. The silhouettes of women walked along the tops of the outer wall and the towers.

As they ran closer, Olivia headed for the bridge.

Maria jerked her away from there. "No, go over the water. As long as we keep moving, we won't sink."

Olivia took hesitant steps as they went over the water. She got all wide-eyed as she stared down at the stream and the way they walked on air.

"We're not on the same plane of reality right now," Maria said. "We're more like ghosts."

"I do not like this."

"Well, get us somewhere we can shift back solid. I'm fine, but I'm guessing you'll get lightheaded soon, if we don't."

Olivia tugged them towards the closer of the smaller towers. They stopped outside of it.

"This is going to feel really weird and not necessarily the same as when we went through the chassis of your car. Take a deep breath and plunge through without stopping. Stand in the bricks too long, and you'll suffocate." Olivia took a step, but Maria pulled her back. "Wait. One more thing. Whatever you do, don't lose your grip on my hand while going through the wall. You'll turn solid in the bricks. Do that, and you're dead."

Olivia grimaced. "There might be one or two of my sisters in the tower base. We can't turn solid in there."

"Then take us down the steps into the dungeon."

"How do we use the stairs?"

Maria laughed. "Same as you normally would. The trick is not to think about it."

Olivia grumbled something that sounded like a curse.

"Come on." Maria tugged for Olivia to step into the wall.

Every material felt different. Walking through a person felt like walking through water without getting wet. Wood resembled a layered cake. This blue brick startled her with something close to a cheese grater. The brick didn't draw her blood, but it sent a jolt of phantom pain running through her body. She pushed faster through the wall, determined to end the sensation as fast as possible. In her desperation to return to the open air, she moved faster than

Olivia, whose reaction to the pain had been to jerk back. Maria gripped Olivia's hand more tightly and yanked her through the wall.

Olivia tumbled forward out of Maria's grip and fell to the floor. Her momentum sent her straight towards a dull red tree trunk in the center of the tower. Even with the world slowed to a crawl, the collision created a loud crack as Olivia's body hit the tree. The guards stood across the room by the door. No way they'd missed Olivia appearing out of thin air and cracking against the tree.

They were as good as caught, but with the rest of the world moving slower, Maria considered her surroundings and options.

The slender trunk of the tree reached all the way to the top of the tower. Long, flat branches formed steps leading the way up. From what Olivia had said, these trees acted as antennae to receive power from a nearby power plant and distribute it to the rest of the castle with no wiring involved. Maria wondered how walking up the tree didn't electrocute someone.

The only way around the tree was to the left, because the "steps" blocked her path to the right. No telling what walking through that tree would do to her. Electrical wiring back home tingled, but she decided not to test if the same applied here.

To the left she saw the opening in the floor where the more conventional stone steps led down into the dungeon.

Straight ahead, three guards turned in slow motion towards Olivia. So much for just one or two guards.

Maria considered abandoning Olivia. She didn't like her or trust her, but if Pockets and Ava weren't in the dungeon, she'd have to search this place without any idea of where to go next.

She sprinted at the slow moving Grey Women. She had a second set of brass knuckles she could have used for her left hand, but she couldn't risk losing the time to put them on. They were already reaching for their guns, resting in holsters on their hips.

Two steps from the guards, Maria shifted back into normal space. The two women she targeted never even got a chance to react to her sudden appearance. Her momentum thrust her forward. Her right fist, gripping her brass knuckles smashed into one woman's throat while her other, outstretched arm clothes-lined the second.

Pain shot through Maria's left arm. She hadn't expected that attack to hurt her so much. If she hadn't broken one of the bones in her forearm, she'd come close. The shock of pain distracted her too much to shift back to her intangible state right away.

Even as the first two collapsed, gasping for breath, the remaining guard drew her gun.

Maria's hand-to-hand combat training kicked in. She grabbed the Grey Woman's right wrist to keep her gun from aiming at her. She followed that with a strike to the throat, but the attack missed. The Grey Woman mirrored her defense and grabbed her arm before Maria could hit her.

Maria cursed. They struggled, but not for long. The Grey Woman reacted much faster. She kicked Maria in the stomach, knocking her loose and to the floor.

Two gunshots sounded.

Maria turned intangible before the bullet hit, and it slid through her in slow motion. How she maintained it for the entire time the bullet moved through her, she wasn't sure, but she clung to her power's protection and then rolled away.

The second bullet wasn't aimed at Maria. Olivia's shot struck the Grey Woman in the head. Maria looked away to avoid seeing the horrific results of the headshot play out in slow motion. Instead, she scrambled to her feet. Only one of the two women she'd struck in the throat was still moving. She turned solid as she delivered a kick to the head to knock her out.

Shouts sounded throughout the castle. The door to the tower opened up on a long hallway. A Grey Woman with a gun drawn ran towards Maria. Olivia fired her gun into the hallway, forcing the Grey Woman to dive for cover through the open door of another room.

"Door!" Olivia shouted.

Maria took a moment to realize what she meant. The large door to the tower hung open. She flung it shut and dropped a large bar in place to lock it.

"Summon the dragon now!" Olivia ran for the stairs leading into the dungeon.

Worried the reception might be poor down there, Maria pulled out her radio from her belt before she followed.

"Lynna, they know we're here, and we haven't found the others yet. We need you now!"

Maria didn't wait for the reply. She shifted and ran after Olivia.

Chapter 49: Lynna

Wednesday, 2 February 1983

Lynna flew low over the creek as she rushed towards the Erlking's castle. She'd tried to raise Maria on her radio since the last transmission, but when she didn't answer, Lynna hoped that meant she'd gone intangible again.

Her thoughts split, with half of them focused on her flight path and the other half on connecting with the creek beneath her. Better that it had been a lake or a raging river, not that she could really control that much water, but she'd work with what she had.

Bullets zinged past her as the castle came into view. She swooped up above the outer wall. Grey women armed with rifles shot at her. As fast as she was going, they'd need some phenomenal luck to hit her.

Lynna's attack didn't miss.

At her heels, the creek's water followed in a tight spiral formation. She directed the water to attack the Grey Women and knocked them onto their backs. Some lost their rifles. Two of them plunged from the top of the wall to the brick courtyard.

As she circled the castle, she flew higher. The creek followed her, gallon after gallon. A few gunshots missed her, but not as many compared to her first circle of the castle.

The building spiral of water descended, directed at any Grey Women who got back to their feet. More fell from the walls. Then the rest of the Erlking's private army emerged from the castle. This time, they stayed in the brick courtyard, instead of risking a fall from the outer walls.

That was fine with Lynna. She could do plenty of damage, even if they didn't take a three-story drop. She focused on one at a time. The stream of water hammered into any of them close to a wall. She aimed for their heads, cracking their skulls against the bricks. She landed on one of the abandoned towers, ducking to use the parapets as a shield while she wielded the creek water at the Grey Women.

One of the elven sisters, one with streaks of white in her black hair, shouted something. Lynna wished she could decipher it, but she saw the results fast enough. All of the Grey Women rushed indoors. They'd surrendered the outside of the castle. They'd probably guessed she needed to see where she was sending the water to direct it. They were partially right, but she could have guessed, gone on the psychic equivalent of touch once she directed the water into the castle, but she'd have no way of knowing if her attack had struck an enemy or a friend. It also required a lot more concentration on her part, which meant no flying or defending herself if she was attacked directly.

The water under her command swirled in a loose spiral in the courtyard. She wanted them to see it, a reminder of the threat she posed.

Odds favored they were going to rush her tower. She needed to change position, move to one of the other towers and be ready to strike when the Grey Women emerged onto the roof with her.

Lynna stood. Something struck her right shoulder. She heard the gunshot too late to dodge the bullet. Her scales could handle most projectiles, but that didn't keep them from hurting. She dropped to the roof, landing on her back. Her torso crushed against the joints where her wings met her back.

Distracted, Lynna lost control of the water she'd used to attack the Grey Women. She reached out for it again, but too late. Most of it had already been absorbed into the parts of the courtyard that were ground instead of bricks and down the drains that fed back into the creek.

More shots fired, keeping her from getting back up. She'd forgotten castles sometimes had arrowslits, narrow openings in the walls for archers to shoot through. They also made a perfect spot for a sharpshooter to stay concealed.

The bullets stopped as someone emerged onto the roof. No, at least two of the Grey Women. Lynna scrambled to her feet as they opened fire on her. Another bullet hit her on the forehead. Desperate for escape, Lynna dove off the edge of the tower. Only after the fact did she realize she'd dropped into the courtyard. She didn't land, but so long as she was behind the castle walls, she was trapped in a bowl with bullets raging down on her from all directions. Most of the shots missed. Even the keenest sharpshooter would struggle to hit a fast-moving target in flight.

The courtyard wasn't big enough for her to sustain her flight. She bounced off the walls, latching onto them with her talons and immediately launching back into the air to avoid being a sitting target. Most of the bullets pinged off the bricks. Some lucky shots hit her. One caught her in the left calf and another on her stomach, but most got her wings. None of the bullets pierced her scaled skin, but the longer she stayed in this kill zone, the more likely they'd draw blood.

Her time fighting to escape might have lasted only thirty seconds at most. Her heart pounded, and her lungs fought for every scrap of oxygen. A black hole, just like Pockets' creations, opened in her flight path as she launched into the open sky. She folded in her wings as she ducked beneath the circular void. Gunshots dimmed to faint hisses as they zipped past her, some disappearing into the pocket.

"Maria, not sure if you've got your ears on," she transmitted as she struggled for elevation and back for the creek to reload. "I got their attention, but they ran me off. I'll sweep back in another minute. There are more of them than we expected, so you better hurry."

No answer came. She hoped that was a good sign, but there was no way to know until Maria responded, if she ever did.

Chapter 50: Nevada

Wednesday, 2 February 1983

Dock C23 came into view. As promised, it was a blink-and-you'll-miss-it location in a shipyard with cargo ships larger than three city blocks. By comparison, DeWare's *Hylonome* was closer in size to Lynna's dog.

But the ship was still here.

Judging from the crew's activity on the ship and the dock, the Hylonome wouldn't be here much longer. Nevada didn't see a point in subtlety. She slammed on the brakes, stopping right next to the ship.

A guy wearing a reflective vest walked over to her as she got out.

"You need something, lady?" He said the "lady" in a way that made it clear he suspected she was a kid.

"Yeah, I do."

Nevada grabbed him by the shirt and slammed him against the hood of the car. She bit him in the throat. He screamed and struggled. Instinct asserted itself, and she bit harder, letting the blood flow. She fought against the intoxicating rush of joy that made her want to keep drinking. She only needed enough and didn't want to kill him. No, that wasn't true. Something stirring in her heart very much wanted to take his life. She sated it with a promise for what was to come and released him, shoving him to the ground.

Other shipyard workers ran to their coworker's defense. She ran past them easily enough. One that got too close paid for it. She flung him at two of the others as if he weighed as little as a small twig.

A set of stairs was retracting and already well out of reach for most anyone else. Nevada leaped up twenty feet to grab onto the bottom of the steps. Shouts came from the ship. They knew she was here. Footfalls pounded across the deck.

The white ship stretched out longer than a football field. A three-level structure, each level smaller as it went up, occupied the middle of the main deck. The stairs Nevada had grabbed onto were folding into an opening on the side of the lowest of those three levels. A woman who appeared to be working the controls of the stairs shouted for help.

Nevada hopped off the retracting stairs and onto the deck. The ship quivered beneath her feet as the engines rumbled to life. If the crew on the bridge realized she was aboard, they were opting to deal with her out at sea. Fine by her. If they assumed they could simply toss her overboard, they were in for an unpleasant surprise.

She grabbed the woman in front of her and slammed her against the wall. "Where's DeWare?"

The woman screamed, staring at Nevada as if something horrid had touched her. With the blood from the shipyard worker still on her, Nevada probably resembled a rabid animal. She wiped at her mouth with her sleeve, but she could still feel the blood there, starting to dry and stick to her chin, not to mention the way the front of her shirt clung to her. The scent of blood filled her senses and threatened to distract her.

She couldn't afford that, because the guards the woman had shouted for were here. They drew their guns as they ran out onto the open deck.

Nevada surrendered to the hunger in her. She'd never really let the animal in her loose.

Tonight, she planned to let her inner demon feast.

Chapter 51: Maria

Wednesday, 2 February 1983

Olivia had guessed wrong. There were two guards in the dungeon. The pair of armed Grey Women ran in slow motion past them for the stairs they'd come down, likely to see what the disturbance above had been and expecting to aid their sisters, without realizing the threat was slipping right past them.

As soon as the two disappeared from sight, Maria shifted back solid. Better they breathe while they could.

"Where to?" Maria whispered.

Olivia didn't speak. She let go of Maria's hand and ran down the corridor, past all of the open doors.

While the dungeon lived up to its more claustrophobic expectations in terms of narrow corridors and low ceiling, the space was well lit. Vines adorned with glowing yellow globes ran along the edges of the ceiling.

Olivia stopped when they came to a shut door and looked in through its small, eye-level window. A large, metal bar ran across the front of the door, locking it in place. Olivia slid the bar out of its end cap and pushed the door open.

Unlike the corridor, the tiny room didn't contain any source of light. Maria pulled out a slender black mag lite from her jacket's breast pocket and twisted it on. Pointing the bright beam into the room revealed a round hole about three feet in diameter in the floor.

Maria moved into the room and pointed her light into the hole. The small pit was about fifteen feet deep, and stank of the oil that covered the brick walls of the hole, probably to keep prisoners from climbing out.

"Pockets!"

He grinned up at her, even as he held up his grease-smudged hand to block her light from his eyes. He'd lost his sunglasses, so she shifted her light away from him. "You all right?" she asked.

"Yeah. You?"

"I'll be better once we have you out of there."

Olivia ignored them and moved to the side of the small room with a rope ladder attached to the wall. She grabbed the other end of the rope ladder and flung it into the hole.

"Hurry," Olivia said and went back into the corridor, probably to watch for her sisters.

Pockets did as told, scrambling up the ladder. "Where are we? They put me in a pocket like the kind I create. One minute I'm at the Greenhouse. The next I'm falling into the hallway up here."

"We're in Never-Never Land." Only then did she realize she had no actual idea what the name of this place was.

Pockets reached the top of the hole. Maria grabbed his slick hand and pulled him out the rest of the way. He smelled awful, a mix of the oil and his body odor, but she happily breathed him in. They kissed, keeping the embrace short but long enough to share all the desperation and fear they'd felt in these long hours apart.

His dark eyes, scared and uncertain, stared at her. "My powers aren't working."

"It's this room. It cancels them." She could feel it when she walked through the open door. Something ephemeral had run down her spine and choked her nervous system.

"Get him out of here," Olivia said in a harsh rebuke. She stood with her gun drawn, in the corridor.

"We still need to find Ava," Maria said as they stepped out into the corridor, that feeling of restraint on her powers releasing its grip.

"She's not down here." As if anticipating Maria's question, Olivia said, "All the other cell doors are open."

Maria held up a hand to stop Pockets from saying anything. He looked ready to question why one of these Grey Women was helping them.

"Maria, not sure if you've got your ears on," Lynna's voice came over the radio clipped to Maria's belt. *"I got their attention, but they ran me off. I'll sweep back in another minute. There are more of them than we expected, so you better hurry."*

Maria pulled the radio off her hip and transmitted back, "We've got Pockets, but Ava's not down here in the dungeon. Not sure where she is."

"Most likely she's in one of the room's closer to the Erlking's bedroom," Olivia said.

"Olivia seems to have a rough idea where Ava is," Maria transmitted. "I'm going to give the radio to her while I get Pockets out of here."

"Understood."

"I'm not going anywhere until we've found Ava." Pockets shot Olivia a look that plainly said he trusted her about as far as he could throw this castle.

"This really ain't the time to be all Clint Eastwood, baby." Maria placed the radio in Olivia's hand. "I'll get back as fast as I can."

Olivia nodded. Her eyes narrowed on Pockets. Maria couldn't decide what to make of the way she looked at him. It wasn't exactly distrust, but she seemed uncertain about him. Wasn't time to get into that, though.

Maria took Pockets by the hand and shifted. "Let's move."

Chapter 52: Lynna

Wednesday, 2 February 1983

If time had allowed it, Lynna would have gone for a tidal wave's worth of water. Instead, she swooped in low over the creek and lifted about ten gallons of it. The mass of water followed her in the shape of a sphere. She needed to get back to the castle. Maria moved faster when she was shifted, but getting Pockets far enough away to follow the creek to the car would still leave Olivia exposed for a long time.

Lynna also couldn't afford to give the Erlking and his daughters time to prepare for her next attack.

She kept her distance, swooping in close enough to let the Grey Women get a look at her without scaring the ones on the roof and in the courtyard into seeking cover in the castle.

The gunshots started as soon as they saw her. The distance worked in her favor, and she beat her wings hard to maintain her speed. Even though she flew in a tight circle over the castle, she altered her altitude as much as possible to foil any of the sharpshooters. There was also the potential benefit that getting the Grey Women to shoot straight up might mean they'd end up hitting some of their own when gravity pulled the bullets back down.

To improve her odds, Lynna split the sphere of water into two halves. One half she fashioned into a dense circle floating beneath her. It wouldn't stop any bullets, but the water would slow them and possibly deflect them from hitting her. She sent the other half of the water after the Grey Women.

Even though she could fashion the water she controlled into complicated shapes, the real challenge came from how many separate bodies of water she maintained. That's why Dr. Howard had long ago added juggling to her training. They'd started simple with two balls, but by the time they'd finished, Lynna had learned how to keep as many as ten things in the air, even if they were objects of different shapes and sizes.

Dr. Howard would be proud of her now.

Lynna split the water directed at the Grey Women into three separate spheres. She didn't try to knock the Grey Women off their feet. Instead, she targeted three of them and entrapped their heads in the water, drowning them where they stood. The Grey Women who weren't drowning tried to pull the water off their sisters' heads, but they couldn't rip the water away. If they'd had a straw, they might have helped. They dragged one of the drowning women down into the castle, beyond Lynna's view. That wouldn't help, though. As long as the water was wrapped around someone's head, Lynna could sense it and hold it in place.

The two drowning on the roof collapsed. When the pair passed out, Lynna sent the spheres of water after new targets. The Grey Women retreated back into the castle. Lynna managed to get at least one more woman's head wrapped in water, but the rest got away.

The gunshots continued, coming from the arrowslits.

"I've got their attention," Lynna transmitted over her radio. "They're hiding inside the castle and shooting at me."

Olivia answered. *"They haven't come down into the dungeon yet, but that won't last much longer. They'll eventually figure out that you're distracting them. Your friend hasn't returned either."*

"You're a glass half-empty kind of person, aren't you?"

There was a moment's silence before Olivia answered. *"Is that a sort of strategy you're suggesting? Because I've no idea what you—They're here."*

Lynna didn't respond. If Olivia didn't turn down the volume on her radio, then Lynna could give away her position to her sisters, assuming they hadn't already spotted her down there.

Maria needed more time to get back to Olivia. Lynna couldn't possibly get down into the dungeon, but she could force the Grey Women to focus their forces on her and give Olivia a better chance of surviving.

Summoning all of the water she had at her command, Lynna descended towards one of the smaller towers.

It was time to take her attack inside the castle.

Chapter 53: Maria

Wednesday, 2 February 1983

Maria set Pockets free by the cluster of bushes she and Olivia had used for cover before she turned them invisible. Gunfire sounded from the Erlking's fortress with Lynna circling above it.

"I can draw some of their fire away from her." Pockets wiggled his fingers. "I've got some nasty stuff I can set loose."

"And maybe get Ava killed. We don't know where she is in there. Save the doomsday weapons for when we're ready for all of us to run." They didn't even really know for sure if Ava was in there, but she preferred not to speak that possibility into existence. "Follow that creek over there, away from the castle. You'll come to a washed out bridge where there's a car waiting."

"Where are we?" he asked again.

"We're not on Earth. From what Olivia said, we're in a different dimension."

Even in the dark of night, Maria didn't miss his scowl. "Bullshit."

She pointed up at the two moons above. When he saw them, his jaw dropped open.

"Now, get to the car." She kissed him, a much quicker one this time, and then went intangible to run back for the dungeon. At least this time, she didn't have to take things slow for Olivia.

Loud cracks of thunder reached Maria as she descended into the dungeon. She recognized the sounds as bullets being fired. Even in her intangible state, Maria could sense the vibrations in the air from the gunshots.

A body lay on the floor of the corridor in a small puddle of blood. Three more of the Grey Women had taken cover inside the doorways of the dungeon cells as they shot at Olivia, who'd taken a similar position back where Maria had left her.

Maria considered her options as fast as she could. She couldn't attack the Grey Women while they were in the cells, because the wards in them would turn her solid and leave her unprotected. The same issue prevented her from pulling Olivia out of here since she was also in a warded space.

Maria ran back upstairs into the base of the tower they'd originally entered. Even moving faster than normal, she didn't have much time before Olivia ran out of bullets and her attackers rushed her.

The bodies of the three guards Maria and Olivia had taken out when they first arrived were still on the floor inside the tower. Maria turned tangible long enough to catch her breath and grab one of the fallen women's guns.

When she got back into the dungeon, the three Grey Women were still shooting, taking turns ducking out of the open doors to fire. Maria started with the one furthest back. She pointed the gun in her hand at the woman's head and pulled the trigger. While the bullet was in the barrel of the gun, it remained intangible, but as soon as it reached the open air, it went solid and into the woman's head. By the time the last of the three women turned to see what had happened, Maria had already pulled the trigger on her, too.

Chapter 54: Nevada

Wednesday, 2 February 1983

Blood.

Nevada had spilled a river of it throughout the upper and lower decks of the *Hylonome*. Some of it had been her own, from the cuts and gunshot wounds inflicted by DeWare's crew. The injuries she'd taken had healed almost as fast as they were formed. Oh, they'd hurt like hell, but the pain was short-lived, adding fuel to her rage.

A symphony of life and death flowed through her, and she reveled in it.

The bridge crew had been among the first she'd slain. She killed the engines a few miles out from port, leaving them adrift with the lights of the shipyard and the rest of the coastline at their backs.

She'd expected some sort of alarm to go off through the ship, bringing the lot of them down on her. Only, she'd acted too quickly for them to respond. Right after she'd taken out the bridge crew, she'd shut down the guards' ability to communicate by leaving one of the radios with its transmit button depressed next to a boombox playing the Doors, tying up the channel so that no one else could speak over it.

The music provided the soundtrack to her descent into the ship as she came across people with radios playing *Break on Through*, then *Soul Kitchen* and from there *The Crystal Ship*.

Her search through the *Hylonome* only paused when she came to a cramped room below decks that was filled with small beds with smaller bodies on them. Most of these abducted children were asleep, but a single pair of wide eyes fixed on Nevada as she stepped into the room.

"I'm not going to hurt you," she said. "Which of you has been here the longest?"

The boy took a moment to find his voice. "Me."

She thought back to Taggart's file, which her electrified brain recalled with a disturbing ease. "What's your name? Are your initials G.S.?"

The boy's eyes got even bigger, probably wondering how she'd guessed that. "Gene Sommers."

"How old are you?"

"Three."

She smiled at him, but that only made him pull back and grip his bed cover closer, as if he could hide beneath his blanket now that he'd already been seen. She supposed her smile was a gruesome thing by this point. Best to put it away.

"Don't you worry, Gene. I'm gonna make sure you live to see four and many more." She went back into the corridor. "When I come back, we're going to get you and your friends here somewhere safe."

"Safe from what?"

Nevada didn't answer. She shut the door. Once she finished with the rest of the Hylonome's crew, she'd make sure these kids were safe from ever ending up like her. They'd be safe from DeWare.

Her last stop was the cargo hold.

The door sat partially open. She pushed on it and stepped inside. Dozens of bullets pinged off the metal. One of the bullets shot through her right leg before she could retreat back into the corridor. The bullet went all the way through. Blood seeped out both the front and back of her left thigh. She waited for her powers to seal the wound. The bullets stopped.

"Ms. Brandle, it's a pleasure to have you visit!"

Five years had passed since she'd last heard that voice, but hearing Dr. Rudolph DeWare speak made her feel ten again. An instinct she'd forgotten told her to run and hide.

"I notice you didn't bring any of your friends," he called out from the cargo hold.

He sounded distracted. The reason shocked her. The bastard feared her. He wanted to stall her long enough to get his guards in a position to ambush her.

"Don't worry," he said. "I'm happy to inform you that I've already brought a friend of yours here." That sounded more like the confident monster, a taunt that only he could find funny. "Would you like to see Mr. Bennu? I must say that he's looked better, but if you'll kindly permit me the chance, I think we can remedy that."

She glanced through the crack of the partially open door to the cargo hold. The boxes weren't shoved up against the walls. If she got inside fast enough, she could get into the cover of the crates and work her way closer to ambush DeWare and his mercenaries.

Standing safely to the side, she placed the flat of her hand against the door. When she pushed it open, no bullets answered.

"Don't be shy, Ms. Brandle. I'm quite curious to see what you've become."

She ran into the cargo hold. Bullets chased her as she reached the cover of the crates. The brief instant before her view was blocked, she saw DeWare. He wore a dark brown sports jacket over a white, button-down shirt and stood more than six feet tall. The only thing that looked different about him was the hint of white to his dark blonde hair.

DeWare and three men with machine guns stood around a long, wooden box with the lid pried off. The bastards had shipped Raymond like any other piece of property. DeWare stood behind the crate with his hands resting on top of it.

"Did you see how fast she moved?" one of the gunmen said. He'd whispered it, but her enhanced hearing didn't miss it.

"Oh, yes." DeWare said it with the same kind of pride someone reserved for a compliment on a well-trained dog.

She worked her way around the edges of the room. They might expect this, but she hadn't heard any of the gunmen try to move. She wished they would. If they broke away from DeWare, she could pick them off one at a time.

"I take it you've graduated to human blood, Ms. Brandle?"

Nevada resisted the urge to respond to his taunt. Opening her mouth would only give up her position.

"My my... I find it hard to believe Elyce approved of that."

Typical. He wanted to bait her by denying *Doctor* Howard her title. That ploy probably would've hit the mark with Lynna, tricking her into giving up her position, but he'd wasted it with her.

She reached the part of the room where DeWare and his gunmen were a few crates away from her. Slow and patient had gotten her close.

"I'm curious, Ms. Brandle. How addictive are you finding human blood? I ask, because I've read Elyce's files since she believes she took over the Greenhouse, and there's a reason they've avoided letting you sample human blood. Has she told you about your parents?"

That stopped her cold, making her feet unsteady as her mind swam with this. Doc Howard knew information about her parents. She knew and hadn't told her?

"I can't imagine she would," DeWare said, seemingly oblivious that he'd struck her dumb. "It's a pity what happened to your mother. You see, Lilian Brandle was the unwitting subject in a genetic experiment."

Lilian... Her mother's name was Lilian.

Nevada almost answered him then, hungry to know more. She didn't need to, because he kept talking.

"I always knew you were the one I could count on to develop into something more. Most of your hybrid siblings were most likely happy accidents—though, I suppose some might have been anything but pleasant—but not you. You are a marvel of genetic engineering. Yes, your mother was human and your father a vampire, but I created you. I'm the reason you exist."

She told herself he was full of shit, but the way the words struck her in her soul... She knew. Every word was the stone-cold truth. She heard it in his voice, that arrogant certainty that he always knew more than anyone else in the room.

A guard emerged from behind a crate a few rows over and fired his machine gun. Nevada leaped up the stacked crates next to her. Several bullets hit her in the side as she scrambled to the top.

"I hit her!" the gunman shouted. "She's on top of the containers!"

The crates came so close to the ceiling that she had to hunch over. That made leaping from one stack to another a challenge.

The guards scrambled towards her position.

"Finish her off!" DeWare shouted. She took a brief bit of satisfaction in the panic behind his words. The bastard feared her, and he fucking should. She was going to kill him.

"There!" the guard who'd shot her shouted.

More bullets fired.

She dove for the next row of crates. DeWare's goons chased her with their machine guns, forcing her to hop from one stack of crates to another. She managed to take a leap that landed her two rows over. Her body ached, having taken too many hits. Even her ability to heal struggled against all her bullet wounds. She felt like Swiss cheese. The double leap bought her a few extra seconds, though.

The guards shouted to each other. "I don't see her!"

"Go right! Run!"

Gunshots pinged off the metal ceiling. They were firing at the entire row she'd skipped, gambling she hadn't gotten as far as she had and that she was hiding by lying flat on top of the crates.

"She ain't moving anymore."

"I don't think she's up there!"

"Bullshit! I must've hit her more than a dozen times before she started jumping."

"Then we shoot up this row, too, until we get her or flush her out."

She dropped to the floor of the cargo hold on the far side of the crates. Her right leg wasn't fully healed, though, and as hard as she fought against it, she still shrieked in pain as her bleeding leg rebelled against her putting weight on it.

Even limping, she moved faster than these damn humans.

"I see her!"

She cursed at her body to heal, but it mocked her, demanding more blood for the deed.

One of the guards ran into her. When their bodies collided, she grabbed his rifle. His finger pressed on the trigger. Bullets thundered from its barrel, but this close, they didn't have a chance of hitting her. His partners weren't so lucky. Nevada pointed the barrel towards the other two as they emerged a few rows down. Both of them went down, guns clattering on the floor next to them.

The guard struggling against her screamed, certain he could overpower her.

He was wrong.

She smashed the side of the gun into his face. Blood burst from his nose. His screams choked off.

That's when Nevada went for the jugular. She took him to the floor pinning him there until his body went limp from blood loss.

Chapter 55: Lynna

Wednesday, 2 February 1983

Lynna fought her way into the third floor hallway and left a swirl of water spinning in place to block the doorway from the tower to the hallway. The swirl wouldn't stop anyone from going through the door, but no one could sneak up on her. She folded her wings around her to create a shield against the gunfire. It still hurt, but her wings weren't as sensitive as the rest of her body. She directed the additional water at any of the Grey Women who got too close, drowning in them where they stood. A couple managed to get close enough to hit her. One tried to hold their breath as they fought, but one good punch to her stomach caused her to gasp and choke on the water.

Lynna's progress through the third floor was patient and methodical.

"All I want is my friends," she said during a lull in the fight. The Grey Women had dragged away the bodies of some of their own. "I've no interest in killing anyone else, but Ava Lanier and Rowan Beltrami are leaving with me."

"By all means, dragon." The deep voice belonged to the Grey Man from the cabin in East Germany, the Erlking. "Let us speak."

He stepped out from a room near the end of the hallway. He gestured for his daughters to fall back into the large tower, and once they were out of the hallway, he pointed towards the room he'd stepped out of.

"Your friend, the small Ljósálfr, is in here. Join us."

He retreated back through the door.

Lynna hesitated. The empty hallway didn't reassure her. It meant the Grey Women were out of her sight, likely setting up an ambush while the Erlking distracted her. Still, if Ava was in that room, then she could grab her and get her out of here.

She placed a second swirl of water at the tower entrance the Grey Women had retreated through. If they entered the hallway from either end, she'd sense it once they passed through the water.

Lynna stopped in front of the room the Erlking had entered. He stood behind Ava who was shackled to a chair with her hands behind her. She wasn't gagged, but she stayed silent, smiling at Lynna.

The Erlking stood behind Ava, stroking her brown hair. "As you can see, she is alive and well."

"Well isn't exactly the word I'd use when you've got her chained up."

He grinned. "I have no desire to harm her. She is more valuable to me alive."

"She's leaving with me, even if I have to kill every one of you to get her out of here."

He laughed as one might at the adorable protest of a puppy. "Be certain that if it comes to that, I guarantee she will be dead, too."

The golden hilt of his sword still showed over his shoulder, but he didn't hold a gun or any other weapon. Odds favored he had a gun on him, though.

"However," he said, "I will allow you to leave in peace with your other friend. You can save one of them or neither."

Lynna grinned. He didn't know they'd already gotten Pockets out of the castle.

"What say I let you keep him, and I take her?"

He shook his head. "Her value far exceeds his."

"Then I'll have to take them both."

She launched one of her spheres of water into the room at him, but it collapsed to the floor as soon as it crossed the threshold.

The Erlking waved a hand towards the ceiling. "Wards. No magic will work in here. How else do you think I'd keep something as powerful as this child restrained? Now, if you would be so kind, please join us in here."

He wanted her in the room without any of her powers. "I don't think so."

He reached inside the leather jacket he wore and produced a small dagger. In a flash, he'd grabbed Ava's left ear and placed the edge of the dagger against the top crook "I'd threaten to kill her, but we both know that threat is empty. Instead, if you refuse to enter, I will cut off pieces of her, starting with her ears."

Ava warned Lynna away with a tiny shake of her head, careful not to cut herself on the dagger.

The Erlking grinned at her. "Please, it would be a pity to carve up a child, because you are too stubborn to accept a simple invitation."

Lynna glanced at each end of the hallway. She didn't see the Grey Women in the tower stairwells, but she didn't doubt they were waiting for the water barriers she'd constructed to collapse, which they most certainly would as soon as she entered the room.

"Fine."

"Lynna, no!"

Lynna smiled her apology to Ava and stepped through the open door.

Chapter 56: Lynna

Wednesday, 2 February 1983

T he wards pressed on Lynna as she entered the room. Her connection to the swirls of water vanished, and she heard them splash to the floor.

The Erlking grinned at first, but then his smile vanished.

Lynna glanced down at her hands, still covered in pale blue scales. She was still in her dragon form. That's when she remembered what Olivia had said to her at the Lincoln Memorial.

"Do you really believe the dragon is any less what you look like? Do not be so narrow-minded. We are both."

Being the sea dragon wasn't some trick of magic. It was simply a part of her.

Judging from how the Erlking's stance pulled back into something defensive, he hadn't expected this either. She had only a moment to exploit it and launched at him.

He swatted her to the side but not before she raked her talons across his face. His tough skin parted for her nails. A little faster, and she'd have gouged out his right eye. He scrambled back as she slammed into the brick wall.

When he lunged at her next, he'd drawn his sword. She swatted at it with one of her wings. Then she spun inside its reach and landed an elbow to his temple. He shoved her away.

His sword drew her blue blood from her upper arm, slicing through her scales as easily as if she were made of gelatin. One swing cut through the membrane of a wing when she attempted to block his attack.

She responded with her talons, shredding through his leather jacket and the back of his sword arm. His dark blood spilled across the floor. Pity she hadn't gotten the inside of his wrist, or she'd have done some real damage.

He kept the fight confined to the warded room, though, never letting up enough for her to draw him towards the door and potentially out from the grip of the wards that kept her from manipulating water. She could have suffocated him in an instant, otherwise.

Boots pounded on the floor in the hallway. The Grey Women were coming to defend their father.

Once they entered the room, they'd overwhelm her with numbers, and their guns would probably work fine in here. Lynna screamed as she shoved the Erlking's sword arm against the wall. The shock of pain to his wounds made him scream. She slashed at his throat with her free hand, but he blocked the attack with his other hand.

They showed only the slightest restraint when their fight took them near Ava in the center of the room. Some of the Erlking's dark blood had splattered across her brown hair. Ava struggled within her chains in a vain effort to free herself.

Then the Grey Women appeared in the doorway. The closest one raised her gun and aimed at Lynna.

"Stand down, drag—!" The side of the Grey Woman's head exploded as a bullet from a different gun thundered from the hallway.

More gunshots sounded, impossibly close together, as if someone with a machine gun had joined the fight, but Lynna knew they hadn't brought one. If the Grey Women had one, surely they'd have used it against her by now.

Stunned by what they were witnessing in the hallway, Lynna and the Erlking went still and silent. Even Ava's struggles ceased.

Then everything went silent, except for a faint whine that erupted into a rage-filled scream as Olivia suddenly appeared out of thin air, launching at an impossibly fast speed through the open door with a dagger in her right hand. That's when Lynna realized what Maria had done to finish off the Grey Women.

Olivia's dagger sliced through the Erlking's throat, before he could pull back from Lynna's grip and swing his sword at Olivia.

Dark blood splattered across the back wall of the room. The Erlking's sword clattered to the floor as he grabbed at his throat. Lynna stepped back and caught her breath, something the Erlking could no longer do.

He collapsed to his knees and stared up in horror as Olivia lifted the sword he'd dropped.

"This," Olivia said in a cold whisper, "is for my mother."

She buried the sword in his heart. Then she ripped it back out.

The Erlking fell to his back. The entire time, his pale blue eyes fixed on Olivia in a mix of wide-eyed shock and betrayal. They lost their focus as his hands slipped from his throat and his life melted away.

Maria appeared outside the door with a gun in each hand.

"Tall, grey, and gruesome finally dead?" Maria asked.

Olivia didn't look up from him, as if she thought taking her eyes off of him might undo his death.

"Oh, yeah," Lynna said. "He's done. What about the rest of the Grey Women?"

Maria held up the guns with smoke still wafting out of their barrels. "I definitely got them. Roland Deschain, eat your heart out."

Ava cleared her throat. "Not that I'm unhappy to see all of you, but would someone get me out of this chair?"

Lynna knelt behind Ava and looked at the shackles on her wrists. "Anyone see the key to these things?"

Olivia answered but never took her eyes off of the Erlking's body. "The key is hanging in the hallway on a hook next to the door."

Once they'd gotten Ava loose, Lynna walked up behind Olivia and placed a hand on her shoulder. The dark elf jerked in surprise, but she didn't look away from the Erlking.

"You did it. You're free now."

That pulled Olivia's gaze away from her father. She didn't smile. There was nothing of relief or satisfaction in the hard lines of her narrow face.

"People like us," she said, "we are never free."

Olivia screamed as she swung the Erlking's sword and cut off his head. The rest of them jumped back as she delivered the final blow.

She sneered as she wiped the blood from the sword with her shirt.

"Just to be certain," she said and marched out of the room. "Let's go."

Chapter 57: Nevada

Wednesday, 2 February 1983

Nevada discovered the door leading out of the Hylonome's cargo hold was locked. DeWare had trapped her, but it was only a matter of time before her blood-fueled strength allowed her to pry it open.

The Doors stopped playing over the dead mercenaries' radios, cutting off in mid-song. Then the radios squawked and DeWare's voice transmitted over them.

"Ms. Brandle, there's more I know about your parents," he said.

Her temper bested her, and she snatched up one of the mercenaries' radios to answer. "So does Dr. Howard! You know what that means? It means you're expendable." She laughed. "Should've kept that detail to yourself when you were trying to distract me earlier."

"What do you think will happen when the CIA finds out what you've done here?" He sounded amused. *"You think I was awful? Oh, no. After they toss you in a prison cell, they'll send your beloved Dr. Howard packing along with that besotted agent she's sleeping with. Then every one of your little friends will get handed over to the Pentagon."*

While he ran his mouth, she finally forced the door open and charged into the hallway with one of the guard's machine guns slung over her shoulder.

"Small problem with that scenario," she transmitted over the radio, listening for her own voice, to let her know if she was getting close to him. "They'll never know I was here. All the security cameras on board? Well, thanks to my training, I'll make sure all of that is wiped clean. And the kids you've got stashed on this ship? When I crash this ship back into port with dead bodies and children on board, I'll create a very public mess that the news won't miss and even the government can't sweep it under the rug. The Feds are gonna love you for that."

Hearing her voice from around the corner, she stopped talking and readied the machine gun. When she turned the corner, reaching the stairs, she found her voice had been coming from the radio clipped to the belt of a body she'd left there.

"Agent Mills will be waiting back at the dock, too," she transmitted as she climbed the stairs. "He happens to be there following up on our investigation into Taggart. He'll conveniently find the kids and Raymond's body on this ship. Well, of course, the only logical thing for him to do is take them all back to the Greenhouse. After all, that's where freaks like us belong, right?"

"Bravo, Ms. Brandle. You do make me proud, but do you really think they'll take you back like this? You're a blood-covered murderer who'll never get that hunger growing in you under control. You are a monster."

Her hand shook as she shouted into the radio. "Fucking takes one to know one!" She growled—a guttural rumble that started at the back of her throat that felt as natural as laughter. "The only reason I'm not gonna drink you dry is because I don't want that crap in your veins in mine, but I am gonna kill you!"

There was a long pause then. Right before she transmitted again, DeWare came over the radio. *"That, you'll find, is an empty threat."* His transmission included a noise in the background, what sounded like the grinding of an engine.

"No!" she shouted as she sprinted up to the Hylonome's deck and ran to the railing.

A motorboat bounced across the ocean waves, fleeing towards the Atlantic's black horizon. She pointed the machine gun, balancing it on the ship's railing to steady it as she aimed, and fired. Even as she pulled the trigger, she knew DeWare was too far out, but she shot at him until she emptied the clip.

Throwing down the machine gun, she shouted into the radio again. "You're gonna spend the rest of your life running, bastard! I will find you and kill you!"

"I look forward to our next encounter, Ms. Brandle. Do take care."

She screamed as the boat disappeared into the distance. For a moment, she considered using the Hylonome to pursue him, but as she climbed up to the bridge, she knew it was too late for that. Instead, she turned the ship back towards the Algonquian Shipyards. She needed to make good on her threats, creating a mess so big that it would leave anyone connected to DeWare scrambling to disavow him and cover any connections they had to him.

Chapter 58: Lynna

Friday, 4 February 1983

A black 1982 Ford Crown Victoria with government plates sat in the driveway when Lynna and the others got home from school. Lynna, Ava, Pockets, and Maria all ran straight for the billiards table inside the mansion. It was easier for Pockets to reopen an old portal in the same place.

Pockets held a finger to his lips. As he opened the hole beneath the table, the shouts of Associate Deputy Director Donald Brand filled the room.

"—gan is having a fit! That damn boat has been on every newscast for more than forty-eight hours! There were more than fifty dead bodies on that boat! The New York Times is sniffing around asking about those children."

Agent Mills answered in a much calmer voice than Brand's. "You're lucky Vale and I were there when it happened or those news crews would have gotten film of the kids coming off the boat."

"Do you really think I'm dumb enough to believe your being there at the same time was a coincidence?"

Pockets covered his mouth with both hands to muffle his laughter. Maria slapped him on the arm to get a grip.

"I was there for one reason." Mills' tone shifted from relaxed to steel. "We got a tip from one of our agents in West Berlin that our suspect Taggart had somehow intercepted Raymond Bennu's body."

"Yes," Dr. Howard jumped in, "we're still waiting for an explanation as to how Taggart managed that. Since he got away, we certainly won't be getting any answers from him. We'd also like to know why he delivered Raymond's body to a Chinese science vessel. I'd have thought that would concern you, too?"

"You know damn well—!" Brand stopped short, probably realizing he was about to give up the fact the ship didn't belong to the Chinese.

Ava pumped her fists at that. Lynna grinned to her.

When Brand continued, his volume had lowered significantly. "I'm not at liberty to divulge any of the information we have on that vessel or its crew. Neither of you has the security clearance for that."

"Wait. Are you saying that was a U.S. vessel?" Agent Mills asked making a good show of sounding shocked.

Maria mouthed to Lynna 'Oh, he is good.'

"I'm not confirming anything!" The way Brand's voice cracked on that last word almost made Lynna laugh.

"I would think you'd want us involved," Dr. Howard said. "From what Agent Mills gathered while searching the ship, those thirteen children he found on board are hybrids. Given the ship they were on, it sounds as if the Chinese are attempting to duplicate our work here."

"As I said, all information on this has been deemed top secret, so I won't be discussing that with either of you."

Something in Brand's tone made it sound as though he was winding down. Maria grabbed hold of Pockets' hand.

"So does this mean you plan to move those children somewhere else, perhaps return them to their parents?"

There was another pause that ended after someone sighed. "Unfortunately, we might never be able to figure out who their parents are, so given their unique nature, the president has decided it best to leave them in your custody here—for now."

Lynna and the others exchanged smiles.

The chairs in the conference room squeaked, sounding as though Brand, Agent Mills, and Dr. Howard had all stood. They also heard the clicking sounds of a briefcase being shut.

"Let's be clear," Brand said. "The president wants monthly updates on the progress of these new hybrids. They're to be trained with the idea that they will eventually be operational, and we expect your current crop to remain mission ready at all times. The past few weeks have made it clear how vital this program is to our mission to defeat the Soviets."

"We'll make the children aware of that." Dr. Howard's voice had an edge to it.

"Oh, and I'd like to know what you intend to do with the Bennu boy's body?" There was no missing the suspicion behind Brand's question.

"A proper funeral," Agent Mills said without a hint of hesitation. "He deserves nothing less, and I think it'll be good for the children to have a chance to say goodbye to him."

"Ah," Brand said, "what a pity. He was one of the best operatives this unit has produced."

The voices trailed off after that, at least until the adults made it to the stairs leading down into the foyer.

"—preciate it if you'd let us know of any word on Taggart or if the intelligence on that Chinese vessel becomes cleared for us," Dr. Howard said. "There might be research the Chinese have done that could benefit our unit, too."

"I'll mention that to the president," Brand said in that way that suggested he considered it as likely as a snow storm in Hell.

Lynna and the others hid around the corner from the door frame. This time, they weren't dumb enough to try to sneak any peeks at the adults.

Brand didn't linger. As soon as he walked out of the mansion, Agent Mills closed the door and sighed his relief.

"You get all that, Rowan," Agent Mills called over to where they were hiding, "or do we need to fill in anything you might have missed?"

"How did you know?" Ava poked her head out from around the door frame.

"The silver plate hanging on the far wall in there gives a distorted reflection of you." Dr. Howard sighed, apparently disappointed none of them had figured it out yet.

"Do you really have to give up all my secrets?" Agent Mills said.

Dr. Howard grinned at him in a way that was borderline mischievous.

"In the meantime," Dr. Howard said, directing this to Lynna and her friends, "some of you have a training exercise in a half hour."

Pockets delivered a mock salute to her and grabbed Maria's hand to walk towards the barracks.

"And I'm guessing you have homework?" Dr. Howard directed that to Ava who ran for her room.

Agent Mills looked between Dr. Howard and Lynna. "I take it you don't need me for whatever this is?"

Dr. Howard shook her head and whispered to him, "I'll see you later."

She cocked her head for Lynna to follow her outside. Brand's black Crown Vic was already disappearing down the driveway.

"Your note said you wanted to talk."

Lynna nodded. "Any word on Nevada?"

"No, I'm sorry." She didn't meet Lynna's eyes as she said that, and Lynna wished she could decide if that was a sign of sadness or guilt. "But given what happened at the shipyard, I think it's safe to say she isn't coming back. Agent Mills and I are working on a plan to claim she goes AWOL from school next week. We can't risk the CIA figuring out she killed all those people on DeWare's ship."

"You don't think DeWare will give her up?"

"Assuming he's still alive, I suspect he views what Nevada did as a success, but he's not foolish enough to think the government blment will see it that way. Hopefully, anyone in a position of power will treat him as radioactive."

"And what about Olivia?"

"Agent Mills is working on that. We certainly can't tell Brand she's a refugee from another dimension." Dr. Howard shrugged. "Odds favor we'll claim she's a specialist brought in to oversee part of your training."

That wouldn't be a difficult sell, considering how good a hand-to-hand combatant Olivia was.

"And when are you going to try to revive Raymond?" That had been the real reason she'd wanted to meet with Dr. Howard.

"Tonight." She glanced towards the mansion, where Raymond's body was currently resting in one of the infirmary's morgue lockers. "Agent Mills made the arrangements."

"Ava and I would like to be there."

"It's all too probable this won't work. Are you sure?"

Lynna hesitated, surprised when her emotions choked her, making it difficult to speak. Once she'd wrestled them back under control, she nodded. "We were there when he died. It's not that we don't trust you, but we need to know for ourselves."

Dr. Howard walked over to her and pulled her into a hug, kissing the top of her head. "Okay. Tell Ava to be ready to leave at ten, and meet us at the front gate." When she pulled back, she studied Lynna for a moment. "Something else?"

"Um, yeah." Somehow, it seemed weird that this part made her the most nervous, but after everything that had happened, she wasn't optimistic about what Dr. Howard's response would be. "Tomorrow night... Patrick has four tickets to see Prince in concert. Is there any chance Pockets and Maria could go with us on a double date?"

Dr. Howard barked out a laugh. "Are you mad?"

She winced. "Is that a 'no'?"

"God help me." Dr. Howard rolled her eyes. "Yes, you can all go, but you have to be back right after the concert, no making out in the car or going anywhere else. Are we clear?"

Lynna was so busy dancing with joy in the driveway that she took a moment to realize she hadn't answered Dr. Howard's question.

"Oh! Yes!" Lynna saluted to her. "Yes, ma'am. Totally clear."

Dr. Howard tapped her on the shoulder as she walked past her and back towards the mansion's front door. "Go get your homework finished and make sure you and Ava are ready to go at ten."

Chapter 59: Lynna

Friday, 4 February 1983

The clouds hid the moon as Agent Mills drove the Greenhouse's van up Staples Mill Road. Lynna had heard the road mentioned in traffic reports on the radio, but she'd never actually ventured into this part of Henrico County, north of Richmond.

Dr. Howard sat in the front passenger seat. Lynna and Ava took the seat directly behind them. No one dared discuss what they were doing here. Somehow, Lynna didn't think they'd have spoken, even if there wasn't a risk of listening devices in the van. Agent Mills had lowered the two back rows of seats to make room for the long, wooden crate. Raymond's body sucked out all of the air in the van.

The time was close to 22:45 by the time the van made a slight u-turn and then pulled into the parking lot of a building without any of its lights on. The concrete sign out front identified the place as a funeral home.

Agent Mills drove all the way to the back of the building and backed up to what looked like a lowered garage door. After he honked the horn on the van, the door to the garage rolled up. He backed inside next to a long black hearse. Someone stood next to a door in the back of the garage and pressed a panel on the wall, shutting the garage door.

Fluorescent lights turned on as the door closed. Agent Mills climbed out of the van first and then cued the rest of them to do the same.

"You're late," the man waiting in the garage said in a gruff voice that was more teasing than critical. He didn't look much taller than Lynna. His black hair was starting to go bald in that way that managed to be dignified instead of pitiful. He wore a white shirt with the top button undone and a black tie hanging loose. He walked with a cane in his right hand, so Agent Mills shook his left.

"Appreciate you doing this." Agent Mills pointed with a thumb towards the back of the van.

The guy with the cane flashed a flirtatious smile at Dr. Howard. "Pleasure to meet you, ma'am."

She smiled back. "Lucas says we can trust your discretion."

He pulled out a cigarette and lit it. "Lady, some of the secrets I got would make your toenails fall out."

He offered his pack of cigarettes towards Dr. Howard and Agent Mills, but they both passed.

"Can I try one?" Ava asked.

The old man said, "Sure!" as Agent Mills and Dr. Howard both said, "No!"

Ava crossed her arms as she pouted.

"Sorry, kid." Turning his attention back to Agent Mills, he pointed at Lynna and Ava. "You didn't mention this was going to be a field trip."

"I know. It's also best we avoid any names." The way Agent Mills said that while looking at Lynna and Ava made it clear that went for all of them.

Agent Mills and the man Lynna assumed was the funeral home director got to work carrying Raymond's body from the back of the van and into the room with the funeral home's cremator. Ava, being her usual nosy self, had insisted on going in to watch as the funeral home director worked the controls on the cremator. Lynna doubted she was learning anything, because Ava seemed to be doing most of the talking.

"How does Agent Mills know this guy?" Lynna whispered to Dr. Howard while they waited outside of the cremator room.

"Friend of a friend," she whispered back. "One of his mentors in the CIA says this man got him out of a tight spot in Hong Kong more than a decade ago. That's all I know, and that's probably for the best."

They didn't talk again for several minutes, not until after the funeral home director announced they were ready to slide the body into the cremator.

Dr. Howard reached over and took Lynna's hand in hers. "I'm such a hypocrite."

"I don't understand."

"About everything." She winced before she continued, keeping her voice too low for the others in the cremator room to hear her. "I tell you not to get your hopes up about what we're trying tonight, but dear God, I need this to work. We just told you two not to share too much to a stranger, and I'm the one who endangered all of you by contacting the elves. I thought I could bargain a way to freedom for all of you, and all I did was get Raymond killed. And Heaven knows where Nevada is."

"Nevada chose to leave, and you should respect that." The truth behind those words surprised Lynna, even as she spoke them. She tightened her grip on Dr. Howard's hand as if to press that truth into her palm. "We're going to choose where we want to be and when we want to go there. I've had these wings for five years now. If I'd really wanted to go, I'd have been gone."

"You should get away from this. All of you should."

"And we will, but you've got to trust that we'll do it when we're ready."

Dr. Howard stared back at her as if seeing her for the first time. "Why are you still here?"

"Because the people I love are here, and they need me. Here might suck, but I can make it better. I know I can. While I'm here, I can change the whole world, and I want a chance to make that happen. Nevada saw an opportunity to make life better for those thirteen kids by getting them away from DeWare and sending them here to you—to us. We'll see her again, because the Greenhouse is her home, too.

"No one gets to take that away from us, not even you."

Ava scrambled out of the room to stand between Lynna and Dr. Howard. "Here we go!" she said. They each placed a hand on the smaller girl's shoulders.

"Trust me," Agent Mills said as he escorted the funeral home director out into the hallway with them, "probably best if we aren't in there, if this works."

They waited there with the funeral home director as he lit up another cigarette. He managed to get all of them laughing, sharing stories about some of the stranger funerals he'd handled here and even some stories from his teenage years, including the time he and his friends drove around town tossing powerful fireworks into people's mailboxes.

"Was a lot of fun right up until we got onto Pine Hill Road. Albert was in the passenger seat up front at that point with the cigar box still half full of those little grenades. He lights one up and tosses it out the window. Only it didn't go out the window. Damn thing hit the top of the door frame and bounced back into the box.

"We all start screaming like idiots thinking we're about to get blown straight to the hot place. Then Al tosses the cigar box out the window. Bet that left a crater in the ground, not that we ever saw the which way of it. We're all breathing easier until Al starts screaming again, because three of those suckers had fallen out of the cigar box and were still in the seat between his legs.

"And *BOOM!*

"Blew the poor devil's pants clean off of him. I drove him to the ER, and the whole time the doctor is asking what the heck happened to him. Only, I'm half deaf and spent the entire time yelling at the doctor to talk louder."

That's when a loud bang came from inside the cremator. Then something pounded against the inside of the cremator door.

"Sweet fucking Jesus!" The funeral home director ran, as best he could with a cane, back into the cremator room.

"Turn it off and open it!" Agent Mills ran in behind him, standing at the foot of the conveyer belt like an expectant father waiting to see his wife give birth.

Lynna followed them into the room, pulling off her jacket and ready to turn into her dragon form, if needed. Something banged on the inside of the cremator's door again.

"That's killed the fire," the funeral home director said. "I'm opening her up."

As soon as the door slid open, a rush of heat filled the room and flames burst two feet out of it. Both the funeral home director and Agent Mills retreated as far as the confines of the room allowed.

But Lynna new those flames, bright white like a soul on fire, because that's exactly what it was.

The conveyer belt pulled Raymond out feet first, and once he'd made it far enough, Raymond's hands still bathed in fire grabbed hold of the edge of the door and pulled him out the rest of the way.

He fell several feet off the side of the conveyer belt and onto his ass on the linoleum floor.

"Ow!"

"Douse your flames!" Lynna approached him with her hands held up in a position to keep his fire from blinding her. "You're safe."

The flames vanished, and in their place was Raymond, completely naked. His skin looked lobster red as if sunburned. His blond hair had survived, though, looking bright like an angel's halo.

"What happened?" he asked.

"Well, I'll be damned." The funeral home director laughed and looked over at Agent Mills. "I don't suppose you're ever going to explain this to me, are you?"

"You know the old saying. I'd tell you, but then I'd have to kill you."

Agent Mills knelt next to Raymond and offered him his jacket to at least partially cover himself.

Raymond looked up at the funeral home director as if to ask who the heck he was and then turned his attention back to Lynna and Agent Mills. "Okay, someone here needs to tell me what happened, because two minutes ago, I was getting drowned in a lake by the Not-So-Jolly Grey Giant, and next thing I know I'm in a burning box."

"Long story short," Agent Mills said, smiling over to Dr. Howard, who was standing in the doorway with tears in her eyes, "you're alive, and you're home. We'll fill you in on the rest of it later. For now, no names and no more details."

Chapter 60: Lynna

Saturday, 5 February 1983

Lynna and Patrick's double date with Maria and Pockets ended up more like a quadruple date. Agent Mills snagged four additional tickets to the Prince concert, although the seats he got weren't anywhere near as good as the ones Patrick had.

They all rode together in the Greenhouse van with Agent Mills driving and Dr. Howard sitting next to him. Lynna didn't doubt this was a date for them, too, but she didn't out them. They told the others they came along as chaperones.

Lynna and Patrick had taken the very back seat of the van, holding hands the entire time. He'd met them at the Greenhouse, and seeing him on the campus was one of the most surreal moments of her life.

After they'd sung *1999* for the fourth time in the van on the way back home, Agent Mills had finally told them to give the singing a break.

"You've got to tell me what it was like." When Patrick saw the confusion on her face, he said, "I mean, when you went through the shadow portal to Audur."

"Is that what it's called?" She glanced at Olivia, who was chatting with Raymond. "She never told us the name of the place."

She had a hard time putting the words together, because she was distracted by the sight of Olivia actually smiling. At Raymond? No... Sure he could be charming when he wanted, but if there was anyone it wouldn't work on, she'd have placed money on it being Olivia.

"Yeah, I've never been there," Patrick said, oblivious to the abnormality occurring directly in front of them.

"Wait," she stared at him in surprise as what he'd said managed to get through her distracted thoughts. "You've never been there?"

"No, my mom is an exile. She accepted it to be with my dad." As he said that, she remembered how Olivia had explained Pockets being abducted to potentially blackmail whoever his dark elven parent had been. "So," he continued, "what was it like?"

"It was really cool. The whole thing reminded me a bit of *Blade Runner*, only without the flying cars and a lot cleaner. You really can't go?"

He shook his head, which was hard to see in the dark as they turned off of Midlothian Turnpike onto the driveway of the Greenhouse campus. It was after eleven as they hopped out of the van. Even though Agent Mills had dropped them off by the barracks, Lynna didn't go to her room yet. Instead, she walked Patrick over to his car—or rather, his mom's Corolla. The Buick was still in the shop getting repaired.

"I'm surprised your mom and dad didn't kill you for smashing up your car," she said as they walked up to his borrowed ride.

"Are you kidding?" He laughed. "When I told them why, Dad even gave me a high five... well, after Mom had left with Olivia to bring her here."

Sadly, the parking spaces in front of the mansion were well lit, not that it stopped them from kissing. A lot.

"You think we might get to do this sort of thing more often, but just the two of us?" he asked.

She nodded. "I think the inmates are finally running the asylum."

"Then can I give you a ride to your barracks?" he said with a playful grin.

She snort laughed at that. "All thirty feet? Sure."

He held the door for her as she got into the car. As he climbed into the driver's seat, he reached between the seats and pulled out something big and white from the floor of the back seat.

"This showed up at my house before I left to pick you up." He held it out to her. "My mom thought it might be best if I waited to give it to you at the end of the evening."

As she took it, Lynna saw it was an unopened FedEx envelope sent to Patrick's address, but with her name on it.

She leaned over as if to hug him and whispered in his ear. "You took a big risk bringing this here. Thank you, but in the future, bring it to me at school. Okay?"

When they pulled back he nodded.

She ripped open the envelope. It contained a postcard of Big Ben in London. When she flipped it over, there were two words written with a red ballpoint pen: "Made it."

Beneath it was a smiley face with a pair of fangs.

Lynna's breath caught as she fought back tears. Despite her words the night before to Dr. Howard, she'd been worried to death about Nevada.

Patrick reached over and wiped away a tear sliding down her cheek. "You okay?"

She nodded and hugged him for real this time. "Thank you."

He held her tight, his warmth passing to her in the embrace. "So everything is all right?"

"Not yet, but things are getting better."

Acknowledgements

As always, I need to first thank my wife Sheri. She's been my biggest supporter in my writing since we met in high school. Part of the fun of writing this book was channeling certain parts of who we were back in those early days of our relationship.

I also want to thank Katharine Herndon and Phil Hilliker. They're two of my best friends, and they've had my back for years. They helped make this book possible, providing beta feedback, editing, much discussion on potential titles, and the cover design.

Writer and consultant Kristi Tuck Austin and the folks at Fountain Bookstore (especially Kelly and Andi) have done so much to help me in my writing journey. Can't thank them enough.

I'd also like to thank press spokesperson Kathrin Westhölter and planning architect Rudolf Wehn who provided invaluable help in researching what Tegel Airport looked like in 1983. Their input changed a lot of my plans for that sequence (for the better).

Thanks to Trudy Hale for the Porches. As with many of my books, important pieces of this novel were written there. Not only does that place overflow with creative energy, it's where I gather with many of my closest friends, including Sheri, Katharine, Phil, Kristi & Adam Austin, Mike & Shawna Christos, Leila

Gaskin, Denise Golinowski, and Eric Smith. They're almost all people I've befriended through my experiences with James River Writers.

I hope I haven't forgotten anyone, but I likely have. The arts community is full of generous spirits, and I've been blessed to meet so many wonderful people who inhabit it.

About the author

Bill Blume's love for the written word started in high school with an addiction to comic books that was later hijacked by novels such as *Frankenstein* and *Dragonflight*. His short stories have been published in many fantasy anthologies and ezines. Like the father figure in his *Gidion Keep, Vampire Hunter* series, he's worked as a 911 dispatcher for more than 20 years.

To learn more about Bill and his books, visit his website at www.billblume.net.

Trigger Warnings

While I had a lot of fun writing this book and hope you will enjoy reading it, be warned there is some difficult content included. With that in mind, here's a list of some trigger warnings.

Animal Abuse (Mentioned)

Animal Death (Mentioned)

Assault

Blood

Child Abuse

Death

Decapitation

Drowning

Drugs

Gun Violence

Hostages

Kidnapping

Knife and Sword Violence

Murder

Profanity

Racism

Sexism

Teen Suicide

I've tried to include everything I could think of, so if I've missed anything, please feel free to contact me via my social media and let me know. I keep a mirror list on my website for this book, and will update that with additional items, if needed. If there are future editions of this book, I will update those, as well.

www.ingramcontent.com/pod-product-compliance
Lightning Source LLC
Chambersburg PA
CBHW022019310726
48972CB00006B/1727